ANDREW J. FENADY,
Winner of Western Writers of America's
Owen Wister Award for Lifetime Achievement

THE MOMENT OF TRUTH

Three of the Apaches concentrated their attack on Ike and Ben. Fists flew and knives flashed. It happened before the two men had a chance to wield and fire their weapons. Both Ike and Ben fell off the wagon with the three Apaches on them.

Quemada and Secorro rode off on the wagon with the Henry rifle still on board.

On the ground over and under the bodies tumbled, grappling in the dirt, twisting, with Ike and Ben warding off thrust after thrust of Apache knife blades while delivering blow after blow—smashing noses, jaws and throats of the Red Men until two of them lay unconscious while Ben grabbled hold of the third and pinned his arms behind him.

Ike drew his gun, cocked the hammer and pointed it directly at the temple of the Apache, who was certain he was about to be killed.

Instead, Ike's other hand clutched the thong at his throat and held out the eagle claw.

Ike said only one word....

Other *Leisure* books by Andrew J. Fenady:

THE REBEL: JOHNNY YUMA
RIDERS TO MOON ROCK
DOUBLE EAGLES

BIG IKE

ANDREW J. FENADY

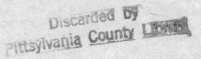
LEISURE BOOKS   NEW YORK CITY

BIG IKE

PRELUDE

A scimitar moon sliced through lingering clouds against the flat star-studded Arizona sky. The night was warm and ripe for autumn. Leaves, crisp and sere, curled into the rusty earth.

Not a bad night for hunting.

Unless you were the hunted.

A brace of leashed bloodhounds yapped and strained with the scent strong in their flared black nostrils.

On the other end of the leash was a uniformed prison guard, and on his heels a flock of other guards, winded and weary, carrying rifles and shotguns on a chase that had covered more miles and hours than any of the pursuers could ever remember.

Somewhere ahead—the pursued. Two prisoners. Two prisoners, still in striped convict clothes torn and wet with sweat; two men trying to do what had never been done before—escape from the Arizona Territorial Prison.

In the lead by more than a dozen yards was an ex-sailor, Convict 2732, named Dawson—a man with abundant muscle, a frying pan face, one blue eye and a puckered shell where the other eye used to be. Dawson heaved for air and was losing the battle with each uneven stride. His face was turning blue, his tongue thick and dry, the pupil of his eye tilted upward.

Behind him, Colorados, an Indian, Convict 2888, tall, lean and hard, breathed and ran smooth and even as the sounds of the dogs yapping grew closer and louder.

It appeared that the two convicts would end up the same as the rest of the prisoners who had tried to escape—either dead and buried or captured and returned to serve the remainder of their time in hell. Which of the two fates was worse was an undetermined matter of opinion.

But suddenly Colorados surged past Dawson, broke sharply to the right and burst forth in a new fury of speed.

Colorados had paced himself. He knew the river was ahead. The rocks were cooler near the river. The earth damper. The crickets louder.

Above the yelping of the dogs a guard's voice roared.

"Over there!"

A fusillade of gunfire shattered the night. Something fell.

Half a dozen guards rushed to the fallen form of one of the convicts.

"Dead?"

"Yeah."

"Colorados?"

"No. It's Dawson."

From a distance, the voice of the guard with the dogs.

"There's blood here. The Indian's been hit . . . and from the looks of it, bad."

"He's heading for the river."

"He won't make it."

"Even if he does, he won't live long."

"Nothin' human could."

"Yeah . . . but Colorados is only part human."

"Part human . . . part panther . . . and all sonofa-bitch."

"Took more punishment than I ever . . ."

"You ever what?"

"Never mind."

"It's gonna be a lot more peaceable without him."

"A-men, brother."

In the distance, out of sight and sound of the prison guards, the Apache chief, Colorados, bleeding and barely able to stand, dove into the reddish-brown waters of the Colorado River and vanished beneath the flowing surface.

CHAPTER ONE

America's rivers carried lifeblood to the nation's heartland.

The great mass of earth between the Atlantic and Pacific Oceans was being conquered by pilgrims, pioneers, settlers and speculators, by way of water first and then by land.

Villages, towns and cities sprang up primarily along the navigable rivers, and later, the Erie Canal linked the eastern seaboard to the entire Midwest.

The nearby land was developed—homesteaded, farmed and formed into communities that stretched out toward America's Manifest Destiny from coast to coast.

That destiny followed and flowed along the course of the great rivers: the Allegheny, the Monongahela, the Shenandoah, the Ohio, the Mississippi, the Missouri, the Red, the Columbia and finally the Colorado—the primary river of the American Southwest, draining somewhere in the neighborhood of 245,000 square miles of land from the states and territories of Wyoming, Colorado, Utah, New Mexico, Arizona, Nevada and California—with headwaters in Colorado at an altitude of over nine thousand feet—flowing southwest toward the Gulf of California and the Pacific Ocean.

The Colorado was the bloodline to the civilized and savage Southwest. Since 1852 the main traffic along the Colorado consisted of steamboats, the first of which appeared in 1852 and scared the hell out of the Indians who thought they had been crafted by some belching white devil. They figured it was an omen of something worse to come—and from their perspective they weren't so very far from wrong. Soon white men and women and children closed in like coyotes over a kill.

The night of the attempted escape from the Arizona Territorial Prison was no different than any other night on the Colorado.

The river traffic moved north and south and across. Part of that traffic consisted of a paddle wheeler, the *Colorado Queen*, sparkling like a bejeweled tiara and leaving gurgling white foam in its wake.

Aptly named, she was the queen of the Colorado, carrying over sixty tons of goods and over fifty thousand pounds of passengers. Two of those passengers collectively weighed just over one hundred pounds and were leaning along the steamboat's rail—Jedediah, age twelve, and Obadiah, age nine.

Jed was fair-complexioned with corn silk hair parted precisely and combed neatly, blue eyes circled by steel-rimmed glasses. His suit seemed freshly pressed and without a speck of dust on it, his aspect serious.

Obie was darker but with a lighter mien, a mischievous laughing moonface framed by circlets of raven hair. His clothes were rumpled and the seam up his left elbow had come unstitched.

"Over there, Jed!" Obie pressed against the rail and pointed as far as he could stretch toward what he had seen, or thought he had seen. "It just bobbed up again! See it?"

"No, I don't."

Obie climbed onto a rung of the rail and jabbed his finger into the night.

"Out *there!* Maybe it's a man overboard."

"And maybe it's Moby Dick."

"What's that?"

"Never mind."

"Jed, I'm telling you—"

"Obadiah! Tell *me.*" A smallish, swarthy man in his mid-forties approached. "But first get off from that railing!"

Jacob Silver stepped closer. He too was neatly attired and barbered, rope thin with a hawkish face adorned by a prominent beak, and he spoke with a slight iambic European rhythm.

"I said get off from that railing!"

Despite Jacob Silver's command, Obie leaned farther out for a better, confirming look.

Jacob grabbed him.

"I mean get off from *this* side."

Obie now stood with both feet on the deck, but still looked toward the river.

"Uncle Jake, I saw something out there."

"Sure, you see all sorts of things when it's time to go to bed."

"It's not time yet."

"I say it is."

"But, Uncle Jake—"

"No buts. I say it is, so it is. Boys grow sleeping. Don't you want to be big and strong like your Uncle Jake?"

"Uncle Jake, what's a moby dick?"

"What? Who told you such things?"

Obie pointed to Jed.

"Uncle Jake, he never read Melville."

"Neither have I. . . . Melville, shmelville, it's time to go to bed. Now go. Go!"

Both boys turned and departed amid murmured protests from Obie.

Jacob Silver looked after them and smiled, then started off, but paused for a moment. He glanced out across the river, saw nothing but the river, shrugged and continued.

After the fifth step he stopped, grabbed suddenly at his chest and ducked into a passageway.

As other passengers strolled by, Jacob Silver unbuttoned his jacket and unfastened a safety pin from his inside pocket. He removed a sheaf of bills bound by a rubber band, riffled the currency, put them back inside the pocket, smiled, fastened the safety pin where it had been, then proceeded, whistling and nodding pleasantly at fellow passengers as they walked along the deck of the *Colorado Queen*.

By far the largest and most ornate room of the *Colorado Queen* was the salon, which was lighted by several crystal chandeliers that illuminated more than a dozen tables with Douglas chairs, bordered by a long stool-less bar and peopled by contented passengers talking, laughing, drinking, smoking and playing cards. A distinguished gentleman sat at the bench of a baby grand Chickering piano and provided music to talk, laugh, drink, smoke, and play cards by.

Jacob Silver entered the salon, gently patted the slight bulge in the chest area of his jacket, looked around, then headed toward one of the tables where a poker game was in progress.

Of the original five poker players, three were still in the hand. One of those three, a squat, squirrel-faced man, studied the cards he held, took a puff off the stub of cigar stuck in the left side of his mouth and glanced at the pile of money in the center of the table.

"I'm suckin' eggs," he said, and dropped his cards facedown in front of him.

The dealer, a genial fellow with a smile slashed across his face, dressed completely in black except for a blazing white shirt adorned by a black string tie, nodded, smiled even wider and looked across at the remaining player who sat with his back to where Jake Silver now stood.

Jake looked down at the man with a broad back in a well-tailored gray suit topped by a crop of wavy blond hair, whose cards were in front of him facedown on the table.

"Well, mister,"—the genial dealer nodded again—"it all comes down to the three of us. Just you, me . . . and the pot."

A spectator next to Jake whispered to the newcomer.

"Stranger, you missed some god almighty poker playin'."

"Is that so?" Jake whispered back.

"Both those boys been holdin' phee-nominal cards all night." He pointed to the dealer. " 'Specially that Slade fella."

Slade looked at the cards in his right hand, then at his opponent.

"It'll cost you two hundred to stay."

His opponent said nothing.

"Want to take another look at your cards before you decide?"

The opponent took a heavy gold watch attached to a heavy gold chain from his vest pocket, clicked the lid open and pressed a lever.

Inside the lid was a wedding picture of a big, handsome, wavy-haired young man and a beautiful olive-eyed bride.

The watch played a tune.

The face of the opponent was the same as the bridegroom—older, but still with the same clear blue eyes and handsome features.

He glanced up at Jake, then turned back to the genial dealer.

"Mister Slade, I paid five hundred dollars for this watch in London."

"This ain't London," the genial dealer said, becoming slightly less genial, "and I ain't a pawn shop."

"Wait just a minute!" Jake interrupted. Jacob Silver went through the procedure of unfastening the safety pin, peeling off two hundred dollar bills and placing them in front of the player on the table.

"Here's the two hundred. I'll take that watch."

He did.

The player pushed the two hundred dollar bills toward the pot at the center of the table.

A blanket of silence fell across the salon.

The piano player stopped playing.

The people in the room stopped talking, laughing, drinking and even smoking.

"Well, big fella," the genial dealer said, breaking the silence and the suspense, "you just lost the pot *and* the watch."

He turned over his cards.

"I'm all blue."

Five spades. He started to reach for the money.

"Full up." The opponent turned up his cards.

Three kings, two aces.

The genial gambler was no longer at all genial.

He rose to leave, took a couple of steps, but stopped and grabbed hold of Jake. "Listen, you Jew money lender, why don't you keep your big nose out of other people's business?"

"That again," Jake said.

"Let him go," the winner spoke softly.

"This is between me and him," the loser said, not softly. "I know his kind."

In a swift motion the winner rose, gripped the loser, slammed him against a post and held him pinned there.

"So do I. His name's Jacob Silver. Mine's Isaac Silver. He's my brother."

"Your what?"

"I said he's my brother. Now, what were you saying?"

"I . . . I . . . what I meant . . . Well, you don't look—"

"I don't look *what*?"

"You don't look . . . like his brother."

"Look closer. Now do you see the resemblance?"

"Yeah . . . sure."

Isaac Silver let go of Slade, who departed straightaway with what was left of his dignity.

The piano player played and the passengers went back to talking, laughing, drinking, smoking and playing cards.

Isaac Silver walked back to the table, where Jake stood stacking money.

"Ike, why do you play cards with bad losers?"

"Beats playing with winners." Ike smiled. "Give me back my watch."

"How much did you win?" Jake also smiled.

"You know I never count while I'm playing."

"Well, we're through playing, so I'll count. Here's the watch. The boys are waiting for you."

Big Ike took the watch, clicked the lid open and pressed a lever.

He listened to the tune and remembered.

CHAPTER TWO

As Isaac walked along the deck of the *Colorado Queen*, mostly he remembered her, Rachel, as he had with the blossom of each dawn, the descent of each sun and much of the time in between.

Isaac Silver was one of six sons born to Ephraim and Sarah Silver, Polish Jews in the province of Lubin, then ruled by Czarist Russia. On the day after his sixteenth birthday, his mother, father and four of his brothers were slain by Cossacks for their part in an attempted revolution; Isaac and his surviving older brother, Jacob, fled across Poland, Germany and France before finally arriving in England, where the prime minister happened to be a Jew named Benjamin Disraeli.

Isaac was tall, handsome, broad-shouldered, blue-eyed and fair-haired; Jacob, the antithesis of his brother, was small, dark, feisty and funny. The two brothers worked together, saved together and stuck together, but they did not study together— Jake was schooled in the streets and alleys, while Isaac put himself through the University of London.

There he met and fell in love with Rachel Morgenstern. She was tall, slender, intelligent, and beautiful, so beautiful that Isaac's heart and brain hammered at the first sight of her and within minutes of their meeting he knew, they both knew, that for each, there could be no other. There were three years of married harmony and bliss. She bore him two sons: first Jedediah, and last, Obadiah—last because Rachel died while delivering her second son.

Life in England could never be the same for Isaac after the death of his beloved Rachel.

This time he fled halfway around the world— he and Jacob and the two infants, Jedediah and Obadiah—across the Atlantic, then around the Horn to the gold coast of California.

That was where and when Isaac Silver became "Big Ike" and Jacob Silver became "Uncle Jake." They went into the business of providing the booming mining camps with food and goods, and prospered doing so. It was a hard life, but rewarding. Then Abraham Lincoln became President of the United States, but the states were far from united.

Big Ike left his brother to take care of his sons and went to fight so there would be a United States, earning the rank of captain and fighting until he was wounded at Shiloh.

And now, a fistful of years after the Civil War, the four of them, Jake, Big Ike, Jedediah and Obadiah, were heading for a new frontier, dangerous and unsettled—but at that moment he was heading for a stateroom to say good night to his two sons.

CHAPTER THREE

Big Ike unlocked, then opened the door and stepped into a cabin barely illuminated by a hanging oil lamp. As he walked in, something flew across the cabin and plopped with a fluffy impact against the wall inches from Ike's head. He grabbed the pillow just before it fell to the floor.

There were more missiles that soon followed, including another pillow, socks and shoes, used as weapons of warfare in the riverboat arena.

"Fellows!"

The combatants froze, but just for a beat.

"Dad,"—Jedediah pointed from the bunk to his younger brother on the floor—"he started it!"

"Did not! Did not! *He did!*"

"I didn't ask who started it."

"I was putting on my nightshirt and Obie whopped me with a pillow—"

"Yeah, but before that he—"

"Never mind before that . . . the war's over. Peace is declared."

With that declaration Ike hit Jed on the shoulder with the pillow, then tossed it on the upper bunk.

"Now both of you help me clear up this battlefield."

Jedediah jumped off the bunk and Obadiah got off the deck and both began to gather up pillows, socks, shoes and other assorted items as their father stood smiling at the familiar procedure that had taken place many other times in many other places.

"Dad," Obie said, looking up, "what's it like in Azirona?"

"Arizona," Jed corrected.

"What's it like, Dad?"

"I've never been there, Obie."

"Has Uncle Jake?"

"Nope."

"Then why are we going?"

"For the same reason why your Uncle Jake and I left Europe and went to England, then left there and came to California."

"What reason is that?"

"To find something better."

"Like what?"

"Well, in this case, it's a store that we're buying."

"A store?"

"That's right, a store that provides supplies that people need to make a better life for everybody."

"I like the life we have since you come back from the war."

"Came back," Jed corrected.

"Are there Indians there?" Obie's eyes widened.

"Yes."

"And soldiers?"

"Yes."

"You were a soldier, weren't you, Dad?"

"Yes, I was, Obie."

"Are there—"

"Obie," Jedediah said, "don't ask so many questions."

"Why not? Do you want to go to bed?"

"You'll both be going soon enough, but what was it you were going to ask, Obie?"

"Are you going to fight the Indians?"

"No, I'm not a soldier anymore, and anyhow, peace has been declared in the Territory. There's a treaty."

"What's a treaty?"

"It's an agreement not to fight each other anymore. That's the kind of agreement you two ought to make."

"Are there kids to play with in Azirona?"

"Uh-huh."

"What kind of kids?"

"Well, Obie, kids are pretty much the same all over the world."

"Then why are older people so different?"

"They're not, really. Obie, you've got your nightshirt on backwards."

"I like it better this way."

"Sure you do. All right now, say your prayers, boys, and you'll wake up in La Paz."

"Is that where the store is?"

"Obie," Jed sighed, "the store is in Prescott."

"Then why are we going to La Paz?"

"We're going there to catch the stagecoach, right, Dad?"

"Right. Now say your prayers."

Jedediah and Obadiah knelt at the side of the lower bunk. Ike stood by and listened as both boys spoke together:

"I thank Thee, O God
For the blessings of this day.
Thou art my Shepherd: I shall not want.
I fear no evil, for Thou art with me.
In peace, I lay me down to sleep.

Bless my home and all who are dear to me.
Sh'ma Yis-ro-el,
Hear, O Israel,
A-do-noy Elo-ne-nu.
The Lord is our God.
A-do-noy E-chod.
The Lord is One.
And please, God, bless Mommy who is with you.
Good night, Dad."

Jedediah and Obadiah climbed into their bunks as Big Ike turned the oil lamp even lower.

"Good night, my boys."

Later, just past midnight, Ike Silver stood at the rail of the *Colorado Queen*, smoking what was left of the tobacco he had loaded into one of the pipes he had brought from England years ago. Rachel had loved the aroma of pipe tobacco and would watch from her chair as he smoked and read one of Dostoyevsky's novels. When she became pregnant the first time, Ike told her he would give up smoking until the baby was born. But Rachel wouldn't hear of it.

"It doesn't bother me one bit, Isaac, and besides, I want our son to grow up and smoke a pipe just like his father."

"What if he turns out to be our daughter?"

"We'll have a son first. Three sons and then a daughter."

It was one of the few times that Rachel was wrong about anything.

Ike tapped the bowl of his pipe against the palm of his hand and let the ash scatter into the night and drift down toward the river.

He let the bowl cool off for more than a minute, put the pipe into the pocket of his jacket and walked toward the stern of the ship.

As he turned the corner, in the distance he saw Jake standing alone looking toward the shore. Ike was about to call out when from the shadows a figure appeared holding something in his right hand. The hand swung hard, hit Jake behind his left ear, and as Jake collapsed, the figure bent and reached down.

Ike sprang across the deck, grabbed the figure, pulled him up and smashed his fist into Slade's face. Ike slammed him against the wall and hit him again. The sap dropped from Slade's hand.

"No! Please!!" Slade screamed.

"If he's hurt bad I'll kill you!!"

"Ike! Don't!" Jake managed to get to one knee and hold out his hand.

Ike turned toward his brother while still holding on to Slade.

"I'm all right, Ike. . . . Don't kill him."

"Slade, you don't know how lucky you are." Ike shoved the bleeding man away. "Get out of here!"

"I-I'm sorry." Slade slobbered and staggered along the deck.

Ike helped his brother to his feet.

Jake patted the bulge in his jacket to make sure the contents were still there.

"I told you . . . he was a bad loser . . . six hundred . . ."

"What?"

"I counted it." Jake smiled and rubbed the back of his head. "Six hundred dollars. That's how much we won."

"Never mind that. How's your head?"

"I won't have any trouble falling asleep tonight, but I'm all right." He smiled. "Thanks to your fists and my hard head. Speaking of hard heads, Ike . . ."

"What?"

"What do you really know about Prescott?"

"I know we own a store there . . . or soon will. I know there's opportunity there . . . and I hope it's a place for the boys to settle and live. . . ."

"For how many centuries have we all been looking for a place to settle . . . and live?"

"That's one reason,"—Ike nodded—"they call us Wandering Jews."

"My brother," Jake said, smiling, "they call us worse than that."

"Maybe not in Prescott."

Chapter Four

It was the dawn of the seventh decade of the nineteenth century, five years after Lee had surrendered to Grant at Appomattox on Palm Sunday, April 9, 1865—a victory President Abraham Lincoln did not live to savor. The single cartridge fired by John Wilkes Booth succeeded where all the firepower of the Confederacy had failed.

With that single shot Abraham Lincoln belonged to the ages and the presidency of the United States belonged to the man who had been elected vice president in 1864, Andrew Johnson. A former Tennessee tailor, small-town mayor, state legislator, member of the House of Representatives and Lincoln's choice on his ticket for reelection, Johnson was also dubbed "Andy the Sot" after he showed up drunk during Lincoln's inauguration ceremony.

The South looked upon Johnson as a traitor Tennessean who had sided with the North during the war, and the North considered him a turncoat who was too soft on the South after the war. In fact, Johnson was only trying to carry out Lincoln's stated policy toward the South, but Andrew Johnson was no Abraham Lincoln. So, in the presidential election of 1868, the voters turned to a true hero of the North, Ulysses Simpson Grant, who had been nominated on a wave of acclamation on the first ballot at the Republican Convention in Chicago and succeeded in defeating his opponent, Horatio Seymour.

President Grant believed that both North and South and the entire United States and Territories would benefit with the expansion and development of the West. He expressed that belief in words and deeds, favoring "appropriations for river and harbor improvements and for fortifications and other advancements in whatever amounts Congress may deem proper."

The East and West were linked by rail two months after Grant's inauguration when the Union Pacific and Central Pacific railroads converged at Promontory Point, Utah, and the Southwest was further flooded by federal disbursements throughout the region.

One of the principal beneficiaries of this bonanza was the Arizona Territory.

Arizona . . . Beautiful. Bountiful. Fertile flatlands. Soaring rock-bound riches. But a battlefield since time remembered. Much of the land was hard and hostile, as hard and hostile as those who dwelled and fought on it—Comanche, Kiowa, Cherokee and Apache.

Then came the conquerors, from this and other continents. Mexicans. Spaniards. Bringing with them horses and gunpowder. And finally those who came to cultivate and stay—Americans. Possibly the most civilized, but definitely the most determined. Lusty. Land hungry. Unyielding. Undaunted. A perpetual procession of seekers. Miners. Cattlemen. Entrepreneurs. Farmers. Runaways. From the defeated South and the victorious North. Outcasts and outlaws. Lawmen and laborers. And with many of them, wives, women who would bear children; and also other women, prostitutes, who would provide the revelry of their profession.

At the western river port of La Paz, Arizona Territory, the steamboat *Colorado Queen* had docked and dropped anchor early that April Monday morning.

La Paz was the passageway to America's last great frontier, one of the Creator's most rugged, vast and complex creations. Dull, flat, monotonous in the places where the devil stomped the dust off his boots; spectacular, craggy and colorful in other places that were akin to paradise.

It was a place peopled by tough, sweat-stained miners who worked the tunnels and veins of the Wickenberg, the Congress, the Constellation and the MacMorris—men who dug up the earth's treasure and raised a lot of hell in the process.

It was a place peopled by Indians, who in spite of treaties were still resentful, fierce and defiant, and who raised a lot of hell—and scalps.

It was a place peopled by soldiers—riding out of Fort McDowell, Fort Apace, Fort Thomas, Fort Breckenridge, Fort Whipple and Fort Lowell—men who swore to keep the peace, but who also raised a lot of hell in the process.

And it was a place where the *Colorado Queen* was unloading passengers and cargo.

The first passenger to leave the ship was a man with a bruised face and body who had lost six hundred dollars in a card game, who tried to get it back with a blackjack, who had instead been beaten almost senseless—a man named Slade, who wanted nothing to do with anyone named Silver.

He was followed by dozens of other passengers, among them four passengers named Silver.

Ike, Jake and the boys made their way down the gangplank.

"Are we in Azirona?" Obie inquired.

"Arizona," Jed corrected.

"We're here." Jake grinned.

"I don't see any Indians," Obie remarked.

"Jake," Ike said, "you and the boys wait 'til they unload the baggage. I'll get the tickets and be right back."

Ike Silver had changed from the gray suit of the previous night to more suitable duds for traveling through rugged country. He wore a wide-brimmed trail hat, light blue denim shirt, leather vest with a heavy gold watch and chain attached, a tan canvas jacket, bugger-red pants and round-toed McInery boots with three inch heels, placing the top of his head more than six and a half feet from the ground on which he walked with panther-like grace.

Ike Silver wore something else. Around his narrow waist was strapped a black cartridge belt and holster housing the latest model Remington handgun. Traveling by stagecoach wearing a holstered handgun might not be comfortable, but it might be prudent—particularly since just about all the Silver brothers' monetary fortune was deposited in Jake Silver's jacket.

Ike moved away from the wharf, where the air was redolent with the riverfront odors, toward the teeming center of town, where the aroma of tortillas, tacos, frijoles and other Mexican dishes mingled with the fragrance of manure. Dogs barked and scampered along with cats, and even chickens, among the polyglot of people, horses and mules.

Despite the early morning hour, several saloons

were already in session with streams of thirsty customers entering and sated patrons exiting through the swinging doors.

At the stage depot a sign hung on the glass door—CLOSED.

A considerable crowd had assembled, waiting for the sign to be flipped and the door to be opened for business. Ike Silver joined the crowd and also waited.

Just as he started to reach for the watch and chain to check the time, a huge hand banged him on the back. Ike made a sharp turn ready for come-what-may.

A sturdy six-footer with green eyes peering out of a catgut face stood inches away, along with a half-dozen other sturdy specimens.

"Big Ike Silver, you son of a bonanza, how are ya!!"

"Sean Dolan!" Ike grinned. "You fugitive from a fistfight! How are *you?*"

"First-rate!" Dolan turned to the men close by. "Boys, this here's Big Ike Silver. He delivers the goods. Weren't for him, many a mining camp in California woulda been without beans, bacon and mountain dew. We cut up a few touches in our time too, didn't we, Big Ike?"

"You might say that."

"I just did. Sure am glad our trails crossed. . . ."

"So am I, Sean. What're you doing in La Paz?"

"Passin' through, I hope. Been three days trying to get out."

"Out to where?"

"Prescott. You're looking at the new partner–foreman of the Rattlesnake Mine—if he ever gets there. . . . Where you heading?"

"Well . . ."

The crowd reacted as the depot door opened and a

bony hand flipped the sign to the opposite side—
OPEN.

The hand was attached to a bald-headed cadaverous fellow who stepped onto the boardwalk and was greeted by a chorus of questions.

"What's the word, Curly?"

"When's the stage gonna run?"

"Are you selling tickets yet?"

"I gotta get outta this rat hole."

"Good news us, Curly . . ."

"There ain't no good news," Curly shouted back. "The 'word' is *injuns*—and there ain't gonna be any stage runnin' to Prescott or any place else 'til an army escort shows up."

"When's that?"

"Yeah, dammit, *when?*"

"Could be in an hour or so. . . ." Curly grinned.

The crowd reacted with smiles, laughter, and even a smattering of applause.

"Or," Curly continued, "could be a week—could be a month—or could be next winter. . . ."

The crowd reacted with displeasure.

"There'll be a notice on that there board." Curly pointed to a bulletin board next to the door. " 'Til then, we're closed."

He turned back toward the door. But standing on the threshold blocking his way was a young nun who had been among the crowd.

"Excuse me, sir."

Curly had no choice.

She was about twenty-one or twenty-two, sunny-faced and pert, with a sprinkle of freckles over the side of her turned-up nose, and wore the habit of the Sisters of Charity.

"Mister Curly"—she couldn't help glancing up at his shiny pate and smiling—"could you please tell me if there is any other way of getting to Prescott?"

Ike and the rest of the assemblage stood by to listen.

"No, ma'am. Not unless you got wings under that outfit. Even then, them Apaches 'ud shoot you down. And things is gonna get a sight worse before they get any better."

"Why is that?"

"I'll *tell* you why is that, ma'am. Last night an Apache Chief called Colorados escaped from the Arizona Territorial Prison. Got hisself wounded. So, there's two eithers."

"Eithers?"

"Either Colorados is dead and there's gonna be trouble—or else he ain't dead and there's gonna be trouble."

"But I was told there was a treaty."

"Yes, ma'am. Sometimes we break it—sometimes the Apaches do."

"I've got to get to Prescott."

"Yes, ma'am. And I've got to get to breakfast. Now, excuse me, lady."

She stepped onto the boardwalk and Curly stepped inside, flipped the sign. CLOSED. And then he slammed the door.

"Oh, my," she murmured, started to walk and bumped directly into Big Ike.

"I beg your pardon, sir."

"Mea culpa, Sister."

"Oh," she said, "you're Catholic."

"No, Sister, my name's Isaac Silver."

"Oh, I see. I'm Sister Mary Boniface and I'm trying to get to Prescott."

"Aren't we all. Are you traveling alone, Sister?"

Sister Mary Boniface nodded.

"I thought nuns always traveled in pairs."

"For a non-Catholic, Mister Silver, you know quite a bit about the ways of the church. I was traveling with Sister Mary Frances, but she took sick and had to turn back—but there's no turning back for me. I'm going to Prescott one way or another."

"I wouldn't bet against you, Sister Boniface."

"That's very reassuring, I'm sure, Mister Silver. Good day."

Ike tipped his hat as Sister Mary Boniface walked away, then he turned and shrugged at Sean Dolan.

"Neither would I." Dolan grinned. "Well, Big Ike, would you care to look down a friendly bottle of bourbon with the boys and me? Cut up a few touches, like the old days?"

"No thanks, Sean. Jake and my boys are waiting at the dock."

"I'd admire to see 'em. Catch up with you later, Big Ike."

"So long, fellas." Ike smiled at the miners and turned toward the river.

When his back was turned he stopped smiling.

He was thinking about those two hundred miles to Prescott.

CHAPTER FIVE

Two hundred miles to Prescott. It might as well have been two thousand. They couldn't walk that far, the four of them couldn't ride by horseback—even if they had horses—there was no railroad to Prescott, but . . . Big Ike stopped walking.

Just a few feet away, a livery barn and corral. Inside the corral were dozens of horses, and outside, over a dozen wagons in different degrees of disrepair. In front, a black man talking to a white man who appeared to be the proprietor.

The proprietor was short and fat and shook his head negatively as the black man pointed to the wagons. The black man took a deep breath, turned and walked toward a wagon hitched to two mules.

Even from a distance, the black man looked king-size, with a dark brown, handsome face, power-laden shoulders and arms, coal-black eyes glistening out of an unsmiling face. He boarded the wagon, where a woman and little boy about eight years old waited. The little boy appeared to be a miniature version of his father; the man's wife was of lighter complexion, comely, in her late twenties.

Without saying a word, the man took up the reins, snapped them over the mules, and the wagon rolled away.

Ike approached the proprietor.

"Howdy."

"Howdy yourself," the proprietor said, and spat out a stream of tobacco juice.

"Ike Silver."

"Herb Kokernut."

"Mister Kokernut, do you have a wagon and team that could make it to Prescott?"

"And back?"

"No. Just to Prescott."

"For you?"

"And my family."

"Yeah, I got a wagon and team that could make it. Not so sure about you and your family."

"What do you mean?"

"I mean Apaches. Haven't you heard?"

"I've heard. How much for the wagon and team?"

Herb Kokernut spat out another stream of tobacco juice.

"I'm thinkin' it over."

"How long will it take . . . to think it over?"

"I'm done thinkin'."

"How much?"

"Say . . . two hundred."

Ike reached into his pocket and pulled out a roll of bills.

"Here's a hundred on deposit. I'll be back in a few minutes."

Herb Kokernut took the money and shook his head.

"What's wrong?" Ike asked.

"Maybe I shoulda said two fifty."

"Maybe . . . and maybe not." Ike smiled and walked away.

* * *

The passengers had disembarked and most of the cargo had been unloaded from the *Colorado Queen* as Ike Silver walked up to Jake and the boys, who stood next to their luggage on the wharf listening to a discussion that had already turned into an argument.

On one side of the disagreement was Captain Cyrus Medford of the *Colorado Queen*. On the other side, a mountain of a man with buffalo shoulders and a face that almost matched.

"What's going on?" Ike asked his brother.

"Negotiation," Jake answered.

"About what?"

"About none of our business."

Captain Medford pointed to what appeared to be about a hundred barrels labeled FLOUR that had been unloaded from the ship.

"Look, Gallagher, the price has always been ten dollars a barrel."

"Well, Captain, the price is now seven. Unless you want to get stuck with one hundred barrels of flour."

"Lessur gets twenty dollars in Prescott."

"Prescott's two hundred miles away, and Mister Lessur told me not to pay no more than seven."

"I got no time to argue—"

"You got time to load them barrels back on to that boat?" Gallagher looked around at the men with him and grinned.

As the disagreement continued, Jake noticed that Ike was rubbing his chin and glancing from the two men to the barrels and back.

"Ike, let's go."

"Hold on, Jake."

"Hold on to what? I don't like that look in your eye. Come on, let's get to that stage."

"There isn't any stage."

"*What?*"

Ike's attention was still on the two men.

". . . but I'm not authorized to sell this cargo for less than ten dollars a barrel."

"And I'm not authorized to pay more 'n seven."

Ike stepped forward. Jake reached for him but missed.

"Ike, for heaven's sake!"

Jed and Obie looked at each other and shrugged.

"I beg your pardon, Captain." Ike nodded toward the barrels. "Is that cargo for sale?"

"It is at ten dollars a barrel," the captain said.

"You keep out of this, bub." Gallagher pointed a huge forefinger and fist at Ike.

Ike ignored the gesture.

"Captain, you say it sells for twenty dollars in Prescott?"

"Payable by the United States Army at Fort Whipple and glad to get it."

"Butt out," Gallagher growled.

"You in the market, Mister?"

"*No!*" Jake interrupted.

"Silver. Ike Silver." He turned toward Gallagher. "You going to give the captain his price?"

"Wiseass . . . I'll give you something in a minute."

About a dozen of Gallagher's teamsters moved closer.

"I'll ask you just once more," Ike said.

"And my answer, bub, is I'm hauling that cargo to Prescott!"

"Not at seven dollars a barrel," the Captain said and turned to Ike. "Mister, give me a thousand dollars and it's all yours."

"Isaac!" Jake rubbed at his face.

"You do,"—Gallagher doubled both fists—"and I'll break your arm, *Isaac!*"

"A thousand, Jake." Ike reached out.

"It's the money for the store!" Jake was sweating. "Don't worry."

"It's the end of the world and he says 'Don't worry.'"

"Jacob . . ." Ike turned his palm up.

"All right, all right!"

Jake unpinned the pocket, counted out about half of the currency and handed the bills to Ike.

"Here's your money, Captain."

The captain reached into the inside pocket of his uniform and placed a piece of paper in Ike's palm.

"And here's your receipt."

"Just a minute, *Isaac.*" Gallagher looked around at his men, then back at Big Ike. "Don't put that receipt in your pocket."

"Why not?"

"Because I'll tell you what you're going to do instead, *Isaac.*"

"Tell me."

"You're going to sell me that cargo, one hundred barrels, at seven dollars a barrel."

"Before or after you break my arm?"

"That's up to you."

Sean Dolan and his miners, consisting of not quite as large a contingent as Gallagher and his teamsters, had arrived on the wharf and were privy to the latter part of the proceedings.

"Any trouble, Big Ike?" Dolan enquired pleasantly.

"Am I glad to see you," Jake said enthusiastically.

Ike put the cargo receipt within the inner pocket of his tan canvas jacket.

"No trouble."

"Big Ike?" Gallagher chortled. "Did you hear that boys? *Big* Ike! He don't look so *big* to me."

And with that proclamation Gallagher shoved Ike, who responded with a swift left cross to Gallagher's jaw.

Gallagher almost went down—almost—but not quite. He rushed back at Ike and that ignited a battle worthy of Ares, Mars, Odin, Tyr and all the war gods combined. The best knuckle-buster the port of La Paz could remember. Fists against flesh. Boards against bone. Heads against heads. Elbows, boots and blood. Dolan's miners against Gallagher's teamsters.

On the wharf and into the water, men dropped, got up and dropped again. And all the while Ike was outpunching Gallagher.

Obie tugged at Jake's sleeve as Jake picked up an axe handle.

"Uncle Jake, is Daddy going to hurt that man?"

"I hope so!"

A fight is not about who is right, a philosopher once noted, it is about who is left. There weren't many of Gallagher's men left on their feet when the shotgun blast went off into the air.

A man wearing a marshal's badge stepped forward holding a double-barreled scattergun with his finger on the second trigger of the weapon. He would have been a noticeable man even if he weren't carrying a shotgun, but with the weapon he commanded immediate attention and respect.

He was a square-built man with a square-built face, hunter green eyes between a prominent nose, under which flourished an even more prominent winged mustache.

"That'll do, boys. My name's Jonas Trapp. Marshal Jonas Trapp. Now you can quit fightin' and go to drinkin', *or* you can go to jail."

Peace prevailed.

Marshal Jonas Trapp turned and walked away as the sea of spectators parted in respectful silence.

Ike smiled at Dolan.

"Thanks."

"Any time." Dolan wiped the blood from his mouth.

"Well, Jake,"—Ike turned to his brother—"looks like we own a hundred barrels of flour."

"Congratulations." Jake nodded. "How are we going to get 'em to Prescott?"

"I've got an idea."

"You and your ideas got us into this pickle in the first place."

"Sean," Ike said, "you and your boys might want to come along."

"Sure. Where to?"

"A journey of two hundred miles starts with a first step."

CHAPTER SIX

Herb Kokernut put the roll of bills into his pocket and smiled.

"Mister Silver, you just bought yourself some wagons and teams."

"And left us bankrupt," Jake added.

"Not quite." Ike smiled.

"Close enough. Good thing we won that poker game last night."

"'Course," Herb Kokernut added with a wry glance at the wagons, "they do need a little repair."

"So does his head," Jake said.

"But," Kokernut shrugged, "they *were* the only wagons for sale in La Paz."

"I repeat," Jake said, "we're—"

"Never mind, Jake, just wait 'til we get to Fort Whipple."

"*If.*"

Jake kicked the wheel of one of the wagons. The wheel collapsed, bringing down part of the wagon.

"I can fix those wagons," a voice said from behind them.

Ike, Jake, Jed, Obie, Dolan and his men all reacted as the man stepped forward.

Ike recognized him as the black man who had been at the livery earlier. Behind him in the distance, the man's wife and son watched from their wagon.

The man came closer and stopped in front of Ike and Jake.

"What are you?" Jake asked. "A magician?"

"I'm a blacksmith."

"Maybe he is." Herb Kokernut shrugged. "Been tryin' to talk me into lettin' him fix them wagons all morning."

Ike looked from Kokernut to the black man.

"I'm Ike Silver. My brother and my boys."

"Ben Brown." He motioned toward the wagon. "My wife and son."

"How much do you want," Jake inquired, "to fix these junk piles?"

"Understand you're going to Prescott. We'd like to ride along that far."

"What do you need us for?" Jake said. "You've got a wagon."

"Better odds against . . ."

"Apaches?" Ike smiled.

Ben nodded.

"Okay." Jake nodded toward the wagons. "But how much to fix them?"

"That's the price." Ben shrugged.

"That's more than fair," Ike said. "How long will it take to get them rolling?"

"Tomorrow soon enough?"

"Too soon." Ike smiled. "Can't be done."

"Yes, it can." Dolan stepped up next to Ben Brown. "If he has some help. Me and the boys'll pitch in. We want to roll just as soon as you do."

"You don't object to that, do you?" Ike looked at the blacksmith.

"No, sir, Mister Silver."

"They call me Ike." He smiled.

"I'd rather call you Mister Silver."

"All right . . . Mister Brown."

CHAPTER SEVEN

The lobby of the Grand Eden Hotel—which was less than grand and certainly no Eden—was filled with guests and others who wanted to register as guests.

Ike, Jake and the boys stood listening as Sister Mary Boniface spoke to the owner of the Grand Eden Hotel, a man who had the appearance of a well-dressed scarecrow.

"But Mister Peevy, even for just one night until I can make other arrangements . . ."

"You'll have to make other arrangements right now. The Grand Eden doesn't have any vacancies for you or anybody else. Now, please, lady, I'm busy—"

"But, Mister Peevy—"

"Why don't you try the mission? They ought to take you in, you being—"

"The mission is miles away and I've got to be in La Paz in case the stagecoach—"

"I said I'm busy."

"Just a second, Mister Peevy." Ike removed his hat

and stepped up beside Sister Mary Boniface. "Excuse me, Sister."

"Oh, hello again, Mister . . ."

"Silver. Ike Silver." Big Ike took a wallet from his jacket and placed it on the counter next to the registration ledger. "Are you certain that there is nothing available at any price . . . for just one night?"

"Well . . ."

"Please look again."

"For one night, you say?"

"That's right."

"Well . . . there is a master suite I'm holding until tomorrow when the next ship arrives. Mister Kensington has reserved—"

"How much is the master suite?"

"Uh . . ."—Mister Peevy glanced at the wallet next to the registration ledger—". . . one hundred dollars for the night."

"Ike!" Jake shook his head.

"And how many bedrooms in the master suite?"

"Three."

"I see. Jake . . ."

"Isaac! We're down to our last—"

"Jake . . ."—Ike put the wallet back into his jacket pocket—"pay Mister Peevy the money and sign the register."

"Madness!" Jake exclaimed and reached inside his coat.

Sister Mary Boniface lifted the small traveling bag she had placed on the floor and started to turn away.

"Where are you going, Sister?" Ike asked.

"To tell the truth, Mister Silver, I don't really know."

"I do. Mister Peevy, what is the number of the master suite?"

"Why, uh . . . two-twelve."

"Sister, there are three bedrooms in suite two-twelve. Would you consider—"

"Hold on, Mister Silver," sputtered Peevy. "There are certain proprieties at the Grand Eden and—"

"Are there locks on the bedroom doors, Mister Peevy?"

"Yes, but . . . Oh, I see, well—"

"Sister, my brother and I only need one bedroom, the boys another. That leaves one room vacant. Would you care to fill the vacancy?"

"Mister Silver . . ."

"Yes, Sister?"

"The room is no longer vacant . . . on one condition."

"What condition is that, Sister?"

"That I pay my fair share."

"What would you consider fair?"

"Would . . . one dollar be enough?"

"On one condition." Ike smiled.

"What condition is that, Mister Silver?"

"That you donate that dollar to the next poor box you come across."

CHAPTER EIGHT

Later that day, the party of five—Isaac, Jacob, Jedediah, Obadiah Silver and Sister Mary Boniface—had settled into master suite 212. They unpacked only what they needed that night. Sister Mary Boniface had very little to unpack.

"Sister," Ike said, "what are your plans for staying somewhere after tonight? You know, we're all going to have to move out in the morning."

"Yes, I heard what Mister Peevy said."

"And I heard him mention a mission a few miles away. Is that where you're going to stay until a stage—"

"Mister Silver, 'Give us this day . . .' "

"That's very optimistic, Sister."

"And very true."

"Speaking of daily bread, would you care to supper with us at one of the restaurants?"

"No, thank you. I have provisions in my traveling bag."

"You can't have many provisions," Jake said, "in that little—"

"I'll be fine." Sister Mary Boniface looked toward

the boys. "Jedediah, Obadiah, it was nice to meet you—and both Mister Silvers, I thank you for your kindness and hospitality and bid you good night, you'll be in my prayers."

She walked toward her room, opened the door, entered and locked the door behind her.

After supper, Jake and the boys retired to master suite 212. Ike stopped by the livery to see how things were progressing. Under the direction of Ben Brown, things seemed to be progressing satisfactorily. It also seemed that Ben Brown was damn good at his profession.

Ike decided to have a quiet drink before turning in. There was a plethora of saloons to choose from in La Paz. He passed several until he found one that seemed the least noisy, the Appaloosa, and entered.

A curling haze of smoke from cigarettes, pipes and cigars settled against anything it could find—the bar, the tables, the posts that held the place together and the people who stood at the counter or sat at the tables playing cards.

The floor had not been swept from the night before, nor the week before. The customary piano player played the customary songs while nobody seemed to be paying much attention to the musical entertainment.

Ike found a space at the bar and ordered a bourbon. The bartender poured and before Ike could lift the glass someone elbowed his way next to him and spoke in a stentorian tone.

"I beg your pardon, kind sir."

Ike Silver turned and looked at the someone. Though not tall, he was imposing, if a bit bleary-eyed, wearing a once proud suit that had gone to seed, as had the man's face, a face topped by a cocked vintage bowler. Still, there were the remnants of regal bearing and dignity in his mien.

"I am Basil Binkham."

"Ike Silver. Pleased to meet you."

"I hope so, kind sir, I sincerely hope so . . . and if so . . ."—Basil Binkham glanced at the glass of bourbon on the bar—". . . I wonder if I might cadge a drink in exchange for a recitation of any of your favorite quotations . . . since you appear to be, unlike . . ."—Binkham motioned around the room—"the other patrons of this benighted parlor, a gentleman of refinement and appreciation of the arts, I—"

"That's quite all right, Mister Binkham, I'd be pleased to buy you a drink." Ike smiled and nodded to the bartender. "And the recitation is not necessary."

The bartender poured, Binkham swallowed the bourbon, set the glass on the bar and looked from Ike back at the empty glass.

"Oh, no! I insist! *Quid pro quo!* Just one more libation for ballast and we'll sally forth into the libretto."

Ike motioned to the bartender, who poured again and Binkham forthwith swallowed the libation.

"Now then, kind sir, what is your pleasure? Shakespeare? Yes, there is a Shakespearean aspect about you. . . . *Hamlet*, yes, *Hamlet* it shall be!"

Basil Binkham peered at the empty glass.

"And perhaps one more . . . after the curtain goes up. Yes, *Hamlet*, Act Two, Scene Two . . .

'Oh what a rogue and peasant slave am I!
Is it not monstrous, that this player here,
But in a fiction, in a dream of passion,
Could force his soul so to his own conceit,
That from her working, all his visage wann'd;
Tears his eyes, distraction in's aspect . . .'"

Basil Binkham paused and starred at the empty glass. Ike nodded and the bartender poured. Binkham drank and continued even louder.

"'...A broken voice and his whole function suiting—'"

"Hey, Binky! Shut up, goddammit! I'm trying to play poker!"

One of the poker players, a sizable man in a red flannel shirt sitting at the nearest table, pointed at Basil Binkham.

"I can't concentrate with all that bullshit going on!"

Binkham lowered his voice somewhat and continued."

"'...With forms to his conceit?'...and, and... I'm sorry, sir...." Binkham lowered his head "I can't seem to—"

"'And all for nothing.'" Ike smiled and picked up the speech. "'For Hecuba! What's Hecuba to him and he to Hecuba, that he should weep for her? What would he do...'"

"Ah, yes!" Binkham nodded. "I'll, I'll carry on—

"'Had he the motive and the cue for passion that I have? He would drown the stage—'"

"Dammit!" The poker player rose, kicked the chair away and rushed at Binkham. "I'm losing money here and I don't intend to..."—he grabbed Binkham by the shirt with one hand and slapped him hard twice with the other—"listen to your bullshit!"

Ike spun the poker player by the shoulder and slapped him twice, hard.

The poker player swung a heavy right fist. Ike took the blow on his left forearm and countered with a stiff smash to the poker player's jaw that sent him sprawling first onto the card table, then onto the dirty floor.

Once again, Marshal Jonas Trapp appeared out of nowhere, this time without a shotgun, but still with plenty of authority.

"Mister,"—Trapp squinted at Ike Silver—"you seem to gravitate toward trouble."

"Marshal, I—"

"Never mind. I saw it." Trapp looked at the unconscious poker player on the floor. "Schultz is a mean sonofabitch and had it comin', but when are you leavin' La Paz?"

"Tomorrow, Marshal."

"Adios . . . and,"—he pointed at Basil Binkham—"why don't you take Binky with you?"

Marshal Jonas Trapp walked toward the door.

"I'm sorry, sir," Binkham said. "I didn't intend to cause trouble."

"No trouble." Ike smiled.

"Nevertheless. Thank you and . . . good night, sweet prince."

CHAPTER NINE

In La Paz, as in most frontier towns from the Rio Grande to the Canadian River, from the Mississippi to the Colorado, every night was a holiday—a holiday to be celebrated in saloons with whiskey and women. Both made the customers shudder and shake, forget and remember—the best hope this side of the grave; illusions by night to face the demands of the day. But with the morning in those frontier towns, including La Paz, the nightly holiday always ended and the daily dawn of reality began again.

But the previous night had been no holiday for Ben Brown, who with Sean Dolan and the miners at the livery, repaired wagons, wheels, harnesses and traces. Brown spoke to the men only when something needed to be said or done. Unlike Dolan and the miners, he never laughed or even smiled; but he worked and set the pace for the other workers to follow. And just before first light, Melena appeared with baskets containing fried chicken and other edibles.

Ike Silver had provided her with the raw materials and she had done the rest.

And so Ben Brown and the miners had worked by lanterns until there was no need for lanterns to work by—and until the work was done.

The wagons were hitched to animals and driven to the dock, where Ike Silver had hired laborers to help load the cargo of flour.

At the dock, a line of wagons was already strung out. On each wagon, a neatly lettered sign: R. LESSUR—FREIGHTING. R. Lessur's wagons were empty and Gallagher and his men stood nearby watching the patched-up carriers being filled with barrels of flour.

"How the hell did them bastards get them wagons?" Rooster Priner asked his immediate superior, Jim Gallagher.

"How the hell do I know." Gallagher was in no mood for conjecture or conversation. He knew that his superior, R. Lessur, would be in an even darker mood if the cargo of flour was not delivered as anticipated. R. Lessur was not in the habit of having his orders not carried out, and the few times that had happened the consequences were not pleasant.

Jim Gallagher pulled the makings out of his shirt pocket and began to build himself a cigarette.

"Boss, are we—"

"Rooster, just shut up and let me think! I'll let you know when to talk." Gallagher stuck the cigarette into his swollen mouth. "Gimme a match."

"Sure, boss."

Ben Brown drove up to the wharf in his wagon and stepped off, while his wife and son stayed aboard.

Ike, Jake, Jedediah and Obie stood and watched as the other wagons were being loaded.

"Mister Silver . . ."

"Yes, Mister Brown?"

"There's room in my wagon for some of that cargo if you need it."

"Thanks." Ike pointed to the patched-up caravan. "Will those wagons make it to Prescott, Mister Brown?"

"They might."

"They better."

Sean Dolan approached, wiping the sweat from his face.

"Gettin' close, Ike."

"Good. Say, Sean, I meant to ask you, isn't there enough gold for you to dig in California? What made you leave and come to Arizona?"

"Well, Ike, in California I'm just a miner. In Arizona I'm a partner. You're lookin' at the part-owner of the Rattlesnake Mine."

"Very enterprising."

"You bet your boots. I got to start thinkin' about my old age—just in case I have an old age."

He turned and walked back toward the dock.

Ike looked at Ben Brown.

"What about you?"

"What *about* me?"

"Are you going to settle in Prescott?"

Brown shook his head no.

"Heading north?"

Brown looked away from Ike and toward his family on the wagon.

"South?" Ike asked.

Brown just kept looking in silence.

"Don't talk much, do you?"

"Just when I'm talked to."

There was another moment of silence.

"All right. Why don't you ask your family to step down while your wagon gets loaded?"

"I'll do that."

Ben Brown walked toward his family.

"Ike, my dear brother, you know something?"

"What's that?"

"Never mind." Jake shrugged. "You already know."

Yes, Ike already knew, and he thought about it as he watched Ben Brown walk toward his wife and son in the wagon. And as he did, Ike saw a familiar figure coming toward them followed not far behind by another familiar figure.

The first figure carried a sawed-off shotgun. The second figure looked like he was carrying the effects of a monumental hangover.

"Morning, Marshal."

"Good morning, Mister Silver."

"Anything wrong?"

"Nope. And I intend to keep it that way."

"I don't understand."

Marshal Trapp nodded toward Gallagher and his men near Lessur's wagon. "They give you any trouble?"

"Not so far."

"They will."

"What makes you think so?"

"Don't think so—know so. Know them and their kind. It's happened before when Lessur's men didn't get what Lessur wanted."

"Who's this Lessur?"

"You'll find out soon enough. But I'm going to stick around here to make sure nothing unpleasant happens until you leave my territory. After that, Mister Silver, you and your companions are on your own."

"That's very good of you, Marshal."

"It's my job and I'm good at it."

"I don't doubt it." Ike smiled.

"There are those who have . . . temporarily. Now I'm just going to meander over to that bale of cotton over there and smoke my morning cigar. You boys go about your business like nothing's going to happen, because nothing will. Not 'til you leave La Paz anyhow."

Marshal Trapp walked toward the bale of cotton and Basil Binkham took a step forward.

"Good morning, Mister Silver."

"Good morning, Mister Binkham. Oh, this is my brother, Isaac, my two sons, Jed and Obie."

"Grand meeting you all . . . and once again, I am beholden to you, kind sir, for your *beau jeste* last night. . . ."

"What's he talking about, Ike?" Jake asked.

"It was nothing."

"It was gallant and I repeat, I am beholden."

"That why you came to see us off?"

"I'm not here to see you off."

"What then?"

"Don't you remember the marshal's dictum?"

"What dictum is that?"

"That you take me with you, of course."

"He wasn't serious."

"But I am. My carpet bag is all packed and ready for the road to Prescott."

"Mister Binkham—"

"You might as well call me Binky, everybody else does."

"All right then, Binky—"

"Good, I'm glad you say it's all right."

"That's not what I meant. . . ."

"Please, sir, there's nothing for me here in La Paz. I propose to make a new start in Prescott, and in the meanwhile you'll find me of some service on the journey."

"You a teamster, Binky?" Ike said, smiling.

"Hardly."

"Then what service?"

"I play many parts. Hamlet, Macbeth, Othello, Richard, Falstaff—"

"This is not a road show. It's serious and dangerous."

"All the more reason for a court jester. Besides, you probably saved my life last night, and therefore you are responsible for my welfare . . . at least until Prescott. I beseech you . . ."

"Ike, let him come," Jake said. "What's the harm? And we could use a little diversion."

"Bravo, brother Jacob!" Binky proclaimed.

"Okay! Okay! I know when I'm licked. But once we get to Prescott, we bid you *adieu*."

"And parting will be such sweet sorrow . . . meanwhile, there is a nearby emporium where my credit might still be good. I shall return!"

Binky bowed and walked away.

"You think he will? Return, I mean." Jake smiled.

"Depends."

"On what?"

"How good his credit is."

"Dad?"

"Yes, Jed."

"Are those people going to Prescott with us?" Jedediah pointed to Ben Brown and his family near their wagon.

"Yes, they certainly are."

"Can Obie and I go over and say hello to the little boy?"

"Don't see why not."

"Sure, go ahead," Jake said, "I'll be over myself in just a minute."

"Come on, Obie."

Both boys walked toward the Brown's wagon as it was being loaded with three barrels of flour, stacked along with the Brown family's possessions.

Ben Brown and his wife were a few feet away from the wagon talking and on the near side their son played with a homemade yo-yo, making it "walk."

"Hi," the older brother said. "My name's Jed and he's Obie. What's your name?"

The young boy stopped playing with the yo-yo, looked at them for a moment, then made a decision. He decided to put the yo-yo in his pocket.

"What's your name?" Jed asked again.

"Name's Benjie."

"What's that thing, Benjie?" Obie inquired.

"What thing?"

"That thing you just put in your pocket."

"Oh, that." Benjie started to walk away. "I got to go."

"Wait a minute," Obie said.

"It's mine." Benjie put his hand over his pocket.

"We knew that." Jed shrugged. "But what is it?"

"Could we see it?" Obie asked.

"Do you want it?" Benjie's hand was still protecting his pocket.

"Just to see it," Obie answered.

"Yeah, that's what *they* said."

"Who?" Jed looked into Benjie's wide-open eyes.

"Those boys who took it away from me."

"But you still got it."

"This is another one. My Pa made me another one. He can make anything. I got to go. . . ."

"Wait a minute," Jed said. "We've never seen one before. What do you call it?"

"Call it a yo-yo."

"What do you do with it?"

"Do a lot of things."

"Show us."

"I got to go."

"Where are you going?"

"Huh?"

"I said where are you going? You're coming to Prescott with us, aren't you?"

"I guess. Got to go and talk to my Ma and Pa."

Benjie walked away with his hand still over the pocket.

Jake Silver had been watching and listening to most of the exchange. He walked closer to his nephews.

"Uncle Jake," Obie asked, "what's the matter with him?"

"Boys, it would take a couple hundred years to explain."

Ike Silver had just taken his pipe out of his pocket when he saw him coming.

As the poker player from last night approached, Ike put the pipe back into his pocket.

"You remember me?" There was a dire look in the poker player's eyes and a blue swelling on the right side of his jaw.

"Mister Shultz, isn't it?"

"You snuck-punched me last night, you remember that?"

"I remember you were out of line. . . ."

"You snuck-punched me you sonofabitch!"

"I'm nobody's sonofabitch."

"I say you are. You snuck-punched me in front of

my friends." Shultz put up both of his fists. "But I'm lookin' right at you now, you sonofabitch, so what're you gonna do about it?"

"I might walk away. And then again . . . I might not."

Ike feinted a left and crossed with a cannonading right that landed on the exact same swollen blue spot, this time with an audible crunch, and it was all over. Shultz dropped like a shot buffalo. And lay still.

Marshal Jonas Trapp, still smoking his morning cigar, eased closer and peered at the inert form on the dock.

"Marshal, you saw him coming, didn't you?" Ike said. "Knew what he had in mind. Could've stopped him."

"I could've."

"Why didn't you?"

"Don't like him."

Basil Binkham reappeared and Sister Mary Boniface stood next to him. Binky looked down at Shultz.

"I say," he exclaimed, "isn't this where I came in last night?"

Sister Mary Boniface took a step forward.

"Mister Silver, I saw you hit that man."

"Yes, Sister. Just as hard as I could."

Marshal Trapp's boot prodded Shultz as he began to stir.

"Mister Silver, do you want to lodge a complaint against this . . . man?"

"No, Marshal, I don't."

"Shultz, can you hear me?"

"Uh . . . yeah, Marshal, I . . . I hear you."

"Then get outta here before I sic him on you again. Go on, git."

Shultz managed to wobble to his feet and make his way through the crowd and out of sight.

Marshal Trapp took a puff from his cigar and walked back toward the bale of cotton.

By now Ike was surrounded by Jake, Jed, Obie, Sean Dolan and the rest of Dolan's miners, who were all enthusiastically commenting on Ike Silver's one-punch knockout—all but Sister Mary Boniface.

"Dad, you sure socked him one!" Obie.

"A sweeter punch I never seen!" Dolan.

"A veritable ballet!" Binky.

"Ike, one of these days you're gonna hurt your hand!" Jake.

"Mister Silver, I must speak to you now." Sister Mary Boniface.

"All right, Sister Mary Boniface. What about?"

"In the first place, you can call me Sister Bonney, most everybody does—out of the order."

"All right, Sister Bonney, what's the second place?"

"Well, that's the most important thing. I want to go to Prescott with you. . . ."

"Just a minute . . ."

"I can pay the regular stagecoach fare."

Jake, Jedediah, Obadiah and Sean Dolan, who had been listening without too much interest— along with Binky—suddenly became more interested, especially Dolan.

"How do you do, Sister? My name is Dolan, Sean Dolan. Would you believe that I was once a choirboy?"

"Yes, I'm sure you were, and a very good one, too." She turned back to Ike. "But now, Mister Silver, about going to Prescott."

"Well, I . . . I'm sorry. But no."

"Mister Silver, I *have* to get to Prescott!"

"Why?"

"Because the Mother Superior ordered me there."

"And tell us, Sister,"—Sean Dolan smiled,—"what are you going to do in Prescott?"

"Start a school."

"A school!" Dolan nodded and smiled wider. "Did you hear that, Big Ike?"

"No!"

Silence.

Sister Bonney looked at Dolan. Dolan looked at Ike.

"Awww now, Ike." Dolan put on a long face. "You can't say no."

"*No!*"

"Ike!" Dolan all but pleaded.

"It's no trip for a . . . woman."

Sister Bonney looked toward the wagon, where Melena Brown stood beside her husband.

"It appears," Sister Bonney said, "one woman is going."

Ike Silver appeared embarrassed, just for an instant.

"Uh—that's different."

"How different, Mister Silver?"

"Well . . . she's got her man with her."

"So have I," Sister Bonney said softly.

"Ah–ha!" Dolan exclaimed. "She's got you there. And we could use His help, too."

"If I may say a word . . ." Binky took a step forward.

"No, you may not," Ike said.

Binky took a step backward.

Ike looked at Jake.

"What are you looking at me for? You want to start a religious war?"

Silence.

Ike looked back at Sister Bonney and shrugged.

"Where's your luggage?"

"Right here." She held up the traveling bag and started to reach inside. "And here's my fare."

"Never mind the fare. Just say a prayer."

"I already did." Sister Bonney smiled.

"I might've guessed it." Ike nodded. "Oh, by the way, since you two will be traveling together, I suppose you ought to be officially introduced—Mister Basil Binkham, may I present Sister Mary Boniface."

"Sister Boniface." Binkey bowed his curtain call bow while removing his vintage bowler. "On behalf of our entire company, welcome to our vagabond troupe."

"And on behalf of the Order of the Sisters of Charity, I thank you, Mister Binkham."

"Ike," Jake said, "since we've got more passengers than we expected—do you think the provisions we laid in will be enough, or should we—"

"Oh, please," Sister Bonney interrupted, "don't concern yourselves about me. I've enough jerky and salt pork—"

"Pork?" Jake said, surprised.

"Yes, pork, Mister Silver. I hope you don't object."

"Not at all, Sister. What about Fridays? Where you gonna get fish in the desert?"

"On Fridays I'll fast."

"And as for me," Binky smiled, "my diet is mainly liquid."

"We don't carry that kind of liquid," Ike said.

"More's the pity." Binky shrugged. "Howsomever, I'll carry on. Sister . . ."

"Oh, just a minute, Mister Binkham." Sister Bonney had been looking toward the empty wagons where Gallagher and his men were standing. "Mister Silver . . ."

"Please, Sister, call me Ike."

"Yes, Ike, those signs on the wagons over there, they do say Lessur Freighting, don't they? My distant vision is not—"

"Yes, Sister, that's what they say."

"Do you know who's in charge?"

"I do, Sister," Dolan pointed. "That big ugly ape. His name's Gallagher."

"I've got to talk to Mister Gallagher."

"I wouldn't go over there, Sister," Ike counseled.

"Why not?"

"Well, Mister Gallagher is sometimes a little . . . excitable."

"I see. Well, right now he looks quite harmless."

"So does gunpowder," Ike said.

"It'll be quite all right, I just want to ask him something."

"Okay," Ike conceded, "but we'll keep an eye on things."

"I'll be right back," Sister Bonney said, and proceeded toward the empty wagons.

"What do you think all that's about?" Jake asked nobody in particular.

"Don't know," Ike answered, "but I wouldn't worry about it. I don't think she's a spy."

"Neither do I." Dolan smiled. "She reminds me of my fourth grade teacher. That's as far as I got—the fourth grade."

"Excuse me, Mister Gallagher . . ."

"Yeah?" Gallagher turned around with a cigarette in his mouth and faced the young nun.

"I'm Sister Mary Boniface."

"Yeah?"

"I understand that you're employed by Lessur Freighting."

"Yeah, I am." Gallagher looked at the other men near him. "We all are, what about it?"

"Well, I wonder if you can give me some information?"

"What sort of information?" Gallagher cast a suspicious glimpse toward Ike Silver.

"And you do work in Prescott, don't you?"

"Uh . . . most of the time. What sort of information?" he repeated.

"Well, some time ago something was sent from Saint Brendan's in Santa Fe to be delivered by Lessur Freighting to their depot in Prescott."

"What kind of something?"

"A crate containing books and a few personal items."

"What about it?"

"I wonder if you know if it arrived safely? I—"

"How the hell should I know."

"I beg your pardon!"

"I mean, well . . . I mean . . . a lot of stuff gets delivered. . . ."

"I'm only inquiring about this particular crate. It contained—"

"I heard you . . . books and a few personal items."

"That's right. Do you recall—"

"We deliver hundred of crates."

"From Santa Fe?"

"From all over, and I can't keep track of all the junk—"

"Junk? You consider books *junk*?"

"I consider it freight, and I don't know if it got there. Is that where you're going?"

"Yes, it is."

"Then let me ask *you* something."

"Go ahead."

"Do you intend to go with *them?*" Gallagher pointed his cigarette at the patched-up wagons.

"I do."

"I wouldn't."

"Wouldn't what?"

"Go with them."

"Why not?"

"Well ... I just wouldn't ... if I was you. ... That's my advice."

"Thank you for your advice, Mister Gallagher, and I'll see you in Prescott."

When Sean Dolan saw Sister Bonney walk away from Gallagher, he went back to work with the miners and laborers loading the wagons.

Ike left Jake and the boys and moved toward the Brown wagon. Ben was helping the men load the last barrel as Melena and Benjie stood by.

"Morning, Mrs. Brown."

"Morning."

"How you doing, young fella?" Ike smiled at Benjie. "I see you met my two boys."

Benjie barely nodded and looked at the ground.

"He's a little shy," Melena said.

"Mister Brown ..."

Ben Brown made an adjustment on the strap of the last barrel and stepped closer to Ike.

"Yes, Mister Silver? Somethin' I can do?"

"Yes, there is. You can slow down. You've been on your feet all night."

"I'll be sitting on that wagon most of the way to Prescott and—"

"Maybe so and maybe not, it depends. ..."

"On what?"

"On what we come across along the way."

"You mean Apaches?"

Ike nodded. "You have a rifle, Mister Brown?"

"Under the seat of that wagon."

"Cartridges?"

"Some."

"I'll see that you have more before we leave."

"Thanks."

"Mister Silver . . ."

"Yes, Mrs. Brown?"

"I saw the men loading provisions this morning and I was wondering . . ."

"Yes, ma'am?"

"Do you have a cook?"

"Well, some of the miners have done a little cooking . . . not too easy on the stomach, but . . ."

"I've done more than a little cooking, and if it's all right I'd be pleased to do a little more 'til we get to Prescott."

"Well, I'm sure the rest of us would be pleased, too, after the way you fixed things up last night, but only if you let us pay you for your effort."

"Did I hear you say something about cooking?" Sister Bonney said as she approached.

"Oh, Sister Bonney, this is Mister and Mrs. Brown and their son, Benjie."

"How do you do?" Sister Bonney smiled.

"Mrs. Brown has volunteered to take care of the kitchen duties even though we don't have a kitchen."

"And I'd like to volunteer to assist Mrs. Brown. We must all do our share, mustn't we . . . Ike? That is, if Mrs. Brown has no objection. Do you, Mrs. Brown?"

"My name's Melena, and I appreciate your help, Sister."

"Very good. Well, when do we leave, Ike?"

"As soon as the wagons are loaded."

"Good. I'm anxious to get started."

"Yes." Ike smiled. "So am I." He turned and walked back toward Jake and the boys. Sister Bonney followed right behind him.

"Melena?"

"What, Ben?"

"You don't have to do that anymore."

"Do what?"

"Cook for those people."

"I know. Maybe that's why I want to."

Gallagher and Rooster were still watching as all the wagons were nearly loaded.

"Are we gonna deadhead back to Prescott with them empty wagons?"

"No," Gallagher said.

"Then what *are* we gonna do?"

"Leave 'em here and get some horses."

"Horses?"

"Yeah, the kind you ride on."

"Then what?"

"Then we're gonna follow them wagons at a distance." Gallagher tossed away the butt of his cigarette. "We just might get that cargo for Mister Lessur yet."

An hour later the wagons were loaded and ready to roll.

Jake, the boys and Sister Bonney were aboard one of the wagons and Ike was astride a horse next to them.

Marshal Jonas Trapp, carrying his shotgun, approached, not fast, not slow.

"Well, Mister Silver, it appears that you're ready to start."

"That's right, Marshal. And I want to thank you for your help."

"It's my job."

"And you're good at it." Ike smiled.

"I try."

"Not every lawman would've, well . . . we . . . all of us, appreciate the way that you handled this situation, so thanks again."

"Sure. In a way I wish you were staying in La Paz. We could use more people like you around here. Maybe I'll see you again sometime."

"I hope so, Marshal."

Jonas Trapp nodded toward Jake, Sister Bonney and the boys in the wagon, then turned and walked away.

Sean Dolan was also astride a horse. He rode up next to Ike.

"Well, Big Ike, we're ready as we'll ever be."

"Guess so."

Dolan looked around the wharf. Besides the people who worked, or would normally be there, there were dozens of men and women and even children who would normally be someplace else, but had come to watch the caravan leave on what most of them thought was a fool's parade.

Basil Binkham stood up on the wagon just behind Jake's.

"I say there, Ike. Haven't had as large an audience as this since coming to the colonies! Well . . . tallyho!"

Ike looked at his brother.

"All right, Jake, here we go again."

"Just a minute, Ike." Sean Dolan looked at Sister Bonney, who was holding a rosary in her hand. "Would you, Sister?"

Sister Bonney nodded.

"Saint Christopher . . ." she began. The rest of the words were brief and inaudible until she looked up and smiled. "Well, Ike Silver, it's like the Old Testament."

"What do you mean, Sister Bonney?"

"Moses leading his people to the Promised Land."

"It took Moses forty years, Sister."

"But,"—Sister Mary Boniface held up the rosary—"he didn't have Saint Christopher with him."

CHAPTER TEN

"Ike," Jake said, "this is the most cockeyed caravan
that ever existed."

"You think so?"

"I think so—if we were Irish I'd say we got a mulligan stew."

"What's wrong with mulligan stew?"

"Don't interrupt. Look at the ingredients—a
naïve young lady with beads, a couple ex-slaves
with a little *yingl*, an alcoholic actor, a bunch of
rowdy miners—going to a place we've never been
before across country with wild Apaches inclined to
scalp us and likely eat our livers. . . . Yes, brother . . .
a cockeyed caravan!"

Apache is the word for enemy. And the Apaches
were the enemy of those who crossed into their territory. For centuries those enemies were red. Comanches, Kiowas and other tribes who dared
trespass. But with the birth of a new nation came
another enemy—an enemy of a different color—
that encroached on their ancient domain.

And unseen Apache eyes watched as Ike Silver

and his caravan moved deeper into that domain that with every mile became more ragged and wild; and far behind that caravan there were others who waited and watched—Jim Gallagher and company.

"Hold up there! Hold up!" It was Ben Brown's voice and he moved his wagon up alongside the wagon with Jake, the boys and Sister Bonney.

Jake pulled up and looked across at Ben.

"What's wrong?"

"That back wheel of yours looks a little wobbly. I want to check something."

Brown came off his wagon holding a hammer in his hand.

Ike Silver reined up close by.

"Anything wrong?"

"Want to take a look at that wheel."

"Sure thing."

The blacksmith inspected the rear right wheel, then whacked it a couple of times with the hammer.

"Loose pin. Ought to be all right now."

"Much obliged," Ike said.

"Benjie," Sister Bonney called out. "Why don't you ride up here with us for a while?"

The boy looked for a response from his father. There was none.

"Come on," Sister Bonney beckoned. "We're telling stories."

"It's all right, Benjie," Melena affirmed from the wagon. "Go ahead."

Benjie still looked at his father, who stood between the wagons with the hammer in his hand.

Ben Brown nodded.

The boy climbed down and started past his father, hesitated, then stopped. He put his hand in his pocket and whispered.

"Pa, will you hold the yo-yo?"

"No."

"Climb aboard, Benjie," Jake called out. "We're falling behind the rest of the wagons." He reached his hand down to help.

Reluctantly, Benjie moved closer, took Jake's extended hand and made his way up next to the others.

"Thanks again." Jake nodded toward Ben Brown and snapped the reins.

The wagon started to roll.

"Yes, Mister Brown,"—Ike smiled—"thanks."

"You're welcome, Mister Silver." Ben walked toward his wagon as Ike rode forward to the head of the caravan.

"Now then, boys, what kind of a story would you like to hear?"

"Tell us a ghost story this time, Sister Bonney." Obie sprang up and down on the seat.

"Obadiah," Jake said, "be more respectful. I think you boys ought to call her Sister Mary Bon—"

"Oh, no, that's all right. The children at the orphanage all called me Sister Bonney, too."

"Well, then, Sister Bonney,"—Jake nodded,—"go ahead and tell us that ghost story . . . before it gets dark."

"Well, once upon a time there were three little boys—"

"Like us?" Obie asked.

"Just like you, but they lived in a faraway land called Gloomo Loomo. . . ."

Behind the caravan the sun began to cast longer shadows as it dipped toward the saw-tooth boulders to the west. And among the boulders, Gallagher, Rooster and the rest of Lessur's teamsters watched from horseback.

"Looks like they'll be making camp by them rocks," Gallagher said.

"Yeah," Rooster lifted his hat and wiped at the sweat and dirt on his forehead. "What're we gonna do?"

"Nothin' . . . yet."

" '. . . He jests at scars who never felt a wound
But soft what light through yonder window breaks.
It is the east, and Juliet is the sun!
Arise, fair sun and kill the envious moon . . .' "

For nearly half an hour after supper, as they all sat around the campfire, Basil Binkham had been reciting the story of Romeo and Juliet—and playing both roles.

" '. . . It is my lady; O, it is my love!' "

In both voices.

" '. . . O Romeo! Romeo! Wherefore art thou Romeo?
It is my soul that calls upon my name.
Good night, good night: parting is such sweet sorrow,
That I shall say good night till it be morrow.
Sleep dwell upon thine eyes, peace in thy breast!
Would that I were sleep and peace, so sweet to
rest!' "

Basil Binkham bowed.

"And so, ladies and gentlemen . . . and children, Romeo and Juliet were married and lived happily ever after—at least in this abridged version—and so, I bid you all good night. No applause please—you may praise me later."

As usual, Ike heard the boys say their prayers and kissed them good night.

Sister Bonney had stood just far enough and close enough to watch and listen.

Ike waited until the boys settled in under their blankets, then turned and walked toward the campfire.

Sister Bonney followed. "You can be proud of them. They're good kids."

"It hasn't been easy for them."

"Or for you. Being mother and father."

"A man can get used to anything . . . mostly."

"Some men." She smiled.

Ike said nothing for a moment.

"Good night, Sister." He walked away from the fire and Sister Bonney.

As she watched him move into the darkness, Jake came up and stood beside her.

"There was never a man more in love with a woman."

"When did she . . . ?"

"When Obie was born . . . in England. Things were just beginning to go good . . . after all the hell—uh, excuse me, Sister—he went through getting himself, then me out of the old country. He put himself through the University of London, met Rachel there—the sweetest girl in the world, or at least in his world. And so after she died he decided to come to a new world and brought us with him. . . ."

"To California?"

"Until the war broke out."

"He fought in the war?"

Jake nodded.

"He hated slavery . . . you know, Sister, our people, for a long time, were in bondage."

"Yes, I know."

"All the way across the country he went and fought with the Army of the Tennesse under General Grant, now President Grant. Ike was with him when St. Louis fell, then Fort Henry and Fort Donelson . . . rose to the rank of captain, but the most decisive battle was yet to be fought at a place called Shiloh. The Confederates called it Pittsburg Landing . . . and it turned out to be the bloodiest battle, so far, for both sides."

"Yes, I've heard that."

"The commander of Ike's brigade fell dead during the charge. Ike picked up his sword and led that brigade through the holocaust until the Confederate ranks broke and retreated in defeat. But Ike was severely wounded. . . ."

"Oh, Lord."

"Of course, we didn't hear about leading that charge from Ike. One of the other men who was there told us when they both got back. Ike got a medal, and a discharge, and the boys got a father again."

"And you, your brother."

"That's right, Sister. There were close to twenty-five thousand men dead and missing at Shiloh on both sides . . . they say that after Shiloh, the South never smiled again. And you know something, Sister? Shiloh is a Hebrew word."

"No, I didn't know that."

"Twenty-five thousand men dead . . . and something else you didn't know, Sister, in Hebrew—Shiloh means 'place of peace' . . . sometimes . . . I wonder."

"We all do."

"Even you?"

There was a moment of silence. Only a moment.

"If we knew all the answers, Jake, then what would faith be for?"

Jake smiled and nodded.

Neither Jake Silver nor Sister Bonney was aware that Ben Brown had been nearby.

Near enough to hear what had been said.

At the edge of the camp, close to a boulder, Ike Silver stood with his watch in his hand, listening to the melody. He closed the lid, put the watch in his pocket, and turned to face someone an arm's length away.

Eyes searing, a blotch of blood on his body, his face a blazonry of pain, his arm upraised holding a jagged rock poised to strike.

Colorados.

CHAPTER ELEVEN

Ike Silver could have moved. Could have gone for his gun. But he didn't, not yet.

Colorados shuddered, wavered, and collapsed as Ike reached out and grabbed him before he hit the ground.

"Sean! Jake!"

Ike still held on to him as the men he had called out to and a few more, including Ben Brown and Binky, appeared from the darkness, and with them Sister Bonney and Melena.

"Great thunderin' hallelujah!" Sean ran up to help Ike hold on to the unconscious Apache.

"Dead?" Jake asked.

"Not yet."

"Zounds!" Binky leaned closer to get a better look at the red man whose body was even redder with blood from the wound. " 'Tis not so deep as a well, nor wide as a church door, but 'tis enough, 'twil serve."

"Are you all right?" Sister Bonney looked at Ike. Ike nodded.

"Let's see what we can do for him."

Sean Dolan and Ben, with the help of a couple of the other men, lifted the inert form and started to carry him away.

"You know who he is, don't you?" Ben glanced back at Ike.

"I do."

From the distance a howl cut through the night and was answered from another direction.

"Coyotes . . ." Jake blinked at his brother.

"I hope so."

CHAPTER TWELVE

Both Sister Bonney and Melena did what they could to stanch the bleeding and ease the pain. The red man could not be left behind, but the caravan could not stay in the desert and wait for him to heal . . . or die.

Not long after first light and the morning meal, the wagons were on the move again, moving toward the searchlight of sun that rose above the eastern horizon.

Colorados was only one wounded Apache. But Ike knew that the escaped prisoner from a white man's cell was desperately making his way into the Apache homeland—and so was the caravan. And the Apache chief was only one of hundreds of Apache warriors. Ike had heard tales about these Apaches; maybe those tales were exaggerated, maybe not.

The caravan could only cover fifteen or twenty miles a day with their loaded wagons. But it was said that Apache warriors could make forty-five miles a day on foot, seventy-five on horseback, and when his horse fell dead, the Apache would eat it and steal another.

Often the Apache preferred to move and fight on foot. Over much of the terrain the horse was a handicap rather than an asset. The Apache was swift and noiseless and better off without some stupid animal who might snort or whinny at an inappropriate time—or leave tracks. The Apache warrior needed less food and water than the cumbersome mount he rode. He was a smaller, less vulnerable target on foot with cat-like speed and silence. But when he did use the animal in fighting or fleeing, the Apache was almost as good as his Comanche cousin, whose cavalry proficiency was peerless.

Afoot or mounted, in alkali-dry desert or on sun-blanched promontory, the Apache weighed in as the most dreaded, defiant enemy ever encountered by the United States Army.

And the United States Army was nowhere near.

How near the Apaches were was uncertain.

The cargo of Ben's wagon had been shifted to make room for Colorados, who had been ministered to, but still lay unconscious. Sister Bonney was next to him, placing a damp cloth on the Indian's brow.

Melena and Ben looked back, then toward Big Ike, who rode up next to the wagon.

"Has he come to, Sister?"

"Not yet. He lost an awful lot of blood."

"He sure did." Ike looked toward Ben. "Ride him easy, Mister Brown." Ike smiled and rode toward the other wagons.

"That Indian tried to kill him," Ben said to Melena, "and he says 'ride him easy.' He's a peculiar one."

"Maybe not so peculiar."

Sister Bonney turned to get another cloth from a water bucket.

In that instant Colorados's eyes opened. He had heard. His eyes darted toward the nun, then closed just before she moved back to him.

Ike caught up to the wagon with Jake, Jed and Obie, and rode alongside. Jake pointed back toward Ben's wagon.

"How's your friend, the Indian?"

"Can't tell yet."

"Well, I'll tell you something."

"I'm sure you will."

"You're a little nuts. More than a little, Mister Silver."

"Is that so?"

"Yes, that's so . . . and so are the rest of us. If I thought this caravan was cockeyed before, now I know it!"

"What would you have me do? Let him die?"

"It's not just that."

"What else?"

"We shoulda gone to San Francisco like I wanted—where they got pastrami, pickles and people instead of rocks and reptiles. Do you know what today is?"

"I do."

"In San Francisco we could go to temple. You see any temples around here? I don't, brother."

Big Ike looked toward the cathedral-like boulders flanking one side of the caravan, then back at Jake.

"Don't you, brother?" Ike smiled and rode ahead.

"Obie,"—Jed pushed at his brother—"will you quit leaning on me?"

"I'm not." Obie pushed back.

"Yes, you are."

"No, I'm not."

"Obie . . ."

"Jedediah," Jake said, "don't argue with your brother."

"You argue with *your* brother."

"That's different."

"Why?"

"Because . . . because I'm older and wiser."

Jedediah started to answer.

"Don't say anything."

He didn't.

CHAPTER THIRTEEN

That night Colorados managed to sit up and lean against the side of the wagon. Near him, food. Untouched.

From a distance Sister Bonney had watched as he lay in the wagon after the others had left, watched him stir, try to rise, then put his head down again on the rolled blanket she had provided as a pillow.

Later she brought a plate of rabbit stew and a tin cup of coffee, placed it next to him and walked back to the campfire.

Around the campfire were Ike, Jake, the three boys, Ben, Melena, Binky, Dolan and the miners.

Jake had just finished lighting the last candle on the menorah.

"If the rest of you will bear with us, it's Rosh Hashanah, one of our holiest times, the beginning of a new year, a time of introspection. A time to look back at the mistakes of the past year and plan the changes we'll make in the year to come. It is a time of repentance, prayer and good deeds. The common greeting at this time is *L'shanah tovah*. The custom is to drink a little wine . . . we have none. The custom is to eat a special bread . . . we have none. It is also customary to taste something sweet, so it will be a sweet new year. I just happened to have a bag of candy—enough for all—and I will pass it around. And so, friends, please join us, as you have joined us on our journey, in this our celebration of Rosh Hashanah—*L'shanah tovah.*"

"Bravo!" Binky exclaimed. *"L'shanah tovah!"*

The celebration of Rosh Hashanah, such as it was, began.

Later, Sister Bonney walked over to Ike Silver, who stood alone some distance from the others.

"It's amazing. He's regained consciousness, but he's very weak."

Big Ike nodded as he lit his pipe.

"He hasn't touched his food," she said. "Why don't you—"

"I will, Sister." Ike walked toward the wagon.

Colorados did not stir as Ike approached. He stared straight ahead.

"Colorados."

No response.

"Do you understand me? Do you speak our language?"

Nothing.

Ike pointed to the food with his pipe.

"You ought to eat." Ike motioned toward his mouth. "Eat."

"I meant," Colorados said, still staring straight ahead, "to kill you."

"So, you do speak our language—and you came skin-close to doing it, too . . . killing me, I mean."

"Why?"

"I don't know why."

"I mean why didn't you let me die?"

"Would you have let me die if I were in your place?"

"I have killed many soldiers in battle."

"It's not the same. I'm not a soldier, not anymore, and we were not in battle. At least I wasn't."

"And that is why you didn't let me die?"

"Sister Boniface did most of the patching."

"She is your sister?"

"No."

"Is she your woman?"

"No. She's what is called a nun."

"What is a nun?"

"She's dedicated her life to helping people. That's part of her religion, to help people. Look, you better eat."

"Are you a nun?"

"No." Ike smiled. "Like you, I'm from another tribe."

"What do you mean?"

"Well, you're an Apache."

"Apache chief."

"That's right. But the Apaches have many tribes. . . ."

"Yes." Colorados nodded. "Mimbreno. Chiricahua, Tonto . . ."

"My people are called Jews."

"Jews?"

"Yes."

"I do not know of Jews."

"We come from twelve tribes. My family is from the tribe of Joseph."

"Is he here with you?"

"No. He died a long time back in our homeland."

"Where is your homeland?"

"Far away . . . far across the ocean."

"Why are you here?"

"Well, our homeland was taken away from us . . . a long time ago."

"And now Jews come to take ours."

"No. There's just my brother, my two sons and me."

"What do you do here?"

"We're traders . . . merchants."

"You bring guns for the army?"

"No. Food. Supplies for everybody."

"For Apache?"

"If you want."

"The little man . . ."

"My brother. His name is Jacob."

"He looks like Apache."

"I guess." Ike smiled. "He does at that, Colorados."

"You know my name."

"Yes. Everybody around here does."

"I won't go back to prison. I will die first."

"You will if you don't eat. But every living thing wants to go on living."

Ike blew smoke from his pipe, including a couple of smoke rings.

For the first time Colorados moved a little, trying to sniff the smoke without being too obvious.

"You like to smoke?"

Colorados nodded.

"Well, that's something else we have in common."

Ike extended the pipe.

"Smoke."

Colorados hesitated.

"Go ahead. Take it."

Colorados accepted the pipe. He put it to his lips and inhaled deeply, appreciatively.

Ike thought he could detect just the trace of a smile, but he wasn't sure.

"Keep it. I've got another one."

He put a pouch and some matches on the bed of the wagon and started to walk away.

"Your tribe . . ." Colorados said.

Ike stopped and looked back.

"Did your tribe ever fight against the army?"

"In another country." Ike nodded. "But there they were called Cossacks."

When Big Ike was just a few steps away, Sister Bonney stepped out of the shadows.

"I hope you don't mind," she said.

"Mind what?"

"My eavesdropping. I wondered what you'd say to him."

"So did I."

"I found out something."

"About Colorados?"

"No, about you, Isaac Silver. I found out that you're not only a father, a former soldier, a merchant and a Moses, but something else."

"What?"

"A diplomat."

"I don't know about that, but you know he'll try to run away as soon as he's strong enough."

"Of course he will. But after tonight it'll be different."

"How different?"

"Before he runs away, he won't try to kill any of us."

For the next two days and nights Colorados didn't have enough strength to run away.

He never said another word. Not to Sister Bonney, nor to Melena or Ben, or to Benjie, who were all with him in the wagon most of the day—not even to Ike Silver, who occasionally rode alongside.

Sister Bonney would set a tin plate of food and a

container of water next to him. No one ever saw him eat, but when they returned after their meal, the tin plate and the container would be empty. And at night, when the others were around the campfire, Colorados smoked the pipe that Ike had given him.

During those days Ben Brown was almost as silent as the Apache, talking only to Melena and sometimes to Benjie and only giving a terse answer if anyone asked a question.

And during the journey, Benjie never took the yo-yo out of his pocket.

Somehow Jedediah still managed to look neat and proper and Obadiah was still his restless, disorderly self.

In the evening Sean Dolan and some of the miners serenaded the rest of the travelers with surprisingly sweet renditions of "Lorena," "Shenandoah," "I'll Take You Home Again, Kathleen" and other sentimental songs.

Binky regaled his captive audience with abridged interpretations of Shakespearean dramas and sonnets.

Jake grumbled about whatever he could find to grumble about and occasionally counted again what was left of the bankroll, then pinned it back inside his pocket.

Away from the others, Sister Bonney knelt alone with her rosary.

Ike Silver smoked his other pipe, looked at his watch and listened to the melody it played.

On the third day as the sun arced toward its zenith, Sean Dolan rode up next to Ike Silver.

"Well, Big Ike, so far, so good."

Ike Silver nodded.

"What do you intend doing?" Dolan asked.

"Getting to Fort Whipple, what else?"

"I know that. That's not what I mean." Dolan motioned back toward Ben Brown's wagon. "I mean about Colorados. You know there's a reward."

"Not interested in any reward."

"I figured that, but—"

"But what?"

"He's getting to the point where he might do something, I mean, you think we ought to tie him up, or . . ."

"No, we're not going to tie him up, or anything else."

"You gonna let him escape?"

"This is not a prison, Sean. It happens to be his home."

"You're the boss." Dolan grinned. "There's something else you oughta know, boss."

"What's that?"

"I've made this trek before, you know."

"So?"

"So did you see that outcrop of white rocks a ways back?"

"What about it?"

"That was the halfway mark to Fort Whipple. We're past the point of no return."

Near the outcrop of white rocks, Gallagher and his men on horseback watched as the caravan in the distance moved farther ahead.

"Well . . ." Rooster said.

"Well, what?"

"You got any ideas yet? About getting that cargo for Mister Lessur."

"Rooster . . ."

That's when a rifle report cracked through the air and one of Gallagher's men grabbed at the wound in his leg.

There were other shots—and Indian yells.

CHAPTER FOURTEEN

A whirlwind on horseback, they stormed out of the white rocks with ebony eyes blazing out of flat, red faces striped and smeared with yellow, blue and green paint, rifles and guns spitting fire. Shoeless hoofs pounding across the desert, saddleless riders yelping and screaming, they were led by a tall, muscle-knotted, bronze warrior with a hawk face, yelping and screaming the loudest.

Gallagher led the charge, not toward, but away from the attackers, signaling Rooster and the other men to follow. They didn't need any urging, and there was only one destination that made sense— the wagon train that they had been following.

Ike Silver, Dolan and the rest of the caravan heard the shots and saw the riders galloping toward them with the band of Apaches in narrowing pursuit.

Every rifle and pistol in the wagon train was drawn and loaded for the inevitable battle and bloodletting.

Ike spurred his horse close to the wagon with Jake, the boys and Sister Bonney.

"Get down!" he shouted. "Get down!"

Gallagher and his men reached the wagons and vaulted off their mounts to the cover of the wagons with rifles at the ready.

Gunfire exploded from both sides until the Apaches saw something that nobody in the procession had seen.

On Ben Brown's wagon, Colorados stood with both arms uplifted and shouted a command that no one comprehended except the Apaches.

The hawk-faced leader, holding the coup stick of a chief, reined in his animal in a whiffit of dust and the others swirled to a stop around him, murmuring in disbelief, then silence.

If the Apaches were surprised, the people in the caravan were stunned.

Nobody moved, waiting to see what would happen.

Colorados said something else and lowered both arms.

The hawk-faced leader nodded, then moved slowly on his mount. He stopped at the wagon near Colorados and started to speak in the Apache language.

"Talk so all will understand, Quemada."

Quemada looked back at the other Apaches, then to Colorados.

"Since when does the Chief of the Mimbreros ride with his enemies and protect them?"

"Since they stopped the blood that was leaving his body and gave him back his breath."

"So they can take you back to the white man's prison."

"Do you see shackles on these hands?"

"I see *them* on our land."

"If they were not here I would be dead."

"What would you do now, Colorados?"

Colorados jerked the coup stick from the grasp of Quemada and stepped off from the wagon.

"I will take my place—and you will take yours."

Colorados motioned to one of the other braves, who slid off his horse and doubled up on horseback with another buck.

Coup stick in hand, Colorados mounted and rode close to Ike Silver.

"You gave me back my life. I give you yours."

Colorados touched the pipe tucked in at his waist.

"You gave me something else."

He pulled free an ornament from the coup stick and handed it to Ike.

"The claw of an eagle. The token of a friend—from my tribe to yours."

Colorados wheeled his horse and rode off with a savage yell. The Apaches followed, screaming and yelping.

Quemada rode away with them—in silence.

Not until the dust cloud from the Apache riders dissolved on the far horizon did anyone in the caravan move or even speak.

"Now I've seen it all." Gallagher, still holding his rifle, walked up close to Ike Silver and Dolan.

"Why, you big dumb Mick," Dolan said, "you almost got us all killed."

"Jake, boys, Sister Bonney, are you all all right?" Ike asked.

They all nodded and responded affirmatively.

"Everybody else okay?" Ike looked around.

Sister Bonney came off the wagon, put the rosary into her pocket, and pointed to one of Gallagher's men.

"That man is bleeding!"

"Swenson." Gallagher took a step. "How bad?"

Swenson wiped at the blood leaking from his pant leg.

"Just creased the fat, boss. Went right through."

"Mister Swenson, you come with me," Sister Bonney said. "We'll stop that bleeding."

"Odds bodikins!" Binky proclaimed, appearing from behind a wagon. "We few, we happy few, we band of brothers—and sisters—still stand in triumph over all mischance! Thanks to you, brother Isaac!"

"Thanks to Colorados." Ike smiled.

"That one he called Quemada," Dolan said, "didn't seem too happy about the outcome. He wanted blood."

"Yeah,"—Jake nodded—"ours."

"Well, Sean," Ike said, "Let's put away the artillery. We can cover a few more miles before we make camp."

"Right. There's a water hole not too far ahead. Good place to bed down."

"If we had any beds," Jake observed.

"Mister Brown, you ready to roll?" Ike asked.

Ben Brown nodded.

"Look here, Mister Silver." Gallagher wiped at his face. "Would it be all right if me and the boys ride along with you people . . . far as Fort Whipple?"

"Sure, Mister Gallagher. We can always use a few more good men. Saddle up."

"Well, Obie,"—Jake smiled at the boys—"you said you wanted to see some Indians."

Ike opened his hand and looked at the palm that held the token of a friend—the claw of an eagle.

Chapter Fifteen

The caravan had proceeded without further incident toward its destination. Fort Whipple was named after Lieutenant Amiel Weeks Whipple, who came to southern Arizona in 1849 to survey the new border between the United States and Mexico—and who, with the rank of Brigadier General, died during the Civil War at the second battle of Chancellorsville in 1863.

Fort Whipple was one of the hundreds of outposts established by the United States Army in order to protect travelers and settlers who faced and moved ever westward.

Years ago at the Medicine Lodge Council in Kansas, the Kiowa Chief Satanta had said to the commissioners:

> "I have heard that you intend to settle us on a reservation near the mountains. When we settle down we grow pale and die. A long time ago this land belonged to our fathers; but when I go up to the river, I now see camps of soldiers on its banks. These soldiers cut down

our timber; they kill our buffalo; and when I see this, my heart is broken. I feel sorry. I have spoken."

There was good reason why Satanta was known as the Great Orator of the Plains. He was also a prophet of things to come.

The blare of bugles and the hoofbeats of troopers heralded the inevitable change that fell like a dark shadow across the Indian way of life.

Prairie schooners, the Butterfield Stage, steamboats and the iron horse swept westward across the hunting grounds, and with them people from the East and all the nations of Europe—more people than there were buffalo.

The gold strike in California had signaled another tidal wave of immigrants.

"Our great mission," said Senator John C. Calhoun, "is to occupy this vast domain."

And as early as 1845, an article appeared in an Eastern newspaper. *"Our Manifest Destiny is to overspread the continent allotted by Providence for the free development of our yearly multiplying millions. We will realize our Manifest Destiny."*

Little or nothing was mentioned about the Manifest Destiny of the Indians. But some of the Indians would have something to say about it and something to do about it.

After the war broke out in 1861, the Union Army needed all the manpower it could muster— especially if that manpower had prior experience in warfare.

Much of that manpower was in the West, where their experience included warfare with hostile Indians.

Some of the forts were abandoned; others had to

make do with reduced ranks. Fort Whipple's garrison size dropped by eighty percent, from 124 to only twenty-four.

After the war, Indian hostility accelerated through the ensuing years so forcefully that President Grant assigned Colonel George Crook, who during the four-year bloodbath had distinguished himself at South Mountain, Antietam, Chickamagaua, and Appomattox—and before that was already renowned as an Indian fighter—to command the army forces in the Territory with orders to drive the Apaches to their assigned reservations and keep the peace in any manner he deemed necessary.

It was a tall order for a tall man.

Colonel Crook's first move on arriving at Prescott had been to transfer the department headquarters to Fort Whipple.

The sentry at Fort Whipple hollered to the guards at the gate.

"Wagon train!"

The gates swung open and Big Ike's caravan rolled through and into the compound.

Two men came out of the headquarters door.

One of them was Colonel George Crook, the best "wilderness soldier" who ever lived—copper hair scatter-shot with iron strands, tall, erect, spare and sinewy, with a raspy voice, severe and brusque, but not unkind. He wore civilian clothes except for a well-seasoned, well-wrinkled old army jacket.

The other man, Rupert Lessur, also was tall, but smooth, his skin best suited to the parlor; his voice was pleasant and often dripped caramel, but not always. Lessur customarily walked a half or even a full pace ahead of whomever he was walking with. But not when he walked with Colonel Crook.

"Colonel, I told you Gallagher would get through."

"Yes, you did."

The fact that a wagon train had made it from La Paz to Fort Whipple was good news for everybody at the fort, and most everybody who didn't have official duties that would keep them from greeting the caravan made their way to the compound.

The caravan creaked to a stop.

Ike, Dolan, Gallagher and the other riders stepped off their mounts, as did some of the occupants of the wagons.

Lessur approached with a confident, satisfied smile.

"Well, Gallagher, you made good time. Congratulations."

Gallagher said nothing as Lessur looked around at Ike and the others.

"I see you picked up some passengers along the way."

"Uh . . ."—Gallagher fumbled—". . . not exactly."

"See any Apaches?" Crook asked.

"All we wanted, Colonel."

"But you got the cargo through." Lessur still smiled.

"Not exactly," Gallagher repeated.

"Why the devil do you keep saying that?" Lessur took closer notice of Ike and the dilapidated wagons. "What's going on?"

"Well, Mister Lessur, this cargo don't belong to us."

"How's that?! To whom does it belong?"

"To me . . . ," Ike said, "and my partners."

"And who are you, sir?"

"That's Big Ike Silver." Gallagher gulped. "And he outbid us."

"And he outfought you," Dolan added.

"He what?" Rupert Lessur's expression had darkened.

"Well,"—Gallagher gazed at the ground—"you said not to go any higher—"

"Never mind that."

Crook made no attempt to disguise his amusement and pleasure.

"Mister Silver, I'm Colonel Crook." He extended his hand.

So did Ike, and they shook.

"Yes, Colonel, I know. Pleased to meet you, sir."

"Never mind the sir. You're not in the army, and it looks like the army'll be doing business with you."

"Looks like."

"How many barrels?"

"One hundred."

"What are you asking?"

"What's the going price?"

"Twenty dollars a barrel, but if you—"

"Sold."

"Mister Silver," Crook said, "it's a pleasure doing business with you."

"Vice versa, Colonel."

"Gallagher,"—Lessur did his best to shift back to an amiable mode—"you must have misunderstood, I told you—"

"Wait a minute, Mister Lessur." Gallagher squinted. "We're lucky to be alive. That Colorados—"

"*Colorados?*" Crook interrupted. "We heard he'd escaped, but badly wounded. Thought he'd be dead by now."

"Not by a damn sight," Gallagher exclaimed. "We was attacked by his Apaches, but seems like he's a friend of Big Ike here, so he let us go."

Crook noticed around his neck, on a thong, Ike Silver wore an eagle claw—and Colonel Crook was aware of its significance.

"That's interesting. Mister Silver, will you be going back to La Paz?"

"No, Colonel, at least not for a while. Staying in Prescott. Bought a store there."

"That so? Well, I'll make out a bank draft for the cargo . . . if that's agreeable with you . . ."—he glanced at Ike's companions—". . . and your partners."

"Agreeable!" Jake responded. "It's very agreeable!"

"Fine. Is it also agreeable," Colonel Crook asked, "if we unload the wagons?"

"Colonel Crook, as of now those barrels belong to the army and you can do with them as you will."

"I'll start with that bank draft. One hundred barrels at twenty dollars. I make that an even two thousand. Correct?"

"Correct," Jake said.

Crook gave the command to start unloading while the rest of the occupants of the wagons, including Sister Bonney, Binky and Ben Brown and his family debarked.

Without saying another word, Rupert Lessur began to walk away. He was immediately joined by Gallagher, who followed just a pace behind.

"Mister Lessur . . ."

"Gallagher," Lessur said softly, "you're an idiot."

Chapter Sixteen

Prescott was originally known as Granite Creek; the town site was surveyed and laid out in 1864 near the area where gold had just been discovered, and at that time it was renamed.

In the ensuing years Prescott was on its way to becoming the commercial hub of the Arizona Territory. That was inducement enough for Ike Silver to leave California with his family and once again make a new beginning. That new beginning would begin with the purchase of a general store.

They stood near the corner of Bravo and Sun Up Streets outside a large building flanked by a good-sized stable, looking at the sign.

PRESCOTT GENERAL STORE
SUPPLIES—LIVERY

And on the door there was another sign.

TEMPORARILY CLOSED

The onlookers consisted of Big Ike, Jake, the two boys, Sister Bonney, Binky, Ben Brown and his family, Sean Dolan and some of Dolan's men. They had left most of the animals and empty wagons at Fort Whipple to be brought in the next day by army teamsters.

It was almost sundown on Sun Up Street as an older man with a slight limp and a knotted cane came out of the stable door, squinted through a pair of crinkled eyes on a weathered face framed by a neatly trimmed gray beard, and spoke out of the right side of his mouth.

"Howdy there, strangers." He waved the cane and moved closer. "Any of you be called Silver?"

"I be." Ike smiled and pointed. "So be my brother and two sons."

"Scotty. Scotty Simpson. Work for Mrs. Winthrop, sorta. Night watchman, sorta—and all 'round I-don't-know-what. Glad to meet ya. I'll be sure Mrs. Winthrop's here to meet ya tomorrow."

"Appreciate it," Ike said.

"You'll be wantin' a place to stay the night— Hassayampa Hotel. Place to eat—Sweisgood's Restaurant. Place to drink—Brady's Bar. That about covers it."

"Say, Mister Simpson,"—Ben Brown took a step forward—"you think it'd be all right if me and my family camped behind the stable for the night?"

"Camp *in* the stable if you want, if you don't mind my company."

"Mister Brown," Ike said, "why don't you—"

"The stable will be fine, Mister Silver. And thank you, Mister Simpson."

"Mister Simpson." Scotty smiled. "Haven't heard that in years."

"Ike, the boys and I'll be in Brady's Bar," Dolan

said, "wettin' our windpipes, if you care to join us later."

"I'll join you now," Binky said, "and so will my windpipe—if you don't mind."

"Come on."

"Sister, would you come with us?" Ike asked.

"Mister Silver, under the circumstances, I believe I will."

"Fine. Scotty, see you tomorrow."

"You bet."

Sister Bonney wanted to pay for her room at the Hassayampa Hotel, but Ike convinced her otherwise, on account of payment for nursing services rendered to Colorados on the journey to Fort Whipple.

After they checked in, Jake, Sister Bonney and the boys strolled over to Sweisgood's Restaurant, while Ike opted for Brady's Bar and a drink or two with Sean Dolan.

Brady's Bar was a saloon like just about any other frontier saloon—a dozen round tables surrounded by Douglas chairs, a scarred and stained bar, sawdust on a wood floor beneath a tin ceiling.

Big Ike joined Dolan, Binky and the boys at the bar, bought a round, then nodded toward one of the tables, which was occupied by two players and a monumental pile of money. One of the players was male, the other female. Most of the money was in front of the female.

The male looked nervous, sweaty and consumptive; the female was a stone overweight, had orange hair, two raspberry slashes on the surface of her full lips and a confident look in her verdant green eyes. Her face was still beautiful and didn't need all the paint and powder she had laid on to it, but without it she wouldn't look as much like a saloon gal as she was supposed to.

Most of the players at the other tables had stopped playing and now stood among the other spectators watching the high stakes poker game. Among the standing spectators near the table were Rupert Lessur, smoking a long, thin cigar, and Jim Gallagher, a half step behind him with an unlit cigarette in his mouth, watching silently.

"Looks interesting," Ike said. "Who are the players?"

"That's what I asked." Dolan smiled.

"Did you find out?"

"That lunger is Brady. Owns the joint . . . as of now."

"What does that mean?"

"It means I think they're about to play for the bar and everything in it."

"Who's the lady?"

"Name's Belinda. Belinda Millay. She ain't exactly a lady."

"No?"

"No. From what I gather she started out some time ago as one of Brady's saloon gals and worked her way up."

"To what?"

"Junior partner, plyin' her trade, but mostly playin' poker with Brady—to what looks like a showdown tonight."

"That *is* interesting. Think I'll go over and watch."

Ike made his way to the table.

Brady dealt.

Big Ike watched. He didn't like what he saw.

A granite-faced giant stood behind Belinda Millay, looking across at Brady as the owner dealt out the cards. The giant also looked down at Millay's hand, then rubbed his chin with two fingers.

"How many?" Brady asked after he studied his cards and smiled.

"Just a minute." Belinda looked at her cards again.

"Sure. Take your time. Tell you what, Belinda. How about this one game—for the whole shebang?"

"The whole shebang?"

"That's right. Brady's Bar, lock, stock, and key to the door, for what you've got on the table. Must be close to three thousand."

"Or more," Belinda said.

"Is it a bet?"

"It's a bet."

"Then how many cards?" Brady glanced up at granite face.

Just then Ike Silver stepped in front of the giant.

"Hey!" the giant said. "You're obstructin' my view!"

"No." Ike nodded toward Brady. "I'm obstructing *his* view."

"What do you mean by that?"

"I think you know and so does Mister Brady."

"Why, you lousy bastard!" The giant grabbed Ike's shoulder and started to spin him around fast.

Ike spun faster and shot a right uppercut into the giant's chin that snapped his head back, then dropped him hard onto the sawdust.

"Now you can go on with you your game, Mister Brady."

Ike tipped his hat to the lady.

"Good night, ma'am."

CHAPTER SEVENTEEN

The next morning Jake and the boys didn't have the patience to wait for Ike to shave. They went on ahead to Sweisgood's for breakfast and said they'd be at the store to look it over again and wait for him.

On the way to Bravo and Sun Up Streets, Ike Silver paused to take in the activity in front of what used to be Brady's Bar.

Among the crowd were Belinda Millay, Binky, several workmen and over a dozen interested citizens.

The old sign that read BRADY'S BAR lay on the ground and workmen were replacing it with a glistening new sign that spelled out BELINDA'S EMPORIUM.

"Good morning, Big Ike," Binky beamed. "By the by, you two haven't met officially. Ike Silver, may I present Miss Belinda Millay, the new owner of Belinda's Emporium."

Ike smiled and looked at the dirty sign on the ground. "Well, I see there's no need to ask how the game ended last night."

"No." Belinda glanced up at the new sign. "And I thank you for your good intentions, but that wasn't necessary."

"It wasn't? You often play against your opponent—with somebody looking over your back at your cards?"

"I only let that big bastard see what I wanted him to see."

"Oh, I see." Ike smiled. "Sorry I butted in."

"No, I enjoyed it. But he didn't. Left town this morning."

"Uh-huh. What about . . ."

The batwings of the saloon swung open and two men carried out a stretcher with a body covered by a blanket.

"If you were about to inquire after the late Mister Brady . . . ," Binky said "he's just on his way out."

"What happened?"

"Blew out his brains," Miss Millay replied matter-of-factly. "Oh, Tony." She beckoned to a rotund, middle-aged swarthy man who was accompanying the stretcher bearers.

"Yes, Miss Millay?"

"Oh, Antonio Gillardi, this is Ike Silver. He's a new friend in town. Ike, Tony's the barber in town . . . and the undertaker."

The two men nodded at each other.

"I hope to see you again soon, Mister Silver."

"For a haircut?"

"Yes, of course."

"Tony." Belinda pointed at the stretcher. "See that he gets a first-class burial. He was a first-class son of a bitch. Send me the bill."

"Of course, Miss Millay."

Antonio Gillardi and the stretcher bearers went on their way.

"Until this morning, he always called me Belinda."

"Why didn't you have them letter the sign 'Miss Millay's Emporium?' " Ike asked.

"A rose by any other name . . ." Belinda smiled.

"Ah yes, *Romeo and Juliet*," Binky announced, "one of my triumphs . . . a long time ago. By the by, Big Ike, you'll be pleased to know that I've found employment here in Prescott, thanks to Miss Millay, my new employer."

"Congratulations. Doing what?"

"Ahh . . . just what do I do, Miss Millay, besides play the court jester?"

"Why, Binky, you are the Emporium's—"

"Major Domo?"

"That's it. Major Domo."

"Grand. In that case, may I have a small advance for a new wardrobe befitting my position?"

Belinda Millay nodded and turned to Ike.

"Mister Silver, will you be staying in Prescott?"

"He certainly shall," Binky said. "Big Ike's bought the general store."

"Is that so?" Belinda's green eyes swept up, down and across. "He don't look like any storekeeper I ever met. Mister Silver, again I thank you for your good intentions and hope you'll come often and visit Belinda's Emporium."

"On one condition."

"What's that?"

"I never have to play poker with you."

"Oh? Well, Mister Silver, maybe we can think of some other game to play."

"Good day, Miss Millay."

They were waiting for him in front of the general store—Jake, Scotty Simpson and an older lady dressed in black.

"Ike," Jake said, "this is Mrs. Winthrop, the owner."

"Not anymore." Mrs. Winthrop smiled. "That is if

you still want to go through with the arrangement you proposed in our letters."

"We certainly do, Mrs. Winthrop."

Jake pointed to the property. "Well, San Francisco it isn't, but it's better than the letter described."

"It's a good solid building, gentlemen. The stable needs some work."

"That can be taken care of," Ike said.

"I'm just sorry that the inventory might not be as much as you expected. But since Edward died, and what with the cost of freighting . . . well, maybe two thousand is a little high."

"It's a fair price, Mrs. Winthrop. We already agreed on that, and Jake has a bank draft for just that amount from Colonel Crook."

"And here it is, ma'am, already endorsed over to you."

She handed Ike a ring of keys.

"You can take over right now. I'll sign the deed and have Scotty deliver it to you this afternoon. I'm staying with the Tompkins until I can arrange to get to St. Louis."

"What about you, Scotty?" Jake asked. "You want to keep working here?"

"Nope. Retired this morning! Headin' to Albuquerque—old soldier's home."

"Good luck to you, gentlemen," Mrs. Winthrop said, looking at the sign and thinking of her Edward. Then she turned and walked away with Scotty Simpson.

Just then, the caravan of empty wagons with an escort of troopers rounded the corner and rattled to a stop close to the store.

One of the troopers dismounted and approached.

"Ike Silver?"

"Right, Captain."

"I'm Bourke. Colonel Crook's aide-de-camp. Sorry I missed you yesterday. Out on patrol."

"Glad to meet you, Captain Bourke. My brother Jake."

Both men nodded.

"Congratulations on getting through. The colonel said you encountered hostiles along the way."

"They weren't so hostile, thanks to Colorados."

"So I heard. Most of the time that hasn't been the case with us."

"Well, maybe things'll change."

"Maybe. Where do you want us to park the wagons?"

"Right there'll be fine."

Captain Bourke signaled to the teamsters, who debarked from the wagons and mounted the extra horses that had been brought along.

"Be seeing you, Captain," Ike said as Bourke mounted.

"I hope so."

As the troopers rode away, Rupert Lessur approached with Gallagher not quite alongside.

"Well, Mister Silver,"—Lessur nodded toward the ring of keys in Ike's hand—"looks like you're in business."

"Very neighborly," Jake said, "of you to visit us so soon, Mister Lessur."

"I did want to wish you good luck."

"Thanks." Ike smiled.

"Say, that was quite a punch you laid on that kibitzer last night. . . ."

"What?" Jake looked at his brother.

"Never mind, Jake."

"Maybe I do mind."

Lessur looked at the caravan. "By the way, I was wondering if you were thinking of selling those wagons."

"How much you offering?" Jake asked.

"Well . . ."

"Is the freight business that good?" Ike smiled.

A pained expression oozed across Jake's face.

"I-ee-k . . ."

"Well, it has its ups and downs—depending mostly on the Indian situation."

"I heard that Colonel Crook was sent here to bring peace to the territory."

"That," Lessur smiled, "will take a lot of doing."

"Colonel Crook is a lot of soldier."

"Yes, so we've all heard. I'll make you a good offer for those wagons."

"Not for sale, Mister Lessur."

"You thinking of going into the freighting business?"

"Seems we're already in . . . all we have to do is *stay* in."

"Uh-huh. First the store, then the freighting business—all in one day. Very ambitious. I wonder what business you people will be in tomorrow?"

"Who knows? We'll take 'em one day at a time."

"I see. Good day . . . gentlemen."

As Lessur and Gallagher walked away, Jake nudged his brother.

"Ike, it wouldn't've hurt to listen to his offer. . . ."

"It wouldn't've helped either, because we're not . . . well, well," Ike said, "look who else has come to wish us well. . . ."

"Yes," Jake said as Sean Dolan approached, "but this one means it."

"Mornin'," Dolan said. "Say, that was one hell of a punch last night, Big Ike."

"What's all this about a punch?" Jake demanded.

"Never mind, Jake."

"Always never mind. I *do* mind."

"Tell you later."

"Always later!"

"Me and the boys'll be headin' out to the Rattlesnake, Ike. See what shape it's in. From what I heard around town, not so good. Meanwhile, send up a wagon load of the usual supplies."

"That we'll do," Ike said.

"Yessir . . . one hell of a punch." Sean Dolan turned and walked toward Belinda's Emporium.

"*Now* will you tell me about that punch, brother?"

"Let's go inside first."

As Ike and Jake started toward the store, Jed, Obie and Benjie came charging from around the corner.

"Dad!" Jed hollered. "Did we buy the store?"

Jake held up the keys.

"We did!"

"I told you, Benjie."

"And," Jed asked, "does the stable belong to us, too?"

"It does."

Jed pointed. "And the big room in the back, too?"

"That too."

"Wow!" Obie exclaimed.

"And the rooms upstairs?" Jed pointed again.

"And the rooms upstairs."

"And Jed and I are your partners?"

"Boys, there's going to be a new sign up there, a big one. It's going to say 'Silver and Company.' You're part of the 'company.'"

"*Yipppeee!*" Obie yelled.

Ben Brown and his wife had come out of the stable and were walking toward the front of the store.

"What's Benjie and them gonna do, Dad?" Jed asked.

"Well," Ike nodded toward Ben and Melena, "now's a good time to find out. Morning folks."

"Morning." Ben and Melena both responded.

"Army brought us the wagons." Ike pointed.

"So I see," Ben said.

"They took quite a beating on the trip from La Paz." Ike moved a step toward the wagons.

"I can see that, too." Ben followed. "They could stand some fixing up."

"Right. You available for the job?"

"Well, I'm kinda anxious to get going."

"Uh-huh. We're sure going to need those wagons if we're going to go into the freight business . . . and it looks like we are, aren't we, Jake?"

"You're asking *me?*"

"Be worth . . . thirty dollars to get 'em fixed up."

Melena was looking at her husband—not just looking, pleading.

Ben pointed at the stable. "Can we stay in there while I do the job?"

"You sure can."

"Then the job's worth fifteen, Mister Silver."

"We'll compromise. Twenty, Mister Brown."

Mister Brown nodded.

Benjie took the yo-yo out of his pocket, put his finger through the string, looked at Jed and Obie, and smiled.

CHAPTER EIGHTEEN

"It's called a mezuzah, Sister."

Sister Mary Boniface had been passing by on the street when she saw that Ike Silver had just finished attaching a small narrow box on the right side of the entrance to the store.

"Mezuzah?"

"Yes."

"Is that a part of your religion?"

"Yes."

"And is it permissible to tell me what is contained inside?"

"Yes, of course. A scroll containing three verses from Deuteronomy to fulfill the commandment 'Write them on the doorposts of your homes and on your gates,' as prescribed in the Torah."

"I think I understand. We have medals, Saint Christopher, Saint Anthony . . ."

Ike nodded. "It's customary to place a mezuzah on each doorway of each room in a house or business, but out here, just this one will have to make do."

"I'm sure that it will more than suffice." Sister Bonney smiled. "But I wonder if you'd mind . . ."

"Mind what, Sister?"

"If I said a little prayer to go along with it?"

"Not at all, Sister. Not at all. We'd very much appreciate that."

"Good. I have some business to attend to. I'll see you later . . . Big Ike."

Underneath a sign, R. LESSUR, in front of an elaborate and well-equipped office and stable, Rupert Lessur stood lighting a long, slender cigar. Jim Gallagher was nearby, and both men watched Sister Mary Boniface approach at a brisk pace from the direction of the general store.

"Good day, Sister." Lessur smiled.

"It is a good day, Mister Lessur. And I'm in hopes that it will be an even better day if you have something for me."

"Oh, what's that?"

"I asked Mister Gallagher, and at the time he said he didn't know. Has a crate been delivered to you from Sante Fe addressed to me?"

"Why yes it has, in our last shipment."

"Good."

"Quite heavy, as I recall."

"Yes. Books for the new school . . . along with a few personal items."

"I see. Well, as I said, it's quite heavy. Much too heavy for you to carry. If you tell us where, we'd be happy to deliver it to you."

"I'd be happy to tell you . . . if I *knew* where."

"Oh. In that case, we'll be happy to hold it until we get further instructions."

"Very good."

"So, we're going to have a school, are we?"

"We are. If I can find a place to teach in."

"I'm not of your persuasion, but you can count on me for a contribution."

"Thank you."

"And, Sister, there will be no charge whatsoever for the handling and delivery of that crate. Compliments of Lessur Freighting."

"Thank you again."

"Uh . . . Sister,"—Gallagher took a step forward—"are you going to start a church, too?"

"No. Just a school."

"For Catholics?"

"For anybody who wants to learn."

"I never went to school much . . . or to church."

"Well, it's never too late."

"Too many hypocrites."

"In school?"

"In church."

"You're right, Mister Gallagher. But there's always room for one more."

Sister Mary Boniface continued on her way at an even brisker pace.

"What're we gonna do, Mister Lessur?"

"About what?"

Gallagher nodded toward Ike Silver's newly acquired general store and livery.

"About *them.*"

"They're just mice."

"Huh?"

"What do cats usually do with mice? Right now I think I'll pay a little visit to the new proprietor of Belinda's Emporium."

High up, from a hidden vantage point, Quemada and a half-dozen Apaches watched as Captain Bourke and his troop rode back toward Fort Whipple.

Quemada looked at the young brave mounted next to him, then back to the troopers.

"It is no longer Apache land, Quemada. It belongs to them. To the army," the brave said.

"Not just to the army, Secorro." Quemada pointed to a dust cloud in the distance as Sean Dolan and the miners came into view. "Those are not bluecoats."

"What will you do?"

"I know what I will do. But first we will see what Colorados will have us do. We will see if he is still a cougar—or if the white man's prison has turned him into a coyote. We will see."

Even though it was still morning, there were about a dozen customers at Belinda's Emporium, a few drinking at the bar, the rest playing poker at a couple of tables.

Belinda sat at a distant corner table indulging in a glass of whiskey and a game of solitaire. Even just playing solitaire, her fingers looked like they were fashioned for dealing cards.

She wore noticeably less war paint than the night before, almost as if she had just stepped out of a bathtub. And she had, less than half an hour before.

Lessur came through the batwings, long, slender cigar in hand, paused, smiled and walked to the corner table.

"May I join you?"

"You may." Belinda motioned to the bartender "Henry, bring over Mister Lessur's bottle."

Henry did, and poured.

Belinda and Lessur clinked glasses.

"Congratulations,"—Lessur looked around the room—"on your new enterprise and on being the sole owner."

"Confusion to the enemy."

They drank.

Lessur pointed to the deck on the table.

"How did you get so good at cards?"

"It's a long story."

"I have plenty of time."

"Some other time."

"Very well. May I say you look radiant this morning?"

"Thank you. Anything else?"

"Yes. A little business. You and me."

"I'm out of that business, Mister Lessur, as of last night. But one of the ladies upstairs can accommodate you."

"No. That's not what I meant."

"Then what did you mean?"

"About you being the sole owner . . ."

"What about it?"

"The sign in front of my building says 'Freighting.'"

"So?"

"I'm also in many other businesses here in Prescott—without any signs. A sort of silent partner. The bank. A couple of mines. Livestock. Several ranches . . ."

"So?"

"So I would like you to consider making an arrangement with me . . . as your silent partner."

"Why didn't you make such an arrangement with Brady?"

"I knew that sooner or later he'd lose the place to you, so why complicate matters? Besides, I'd rather make such an arrangement with you."

"Why would I consider doing that?"

"For money and other advantages."

"How much money?"

"Say four thousand dollars for twenty percent of the profits. You keep the books. You run the business, with absolutely no interference from me. The sign stays the same, everything stays the same."

"Except my profits. What are the 'other advantages'?"

"I freight in your inventory. From now on that will be at a sizable discount."

"Anything else?"

"Yes. A sizable reduction in your rent. You do know I own this building."

"And you know, Mister Lessur, that Brady had a five-year lease . . . signed over to me."

"Five years is not such a long time."

"In five years I'll be rich and retired."

"Leases have been known to be broken."

"I wouldn't advise that, Mister Lessur. Look what happened to poor Brady."

"I don't play cards the way he did."

"And I don't play games. Not with you. And you know something else, Mister Lessur? Word is you may have some competition in the freighting business."

"We'll see . . . five thousand instead of four?"

"A thousand times, no."

"Suppose I keep the offer open?"

"Suppose we say 'so long.' "

"Very well, Miss Millay." Lessur stood and smiled. "Suppose we do . . . for now." A plume of cigar smoke trailed in his wake as he left.

In a moment Binky stepped from behind one of the corner curtains.

"Ah, yes . . . one can smile and smile and be a villain. At least it's so in . . . Prescott."

"Why, you son of a bitch!" She grinned.

"Yes, ma'am . . . *and* your obedient servant."

* * *

"I appreciate your opening up and letting me in, Mister Silver."

"Well, we're not officially open yet, still taking inventory, but what can I do for you, Mister . . ."

"Knight. Oliver Knight. I publish the newspaper in town, a weekly—*The Prescott Independent*."

Oliver Knight was pale, bone-thin, wore spectacles and smelled of printer's ink.

"Glad to meet you, Mister Knight. Please sit down. You like a cup of coffee?"

"No, thanks. I'm on a deadline, got a little open space right on the front page. Thought I'd do a little story about you coming to town."

"That's fine."

"Could be next edition you'll buy a little ad."

"Could be."

"You own this place alone?"

"Nope. Got a brother, Jake, upstairs and two young sons. They're cleaning up the place."

"Uh-huh. I also heard you might be going into the freight business."

"No, sir. Not 'might be.' We are."

"You're aware of a fellow named Lessur?"

"I am."

"A smiling scorpion. Got his hand in just about everything in town, except my newspaper."

"And my store."

"Has he made you an offer . . . for your wagons?"

"He has."

"Why didn't you sell?"

"Has he made you an offer for your newspaper?"

"He has."

"Why didn't *you* sell?"

"The paper's called *Independent*. That's what I am. Independent."

"So am I, Mister Knight."

"Well, we'll see—"

Gunshots. One. Two. Three. Four. From outside on the street in front of the store.

"Goddammit! It's the Keeler brothers, Claude and Charlie, shooting up the town again. They're crazy and usually drunk."

"Don't you have any law in Prescott? A sheriff, marshal, or—"

"Nope. Mayor Davis is the law and he's got a committee to keep order, drunks and such. If it gets serious, he sends for the army."

Two more gunshots.

"Where *is* the mayor?"

"Outta town today."

"What about the committee?"

"Probably under their blankets."

Another gunshot. This one shattered a second-story window of the store.

"My boys are up there."

"I wouldn't go outside, Mister Silver. They might go away."

Ike strapped on the gun belt lying on top of the rolltop desk.

"They might not."

He started toward the door.

"Mister Silver . . ."

Ike stepped out of the door, past the mezuzah, and stood on the boardwalk.

Claude and Charlie Keeler had dismounted and were tying their horses to the hitching post.

They had leathered their guns and each held a whiskey bottle in his left hand.

"All right!" Ike barked. "That's enough!"

"Who the hell are you?" Claude said.

"I'm the new owner."

"Well, we need some supplies."

"We're closed."

"Open up." Charlie took a swig. "We're comin' in."

"No, you're not."

"Who's gonna stop us?" Claude grinned.

"I am."

"How?" Charlie smirked.

Both Charlie and Claude's right hands inched toward their holsters.

Ike's hand streaked and his gun flashed twice.

Both whiskey bottles shattered. Both men's guns were still leathered. Both brothers trembled where they stood.

"Now get on your animals and get the hell out."

They started to move.

"Just a minute."

They froze.

"That'll be one dollar for the broken window. Put it on the hitching post."

Charlie took a silver dollar out of his vest and complied.

They mounted and spurred away.

Ike holstered his gun, walked to the hitching post and lifted the silver dollar.

Oliver Knight came out of the door, followed by Jake, then the boys.

"Ike, are you all right?" Jake asked.

Ike nodded.

Ben Brown, Melena and Benjie were now out front, and so were several citizens of Prescott.

"I've never seen anything like that!" Knight gasped.

"Would you care to continue the interview, Mister Knight?"

"I've got more than enough material, Mister Silver. By the way, would you consider that job as sheriff?"

"Not interested, Mister Knight, I'm just a store-keeper."

"You're not a *just* anything."

Oliver Knight walked away.

Lessur and Gallagher stood in front of Lessur's office.

"Yes, sir," Knight mumbled as he passed by them, "somebody's come to town."

"In my whole life," Gallagher whispered, "I never seen anybody as fast and accurate."

"There's always somebody faster and more accurate." Lessur smiled. "And I know who."

CHAPTER NINETEEN

"Dad," Jedediah asked, "will you teach us how to shoot a gun like that?"

"No."

"Somebody taught you," Obadiah said.

"That's right."

"Was it your father?" Jedediah.

"No."

"Who?" Obadiah.

"I did," Jake said.

"Ah, come on." Obadiah frowned. "I don't believe it."

"Are you calling your Uncle Jake a fibber?"

"Well," Obadiah said, "I never seen you shoot a gun."

"Never *saw* you shoot a gun," Jedediah corrected.

"Neither of us did." Obadiah nodded.

"I just don't want to show off, but when the time comes, you'll be astonished."

Benjie came from the stable and approached, spinning out his yo-yo.

Both boys' eyes widened. This was the first time they had seen him in action with the yo-yo.

"Geez!" Obadiah blurted.

"Look at that!" Jedediah exclaimed.

"Want me to show you how to do the yo-yo?"

"Would you, Benjie?" Jedediah asked.

"Sure would. Let's go over there by that tree."

They went away together with Benjie doing his stuff.

"They call this 'walkin' the dog,'" Benjie explained.

"What do you say to that, brother?" Jake asked.

"I say 'progress.'"

Before the two brothers could start inside, they heard a familiar voice and saw a familiar figure, but there was something different about that figure.

"All hail, gentlemen! I was witness to that little demonstration, albeit from a distance. A safe distance. So was Belinda Millay. How do you like my new wardrobe?"

Binky's wardrobe *was* new . . . from top to bottom. The latest style bowler, double-breasted dark suit with stovepipe pants, a blazing white shirt with a flowing tie and shiny black patent leather pumps.

"You look elegant." Jake smiled.

"I *am* elegant, thanks to my new employer. Have to play the part, you know . . . lend a little class to the joint. And speaking of my new employer, she wonders if you would be so kind as to come by, Big Ike."

"When?"

"Now."

Even though it was still well before noon, activity at Belinda's Emporium had begun to pick up. A few more customers at the bar, a few more poker players at the tables, and three of the saloon girls— Francine, Alma, and Marisa—were in circulation, displaying their wares to whomever might be in the market for a little daytime diversion.

Belinda sat at the corner table playing solitaire. On the table, a bottle of whiskey and two empty glasses.

Binky led Ike Silver through the bat wings and both men proceeded to Belinda's table.

"Fair lady!" Binky bowed. "In compliance with your request, I bring you Sir Isaac of Silver. Now, if you will excuse me, I haven't had breakfast yet. Henry!"

Binky walked toward the bar.

"Please sit down, Sir Isaac."

Ike sat.

"Would you care for a drink?" Belinda pointed. "It's from Mister Lessur's bottle."

"No thanks."

"Me neither," she smiled. "I guess you know that everybody in town is already talking about that little demonstration you put on this morning."

"I guess it couldn't be kept a secret."

"Those Keelers are crazy. They're likely to come back after you."

"I guess that is likely, but maybe that little demonstration discouraged them."

"Maybe, but if it didn't, may I make a suggestion?"

"Certainly."

"Next time shoot one in the belly. That'll really discourage 'em."

"Is that why you asked me to come over?"

"No."

She pointed to the whiskey bottle on the table.

"He *is* going to come after you."

"Lessur?"

She nodded.

"But not out in the open. He's a devious sonof-abitch."

"Oliver Knight referred to him as a smiling scorpion."

"Not a bad description. He's out to own this

town, this territory . . . made me an offer for part of this saloon. I didn't accept."

"Neither did I." Ike smiled. "Wanted to buy my wagons."

"So, we've got something else in common."

"How's that?"

"We've both got something Lessur wants." She picked up the cards and shuffled.

Ike pointed toward the deck. "I see you keep in practice."

"Don't want my fingers to stiffen—ever since that crooked card game I was in over in St. Louis."

"How did you know it was crooked?"

"I was dealing."

"Oh," Ike smiled. "Tell me, how'd you get so good at cards?"

"Lessur asked me the same thing this morning."

"Did you tell him?"

"No."

"Then I guess you won't tell me."

"Sure I will. My father—"

A man slammed through the bat wings. Big, bearded and dirty.

He let loose a yell.

"*Yeahh-hoo!* Just spent two months up on a line shack for the Bar Seven. Ain't seen nothin' human for sixty days and nights! Got two months pay an' a powerful cravin' for whiskey and . . . well, well, well . . ." He strode across the room to Belinda's table. "If it ain't my old sweetheart Belinda!"

"No," she said. "It ain't your old sweetheart."

"Sure! You remember me. Krantz. Dutch Krantz. We're gonna have a drink—for openers."

"No we're not."

"Sure we are. You know how much money I got in my pocket?"

"Not enough."

"Hey! What the hell's a' matter? Where's Brady?"

"He's gone," Belinda said. "Didn't you notice the sign outside?"

"Hell no, I didn't notice no sign, now come on . . ."

Krantz grabbed Belinda's right arm and started to pull her up. In one swift movement Ike sprang and landed a cannonball fist onto Krantz's jaw, knocking him backward to the floor, where he instantly reached for his holster as a shot rang out and kicked up sawdust between his legs just south of his crotch.

"Guess where the next one'll be," Belinda said, holding a pearl-handled derringer in her right hand. "Now, Mister Krantz, there's another saloon just up the street. Why don't you go over there and try your luck?"

"Yeah. Sure. I didn't mean nothin'." Krantz made it to his feet and started toward the door. "I didn't mean nothin' . . . I just . . ."

He just walked out through the bat wings.

The customers in the saloon watched as Belinda Millay replaced the pearl-handled derringer into her garter.

Binky approached, removed his bowler and bowed.

"Was ever woman in such humor woo'd? Did ever woman in such humor rebuff the wooer? I think not!"

"And I think I better be going." Ike said.

"Don't you want to hear the story of my life?" Belinda smiled.

Ike smiled back. "Don't think I could stand the excitement."

"You are the fellow who painted that sign for Belinda's Emporium, aren't you?"

"Well, I'm the only sign painter in town, so I must be. And you're the fella that did that fancy shootin' this mornin'."

"Ike Silver." Ike extended his hand, as did the sign painter.

"Tom Bixby." They shook. "What can I do for you, Mister Silver?"

"You know that sign above the general store?"

"I ought to. I painted it."

"Well, I'd like you to paint another one to replace it."

"So would I."

"Good."

"What do you want the sign to say?"

"Silver and Co. General Store—Supplies—Freighting."

"Freighting, huh?"

"That's right."

"Does Rupert Lessur know about this?"

"He does."

"This could get interestin'. What colors do you like? On the sign, I mean?"

"Leave that up to you."

"That's smart. Now, about the sign—I'll give you two choices . . . and that'll have to be up to you."

"Go ahead, Mister Bixby."

"Ten dollars for the 'dee-lux' or five dollars for the 'good 'nuff'?"

"Dee-lux."

"That's smart, too. Have it for you tomorrow."

"Fine."

"You know, them Keeler brothers is crazy."

"So I hear."

"You also know I paint markers, too."

"What kind of markers?"

"Boot Hill."

"I'll keep that in mind, Mister Bixby, for the future. The distant future. See you tomorrow."

"Yeah. Freightin', huh? Say, Mister Silver, would you like to pay in advance?"

"Be glad to, Mister Bixby."

Isaac Silver was walking north on Bravo Street when the two of them stepped out of the alley and faced him.

The Keeler brothers.

CHAPTER TWENTY

Ike stopped and made himself ready for whatever was to come.

This time neither brother had a whiskey bottle in his hand.

"You remember us," Claude said.

"Yeah," Charlie added, "we met up earlier this mornin'."

"I remember. What about it?"

Several citizens had already noticed and drifted into doorways, behind posts and other safer havens from what appeared to be inevitable, one way or another.

"Well, we sobered up some since," Claude said.

"So I see."

"Well . . ." Charlie cleared his throat, then paused.

"Well, what?"

"We been thinkin' it over." Charlie nodded.

"And?"

Claude also nodded. "And we figure we was outta line some."

"We ought not'a shot up your store," Charlie said.

"It's not the store I was worried about, fellas—my boys were up there, and my brother."

"Yeah, so we heard," said Charlie.

"We sometimes get a little rambunctious when we drink, particularly in the mornin'," Claude added.

"Ain't never seen anybody shoot like that." Charlie.

"We know you coulda shot us instead of them whiskey bottles . . ." Claude.

"If you'd'a mind to," Charlie. "So, kinda taught us a lesson . . . when we sobered up . . ."

"Just wanted to let you know . . . and not just in private," Claude said.

"That's all right, fellas, just watch out about that drinking." Ike smiled. "Particularly in the morning."

"We'll try," Claude said.

"Good."

"Oh, one more thing . . ." Charlie.

"What's that?"

"Be it all right if me and Claude come trade with you over at your store?"

"It be . . . once we open up in a day or so."

Both Keeler brothers nodded, turned, and walked back into the alley.

"Ike Silver."

He turned and saw Oliver Knight hurrying toward him.

"You just provided me with a finish to that story. For a minute there I thought I was going to write an obituary . . . one way or another."

"For a minute there, so did I."

"Never saw those Keeler boys so tame."

"Well, could be they're not as crazy as everybody said."

"Could be, but Mister Silver, you got more faith in human nature than anybody I ever met. Well, got to get back to that deadline."

"And I've got to get back to the store."

Rupert Lessur, Gallagher and Rooster were standing in front of Lessur's office as Big Ike passed by.

"Hello again, gentlemen." He smiled and continued on his way toward the store.

The Keeler brothers smiled and waved as they rode past Ike Silver.

"Can you beat that?" Gallagher shook his head.

"Yes, I can," Rupert Lessur said and walked into his office.

The hammer smashed down.

Inside the stable, Ben Brown worked the bellows and hammered on a chunk of iron.

"What do you see when you hit like that, Ben?"

He stopped work and looked up at his wife.

"What?"

"I said, what do you see when you hammer like that? It's not just a piece of iron you're hitting."

"Have I ever treated you wrong . . . or the boy? Have I ever—"

"No, Ben. You got a gentle touch for such a powerful man. But—"

"But what?"

"We're free now, Ben."

"Are we?"

"Yes."

"Maybe there's kinds of shackles that can't be seen."

"Maybe there are . . . but not around here. Has Mister Silver ever done you wrong? Or us? Has he?"

"No."

"Then can't you just . . ."

"Just what?"

"Ease up a little, Ben? Just a little? While we're here? For the boy's sake. . . . and mine? Can't you?"

Melena turned.

"Where you going?"

"I'm gonna see if I can't fix supper for those folks."

Ike Silver sat at the rolltop desk in the store going over some papers as Melena came in from the side door.

"Mister Silver . . ."

"Come in, Melena. What is it?"

"You know there's a kitchen back there . . ."

"Yes, I know."

"Well, I was just wondering . . . I thought if it's all right with you, I could fix supper for tonight."

"We'd appreciate that, Melena. Sure could use a home-cooked meal. And help yourself to anything you need from the store."

"Thank you, and there's some fat chickens out back. I think they belong to you."

"Pick out the fattest." He smiled.

Melena Brown started to leave, then hesitated.

Ike Silver rose from his chair and came closer to her.

"There's something else, isn't there? Please tell me."

"About Ben . . ."

"What about him?"

"I know he seems sort of . . . starchy."

"Hadn't noticed."

"You're a good man to say that. You see . . . Ben thought . . . after the war, when we left Georgia . . . well, he's good with his hands, Mister Silver. He can do most anything, but he can't get work—not on his own or for anybody—and he's gonna have to go to sharecropping. It's nigh killing him."

"I understand."

"Back in La Paz . . . we didn't have but fifty cents. We can't travel like other folks, but we was gonna have to sell—"

"Melena, don't you say anything to him. Let me see what I can do."

"That's not why I—"

"I know. There's—"

The front door opened and Sister Mary Boniface stood in the doorway.

"The sign says Closed, but I thought I'd come in anyhow. Is it all right?"

"Sister Bonney, the door is never closed for you. Come in."

"Hello, Melena."

"Sister Bonney . . . uh, excuse me."

Melena moved toward the side door.

"Any luck?" Ike asked.

"Yes." Sister Bonney smiled.

"Good."

"No, bad. All bad. I've been all over town. There's nothing available for a school. At least nothing I could afford."

"Are you going to give up?"

"No."

"I didn't think so. But I have been thinking . . ."

"Do you have any suggestions?"

"That's up to you."

"What is?"

"Come with me. I want to show you something."

Ike lead her to one of the doors.

"What is it?"

"It's a door. Go ahead and open it."

She did. He stepped up next to her.

"You see this big storeroom . . . with its own entrance from the street?"

"Yes, I see it."

"Well, right now it's empty. Got any ideas?"

"God bless you, Big Ike," she said, beaming.

"He always has . . . almost always."

* * *

There was a knock on the door of Rupert Lessur's private office.

"Come in."

The door swung open and Rooster's head and shoulder appeared. "Mister Lessur."

"Yes?"

"Somebody here says she wants to see you."

"She?"

"Uh-huh."

"Who?"

"Sister Bonney." The voice came from the other side of the door. "May I come in?"

"Of course. Rooster, quit blocking the door."

"Yes, sir."

Sister Bonney swept past, entered, nodded at Rupert Lessur sitting at his desk and Jim Gallagher sitting in a chair across from Lessur's desk, then looked around the room.

"Very nice office you have here, Mister Lessur, especially that desk."

Lessur rose, looked at Gallagher, who got the message and also rose and removed his hat.

"It was imported,"—Lessur pointed at the desk—"from France. I'm told it once belonged to Cardinal Richelieu."

"Not one of my favorite people," Sister Bonney said.

"Oh? I hope you won't hold that against me. Rooster, that'll be all."

Rooster nodded, took off his hat, stepped back and closed the door.

"What can I do for you, Sister?"

"You can deliver that crate."

"Oh, really? Then you found somewhere to start the school."

"Yes. Just a few minutes ago."

"Very good. Where shall we deliver it?"

"To the storeroom behind Mister Silver's new place."

Gallagher squinted at his boss.

"That's where you're going to teach?" Lessur smiled.

"And live."

"Well, that is . . . convenient."

"Yes, isn't it? The crate—would tomorrow be . . . convenient?"

"Of course. Gallagher, you'll see to it."

"Sure, boss."

"Oh, one more thing, Mister Lessur."

"What's that, Sister?"

"You said something about a contribution. . . ."

"I did, didn't I?"

"Yes, you did. Would fifty dollars be convenient?"

"Of course."

"And what about you, Mister Gallagher? Say, five dollars?"

"Uh, sure, Sister."

"I thank you both . . . and Mister Lessur, that desk looks right at home. Good day, gentlemen."

Sister Mary Boniface closed the door behind her.

"Well, Mister Lessur," Gallagher said, "seems like they're all settlin' in over there."

"So it seems." Lessur struck a match with his thumbnail and lit a cigar. "For the time being."

Colorados, Quemada, Secoro and a number of other mounted Apaches, all grim, almost funereal, looked down from their vantage point toward the activity at the mouth of the Rattlesnake Mine and the nearby area. Dolan and his men were cutting down trees, hauling and sawing beams for shoring.

The Apaches were looking at what was just a small patch of their once vast empire. From the Mogollan River southward across the dreaded desert waste to the sky-piercing peaks of the Sierra Madre in Mexico—all that the Apache had conquered. They had scattered the Zunis out of the heartland, chased the Comanches to the east and the Yumas to the west and carved their claim in blood and fear.

For more than two hundred years the Apache nation, made up of many tribes—Tonto, Mimbreno, Mescalero, Jicarilla, White Mountain, Lipan, Pinal, Arivarpo, Coyatero, and Chiricahua—had been invincible until the white men and bluecoats with long knives and long guns and large numbers had shrunk what was once an empire to a few pieces of dirt called reservations, and to barren slopes and rocks fit only for goats and snakes.

Quemada pointed and spoke to his chief in the dialect of the Athapascan-Spanish tongue. "They came here, Colorados, while you were in their prison. Not enough they take the land where we live and hunt—now they foul the place where the bones of our fathers and their fathers before them rest. For their yellow metal they desecrate the ground where we will be buried."

Quemada looked at Secorro, then back to Colorados, waiting for him to speak, but the Apache chief remained silent.

"And they will come after you, Colorados, to take you back to their prison, where you will die and be buried in some unremembered grave on their land instead of here with your people . . . what is left of your people." He pointed below. "Look at what is happening even now."

"I have seen," Colorados said softly.

"But what will you *do?*"

"Our tribes are scattered."

"Bring them together. Your father did."

"We have no weapons."

"Take theirs—your father did. All the tribes will follow the son of Mangas Colorados. Gather them together."

"I still feel the weakness of my wounds. First I will gather my own strength."

"Then what will you do?"

Colorados did not answer.

CHAPTER TWENTY-ONE

The late afternoon shadows cast cooling shade along the west side of the street as Ike Silver walked from the Hassayampa Hotel toward Belinda's Emporium, where he had been directed upon inquiring as to the whereabouts of Scotty Simpson.

Belinda's Emporium, formerly Brady's Bar, was one of the better-class saloons on Whiskey Row. The worst of the lot was the Golondrina on the far end of the street, whose customers were almost exclusively Mexicans, Breeds and some Indians who had abandoned the blanket and come closer to the white man's dominion, but not close enough to frequent the other saloons on Whiskey Row.

Occasionally some Anglos would duck into the Golondrina and make straight for the cribs out back, where females of varying hues would provide services of varying fillips.

None of the other saloons had cribs, but all had rooms upstairs, which served the same purpose but with more comfort and cleanliness—and higher fees.

In spite of the early hour, Francine, Alma and Marisa had already made several ascents and descents to and from the second level. Currently, as Ike Silver entered, Francine and Alma were drifting among the customers and card games on the main floor.

Big Ike was barely through the bat wings when greeted by the Major Domo.

"What ho, apothecary!"

"What ho yourself, Binky."

And not far behind, the proprietor herself. "This is an unexpected pleasure, Mister Silver."

"Thank you, but not for long, Miss Millay. I was told that Scotty Simpson might be here."

Belinda nodded. "Yeah, but I'm afraid you're too late to rescue him."

"From what?"

"That poker game."

She pointed to one of the tables, where Scotty sat with three other players, including Rupert Lessur, who had most of the money in front of him.

"Scotty Simpson," Belinda said, "is the worst damn poker player I ever saw."

"Why didn't you sit in and rescue him?" Ike asked.

"A long time ago I made me a rule to never sit in on a poker game unless I'm invited."

"Good rule."

Ike moved toward the table, where Lessur was dealing.

"Good day, gentlemen. How're you doing, Scotty?"

"Just lost my poke, includin' stage fare to Albuquerque."

"Sorry to hear that, Scotty, but I was just going to ask you to stay on at the store for a while. We need more help than I thought with the inventory and . . . things."

Scotty pointed at the pile of money in front of Lessur.

"Looks like I got no choice. Old soljer's home'll have to wait."

"Oh, just a minute, Scotty." Lessur smiled. "I had no idea this was your retirement money. I'll be glad to give it back, old soldier, so you can be on your way."

Scotty Simpson rose.

"I don't play that way. Never have and never will. I'll take that job, Mister Silver."

"Good. You want to come over for supper?"

"Nope." He nodded toward the cold cuts on the counter. "See you in the mornin'."

"Fine. Good night, gentlemen. Mister Lessur."

"Oh, Mister Silver,"—Rupert Lessur tapped the deck of cards on the table—"it might be interesting if you and I played a game sometime."

"I thought we already were."

Ike turned and walked toward the bat wings. As he approached, Binky tipped his bowler.

"Touché."

Sister Bonney had just set a platter of cooked vegetables on the long wooden table, already adorned with three fat roasted chickens and several other platters of worthy culinary accompaniments.

Melena was still at the stove.

Big Ike, Jake and Obie entered and were astounded by the sight and fragrance of the repast.

"Isaac, my brother,"—Jake extended both arms— "upon what oasis have we stumbled? Is this the palace of some mighty potentate? Maybe the banquet hall of the Caliph of Baghdad?"

Jake picked up a plate with a small chip out of it. He ignored the defect.

"Never have these eyes beheld such splendor!"

He set the plate back onto the table and inhaled deeply.

"Never has this nose—and what a nose—inhaled such appetizing aromas!"

Ike winked at Sister Bonney.

"I don't see any pastrami."

"Pastrami is for peasants." Jake lifted a platter containing a chicken. "Isaac, milad, gaze upon this royal bird."

The back door opened and in came Jed, followed by Ben and Benjie.

"Aah-hah! As my brother, the card player, once said, 'a full house.'"

Ben stood by the door with his hand on Benjie's shoulder and looked at Ike.

"Jed said you wanted to see us."

Ike nodded.

"Time for supper. Sit down, everybody."

Ben didn't move. He still held on to his son, not budging. Melena tried not to, but her eyes flitted to, then away from her husband.

Ben stared straight ahead.

"We'll eat later, Mister Silver."

It was not an easy moment as Ike finally spoke, the tone in his voice stronger than most of them had ever heard before. "*Sit down, Mister Brown.*" And then with a difference that seemed to adjure, "cut out all this nonsense and sit down," he added: "Please."

Ben's eyes locked onto his wife's. His grip tightened on the boy's shoulder, then relaxed. "Sit down, Benjie," he said softly.

Everyone else in the room seemed to take a deep breath as Jake reached into his pocket, produced a yarmulke, placed it on his head and looked around.

"An old custom," he shot a glance at Ike, "on some occasions I can't break, or want to."

"Who's gonna say a prayer?" Obie asked.

Jed's eyes circumvolved the diners.

"Well," he remarked, "this ought to be interesting."

Sister Bonney bowed her head.

"Why doesn't each of us say a prayer . . . to himself?"

"A decision, Sister," Jake said, "worthy of Solomon."

They all bowed their heads, each in a private, silent prayer.

After that moment, Melena looked at her husband, then started to rise. Sister Mary Boniface restrained her and rose.

"You cooked. I'll serve."

"I'll carve." Ike picked up a knife.

"And," Jake volunteered, "you know who'll do the dishes?"

He pointed to Jed, Obie and Benjie.

"You three!"

During the darkest part of that night there was heard, above the heart of the desert along the sawtooth peaks of the Mogallons, the ominous rumble of thunder and the promise of a gathering storm.

CHAPTER TWENTY-TWO

The next morning the general store and the area around it were a wellspring of activity.

Tom Bixby and an assistant had taken down the old sign and were affixing the freshly lettered new one.

Scotty had reported for work and he, Big Ike and Ben were collecting items and loading the wagon with supplies to be delivered to the Rattlesnake Mine.

Sister Bonney was in the soon-to-be-schoolroom with Gallagher and Rooster, who had brought over the crate from Santa Fe.

"Sister," Gallagher asked after they had set the crate where she had indicated, "you want me and Rooster to empty it?"

"No, thanks. Just open it, please. I'll empty it. There are some . . . personal items along with the books."

"Yes, ma'am."

Benjie was showing Jed and Obie how to do the yo-yo. When he finished the demonstration he handed it to Jed.

"Now you try."

Jake was sweeping the porch when a well-dressed, heavyset gentleman approached smoking what was left of a cigar.

"Good morning," Jake said.

The gentleman looked up at the new sign. "You one of the new owners?"

"Right. Name's Silver. Jake Silver."

"John Davis. I'm the mayor of Prescott. Also have a real estate business. Just got back into town this morning."

"How do you do, Your Honor?"

His Honor ignored the question, but spat out one of his own. Ben, who had been carrying a heavy sack of beans, could hear this part of the conversation. "You're *Jews*, aren't you?"

"That's right."

"Well, up to now, we haven't had any *Jews* in our little village."

Jake shrugged. "Maybe that's why it's a little village."

The mayor looked Jake up and down and through and through in as deprecating a way as he knew how, dropped his cigar on the porch and proceeded along the street of his little village.

"Watch where you drop your butt,"—Jake swept the cigar off the porch—"Mister Mayor."

Ben Brown was still watching and listening as Obie, followed by Jed and Benjie, walked up to his uncle.

"Uncle Jake, why did he say *Jews* like that?"

Jake looked after the mayor.

"Boys, it would take a couple of thousand years to explain that."

Ben went on his way, carrying the heavy sack of beans.

Jake pointed the handle of the broom. "Now, Sister Bonney is in the storeroom cleaning it up. Why don't you boys see if you can help?"

The boys were agreeable to Uncle Jake's suggestion. They scampered around the corner.

Tom Bixby, who had also heard the conversation with the mayor, came closer to Jake.

"I wouldn't pay too much attention to *His Honor*. He's not as honorable as he makes out, and most everybody knows it, but they don't let on."

"You mean he runs a crooked real estate business?"

"Not that. You heard him say he's been outta town."

Jake nodded.

"He bought a mortgage on Widow Brown's place over in Pinto."

"So?"

"So, he collects payment by spending a couple of · nights there every month."

"I get it." Jake smiled.

"So does he."

Jim Gallagher and Rooster had come back from delivering the crate to Sister Mary Boniface. Rupert Lessur stood outside his office and motioned for Gallagher to follow him inside. The motion did not include Rooster, who waited outside.

Lessur sat behind Cardinal Richelieu's desk and lit one of his long, slim cigars.

"Well, Gallagher, what the hell is going on?"

"Where, boss? What do you mean?"

"At the store over there. Where the hell do you think I mean? What're they doing?"

"Like I said, Mister Lessur, they're settlin' in. Gettin' ready to open up, and the Sister, she's gonna fix that back room into a school."

"Not a very informative report. I knew all that. Anything else?"

"Well, no . . . except ole Scotty went back to work over there."

"I knew that, too. Well, never mind. I think you and the boys better head back to La Paz and pick up a load. . . ."

"La Paz? What about them Apaches?"

"What about them?"

"Well, they're . . . hostile."

"You expect me to wait until they're tame?"

"Well, no sir, but—"

"But what?"

"You ain't the one goin' to La Paz."

"That's right. *You* are. That's what you're paid for. Besides, Colonel Crook said something about providing an escort, he—"

There was a knock on the door; then it was opened by Rooster.

"Mister Lessur. I thought you'd want to know . . ."

"Know what?"

"Colonel Crook and some of his troopers just turned into town and they're comin' this way."

"Very good." Lessur rose, cigar in hand. "Probably wants to talk to me about that escort."

Rupert Lessur, Gallagher and Rooster came out just in time to see Crook ride past without slowing down and head toward Ike Silver's general store.

Gallagher thought it wise to make no comment as Rupert Lessur abruptly turned on his heels and moved swiftly back inside.

As Crook dismounted, Big Ike stood outside the doorway.

"Morning, Mister Silver."

"Good morning, Colonel. You must've been up before dawn."

"Old army habit."

"I know."

"You've done some soldiering?"

"Some."

"I thought so. Were we on the same side, Mister Silver?"

"We were."

"Good. We still are."

"Coffee, Colonel?"

Crook nodded.

"Come on in, sir."

There was a large pot atop a stove close to Ike's rolltop desk, near a corner of the store. His hand reached for it and poured the hot black fluid into a couple of tin cups.

Ike sat at the desk and Crook nearby on a Douglas chair.

As each man drank from his cup, Ike took a closer look at the wilderness soldier. While in California after the war, he had heard tales about how the man now sitting across from him had subdued the Humboldts, then the Rogue Rivers and the Shastas, tribes that had been marauding the mining camps. Crook also had been successful in campaigns against the Kalmuths and the Tolowas, and then the Columbia River tribes.

Ike had heard the tales and now he was sitting across from the man himself.

"There's something I wanted to talk to you about, Mister Silver."

"Ike, please, and I didn't think you came all the way here just to get some coffee."

"You're right, and while we're at it, my name's George."

"Not as long as you're wearing that uniform . . ."—Ike smiled—"or what's left of it. What did you want to talk about, Colonel?"

"That eagle claw Colorados gave you. I see you're still wearing it."

"I am."

"Good idea. Are you aware of its significance as far as the Apache is concerned?"

"Not altogether."

"Of all living things, the Apache holds the golden eagle in the greatest respect and reverence. The eagle embodies those attributes the Apache considers supreme. Courage. Vigilance. Swiftness. Bravery and independence. When an Apache chief bestows the claw of an eagle on a warrior, it means he holds that warrior in the highest regard."

"I'm not a warrior."

"You are in the eyes of Colorados . . . and a friend, close as a brother. Maybe closer. Good coffee. You know much about Colorados?"

"No."

"Neither did I. But I made it my business to find out. His father was Mangas Colorados. Organized all the Apaches some years back. Put on a hell of a war."

"I've heard about that."

"Did you hear about what started that war?"

"No."

"Wars have been started over land . . . over religions . . . even over a pig. This one started over a whipping."

Crook took a deep drink.

"Yes, sir, good coffee . . . Some white men got hold of Mangas, tied him up and whipped him like a dog. Hard to get good coffee out here."

Ike poured another cup. "Have some more."

"Thanks. Mangas hit the army hip and high. Then one day he came in to talk peace. We outnumbered him, outgunned him, but we raised a white flag. So, Mangas came in to talk. That was his mistake and ours."

"Why?"

"Because this time he wasn't whipped. He was tortured with hot bayonets . . . then shot to death."

"Colonel, I'm glad I'm not soldiering anymore."

"But somebody has to. You know what Arizona is?"

"What do you mean?"

"I mean, Arizona is a sort of nature's laboratory, where the Almighty's tried some rewarding experiments. Underneath, there's gold and silver, copper and coal. And on top, land for grazing—land for the plow. Enough for everybody."

"What're you getting at, Colonel?"

"I want to be fair."

"I know that."

"How do you know?"

"You've been fair with the Indians before. The Columbia River tribes in Yakima, the Humboldts in California. I was in California when you were."

Crook took another swallow.

"I went in there with a command of forty men, my uniform and a toothbrush. Didn't see a house for over a year."

"The Indians saw plenty of you."

"Well, that was then and this is now, here and now . . . and here and now there are some people who don't want peace in the Territory, and I'm not just talking about Indians."

"Still don't know what you mean, Colonel."

"I mean as long as the Apaches are stirred up there's contracts to be got. The war department disburses over two million dollars a year inside the Arizona border. Those contracts mean big profits to white men. They supply the army with beef. Then there's beans and bacon at forty and fifty cents a pound, flour at twenty dollars a hundred weight. And it all has to be freighted in. Those men don't want the Apaches to be too quiet."

"You think I'm one of those men?"

"No, I don't. That's the reason I've come to see you." Crook pointed at Ike Silver's throat. "That and the eagle claw Colorados gave you. If you see Colorados again—"

"That's not likely."

"It might be more likely than you think. He'll listen to you. I want you to tell him something."

"That the army wants to talk again?"

"That *I* do."

"He won't go back to prison."

"He won't have to—not if the plan I have in mind works. I'll get him pardoned. But it'll take some time."

"What plan is that, Colonel?"

"It's called a truce. He and his tribe can live and hunt wherever they are now. I'll look the other way. In fact, he'll be under my protection so long as they don't hunt *us* . . . our supply trains, stagecoaches, settlers and troopers. I can be his best friend . . . or his worst enemy."

"I believe that."

"I make damn few promises, but I keep 'em."

"I believe that, too, Colonel."

"I'll meet him any time, anywhere he wants. No weapons. No tricks . . . so we can make a beginning. Will you tell him that?"

"I will . . . if I see him."

Crook drank the last of the coffee from the tin cup.

"Mister Silver, you make good coffee."

"Colonel Crook, you make good sense."

As Colonel Crook and Ike Silver came out of the store, Rupert Lessur approached.

"Colonel."

"Yes, Mister Lessur?"

"I saw you ride in just a little while ago."

"Did you?"

"Were you coming by my office?"

"No."

"Oh. Well, I was wondering if you thought over what we talked about. . . ."

"We talked about a lot of things. What were you wondering about specifically?"

"I, uh . . ." Lessur glanced at Ike.

"You can speak in front of Mister Silver. The army has no secrets where its friends are concerned."

"Yes, well, about army escorts for my . . . for civilian supply trains and—"

"Oh, yes, that, Mister Lessur." Crook also glanced at Ike. "We're working on a plan, aren't we, Mister Silver? I'll do what I can as soon as I can." Crook looked toward Ben Brown's wagon, which was loaded with cargo.

"Mister Silver, I see you're already starting in business."

Ike nodded.

"We're delivering supplies up to the Rattlesnake Mine."

"Uh-huh. In that case, I hope you'll remember what *we* talked about."

"I'll remember."

"Good luck, Mister Silver. Good day, Mister Lessur." Colonel Crook walked to where the other troopers were saddled and waiting. He mounted and led the troopers as they rode off toward Fort Whipple.

Lessur smiled. "Mister Silver, about that trip to the mine . . ."

"What about it?"

"I hope you don't run into any . . . trouble."

"Do you?"

Big Ike walked back toward the store.

Rupert Lessur walked back toward his office.

CHAPTER TWENTY-THREE

"Scotty."

"Yes, sir, Mister Silver."

"Will you please just call me Ike?"

"All those years I worked for Mister Winthrop, I called him Mister Winthrop."

"Well, I'm not Mister Winthrop, but if it'll make you feel better, you can call my brother Mister Silver. He's older than I am. Satisfactory?"

"Satisfactory . . . Ike. What was it you wanted?"

"I wanted to tell you . . . what a help you've already been, tell you how much we appreciate it . . . and discuss your salary."

"Nothin' to discuss. Whatever you think is fair."

"How much was Mister Winthrop paying you?"

"Before he died?"

Ike smiled. "Yes, before he died."

"Thirty dollars a month. That's a dollar a day . . . some months."

"Well, from now on you're getting forty dollars a month. That's about a dollar thirty-three cents day . . . some months. Satisfactory?"

"More 'n satisfactory."

"And since Ben Brown and his family have taken over your . . . accommodations back there, I've also arranged to pay for your room over at the Hassayampa. Is that satisfactory?"

"You bet. And you know somethin' else . . . Ike? I been thinkin' . . ."

"About what?"

"There's them that are a lot more ready for it than I am."

"Ready for what?"

"Old Soldjer's Home. Also, I decided to throw away this cane."

"How're you doing, Sister Bonney?" Ike asked.

"Well, as you can see, I've unloaded the books from the crate, along with a few personal items, which I've put away."

"Good."

"Mister Brown has volunteered to build a partition before he leaves in that corner, where I can sleep as soon as I get a bed."

"I'm sure there's one upstairs you can have."

"Excellent."

"And Mister Knight, he's the newspaper man, you know . . ."

"Yes, I know."

"He's donating a desk and chair from the newspaper office."

"Uh-huh."

"I'm working on chairs for the children."

"You're sure there'll be children?"

"Of course I am. Starting with yours."

"Looks like you're doing just fine. If you need anything, just ask Scotty or Jake. He and the boys are upstairs. I'll be gone for awhile."

"May I ask where?"

"Taking a load of supplies to Sean Dolan up at the Rattlesnake Mine."

"He's a good man."

"That he is, Sister."

"Tell him I pray for his safety and the safety of his men at the mine."

"Should I also tell him that you pray they'll strike gold?"

"I believe the good Lord has more important things on his mind than such temporal matters. A safe journey to you, Ike."

Hammering came from the stable as Ike Silver walked in with his Remington strapped around his waist, carrying a long gun. A beautiful—if any gun can be called beautiful—Henry rifle. A .44 caliber, fifteen shot type that weighed nine and a half pounds with a brass breach.

Ben Brown stopped hammering and looked up. "Looks like you're loaded for bear, Mister Silver."

Ike nodded. "Looks like . . . except there isn't any bear out there."

"Yeah, but there's plenty of somethin' else."

"What're you working on?"

Brown pointed the hammer toward the ceiling of the stable.

Ike smiled. "Looks like a little daylight showing through that roof."

"And starlight."

"And rain, if we ever get any."

"Thought I'd patch it up some, before I get back to work on the rest of those wagons . . . if that's all right with you?"

"Fine . . . and thanks for helping Scotty load up the supplies for the mine."

Ben Brown nodded. "You gonna be leavin' now?"

"Soon as I say so long to Jake and the boys."

"Jake and the boys have come down to say so long to you."

Jake had entered the stable followed by Jed and Obie, and then Melena with Benjie.

"Ike, you look like a one-man army," Jake said.

Jed took a step toward his father. "Dad, you going out there all alone?"

"Oh, I've got Mister Henry here for company,"— he patted the gun in his holster—"and Mister Remington, but I'm sure I won't need them."

"It's good to be sure," Jake said, "but I still think I ought to go with you."

"Nope. You've got to stay here. Somebody's got to be in charge of the store and take care of the boys."

"But Dad," Obie said, "Jed and—"

"No buts. I'll be back before—"

"Mister Silver." Ben Brown looked from his wife back to Ike.

"Yes?"

"I'd care to go along, if you don't mind."

"Well . . ."

"It *is* my wagon . . ."

Melena smiled.

"And it *is* a two-man job. One to teamster and one to . . ."—he pointed to the Henry—" . . . if you don't mind."

"I don't mind, if Melena . . ."

Melena, still smiling, nodded.

"Well, then," Ike said, "I guess that settles that."

From the front window of his office, Rupert Lessur stood watching—with Gallagher just behind him—

as the wagon rolled by with Ben Brown at the reins and Ike Silver alongside.

"It appears," Gallagher said, "that the two of 'em are heading for the Rattlesnake."

"Yes," Lessur nodded, "and you're heading for somewhere else."

"Huh? Where?"

Lessur walked to his desk and picked up a piece of paper.

"To where I told you. La Paz. The *Colorado Queen* is due in, and I've prepared a list of items for you to pick up and bring back to Prescott. I'm not going to let our wagons stay empty in La Paz forever."

"But the Indians . . ."

"The Indians will be occupied with what's going on at that mine . . . and with Mister Silver's wagon. Besides, I've made arrangements with Colonel Crook this morning," he lied.

"What kind of arrangements?"

"Crook's sending out a patrol to escort you back once you get into Indian territory."

"He is?"

"He is. Round up Rooster and the boys, tell them to get ready to ride."

"Sure, boss, but . . ."

"But what?"

"Be all right if I stop over at the saloon and have just one drink first?"

"Go ahead."

"Is this a dagger which I see before me?"

Binky was regaling half a dozen customers at a corner of the saloon.

"The handle toward my hand? Come, let me clutch thee. I have thee not, and yet I see thee still."

He gazed at the empty glass held high in his grasp.

"Art thou not, fatal vision, sensible to feeling as to sight? Or art thou but a dagger of the mind? A false creation proceeding from the heat-oppresse'd brain . . ."

Belinda Millay sat at her usual table playing solitaire as Jim Gallagher walked in, nodded at her and proceeded to the bar.

Belinda rose and strolled over as Henry poured whiskey into a glass in front of Gallagher.

"Hello, Jim." She smiled.

"Miss Millay."

"Kind of early for you, isn't it?"

"Yes, ma'am. Having just one before I leave."

"Where you going?"

"La Paz. Business for Mister Lessur."

"Kind of dangerous business, isn't it?"

"Like he said, that's what I get paid for. Besides, he's made arrangements with Colonel Crook to meet us on the way back with a patrol."

"Does Colonel Crook know that?"

"Huh?"

"Never mind."

"You know your friend, Ike Silver, is on his way to Rattlesnake with a load of supplies?"

"Yeah, somebody told me they saw him go by," she said. "Seems like there's an awful lot of traffic around here lately, all things considered."

"Sure does." Gallagher nodded and swallowed the whiskey in one swift gulp, then stared at the empty glass.

"Henry, maybe I ought to have one for the road."

"Sure," Henry said and started to pour.

"One *pint*," Gallagher added.

Gallagher paid, put the pint of whiskey in his coat pocket and headed for the bat wings.

Binky had finished his oration and moved to the bar next to Belinda as Oliver Knight entered and joined them.

"May I buy you two a drink?"

"Not me," Belinda said.

"In that case," Binky said, "I'll have a double."

"Grand." Knight smiled. "It's time for my weekly celebration. I've just put my sweetheart to bed."

"Your sweetheart?" Binky seemed surprised.

"Yes. *The Prescott Independent*."

"Melena," Sister Bonney said as she came into the kitchen, "I just heard."

"Heard what, Sister?"

"That Ben went along with Ike to deliver those goods to Sean Dolan."

"He sure did, Sister."

"I was away trying to promote some necessities for the school."

"I hope you were successful."

"I think so. Sorry I didn't get a chance to say good-bye. Was it your idea?"

"Was what my idea?"

"That Ben go along."

"Oh, I had the idea, all right, but I knew better."

"What do you mean, 'knew better'?"

"Well, my husband's a man set in his ways, and one of his ways is to do what he thinks is his idea . . . and so I let him think all the ideas are his, without my sayin' anything. But sometimes I just look at him in a certain way, without sayin' a word, mind you, and he gets the idea I was thinkin' about . . . thinkin' it was his idea in the first place. You understand what I'm sayin'?"

"I surely do, Melena, and as a matter of fact, I was sort of hoping, actually more than hoping, that it would work out this way. You understand what *I'm* saying?" She smiled.

"I surely do, Sister." Melena also smiled.

A warm nomad wind whispered around boulders and through brush and jagged rocks and vast expanse as the loaded wagon with Ike and Ben aboard creaked and groaned toward the Rattlesnake Mine.

For miles the two men had ridden in silence. Then Ben spoke without looking at the man next to him.

"We'll make a lot better time on the way back, but I don't want to drive these animals too hard with this load."

"You're the teamster." Ike smiled.

"You know somethin'," Ben said, "you sure aren't like hardly anybody else I ever met up with."

"I'm not sure how you mean that, but neither are you."

"Oh, I meant it kindly."

"So did I."

"What I mean is . . . well, hard to explain, but you don't push people, do you?"

"Only when I'm pushed."

"I've seen that too, like with them Keeler brothers. But you coulda done them a lot worse."

"No. I think we're all better off the way things turned out."

"I guess so."

"Those Keelers, they're all right. Most of us have more in common than we think."

There was a moment of silence; then Ben spoke, still without looking at Ike.

"You know somethin', Mister Silver? You and I do have somethin' more in common."

"What's that?"

"That, Mister Silver . . . seems to be the Rattlesnake Mine just ahead."

CHAPTER TWENTY-FOUR

Gold always is, was, and will be where you find it.

The biggest and most famous find was by James Marshall in January of 1848 at Sutter's Mill, a sawmill owned by John A. Sutter—a find which set off a stampede of prospectors and land pirates, some of whom didn't know their assays from a hole in the ground.

After most of the California claims had been staked out and worked, many of those same prospectors whose prospects hadn't lived up to expectations began to backtrack from west to east in search of diggings that might have been overlooked in the westward stampede.

The first and most fertile finds occurred in the vast and varied expanse of Arizona; in the beginning, along the streams and rivers—the Colorado, the Gila, the Hassayampa—and later through all the mountainous regions of the Territory. Men such as Jacob Snively, Paulino Weaver and Henry Wickenburg hastened to exploit the terrain that had become a part of America's Manifest Destiny by virtue of the Gadsen Purchase in 1854.

But with the breakout of the Civil War in 1861 and the withdrawal of the army, the mines as well as the ranches of Arizona were left virtually defenseless. Apaches surged through the countryside in a rampage of ruination—destroying, burning and killing.

But after the official War Between the States, another less official but still deadly war was fought between the army and the Apaches—Apaches whose numbers were miniscule compared to the Confederates, but who were just as determined to fight, and often to die fighting.

The U.S. Army won that war, too. But some Indians wouldn't believe it. Despite the sporadic Apache rebellions, the Arizona mines were back in business— or trying to get back. Among the latter was the Rattlesnake.

The supplies in the wagon brought in by Ike and Ben were being unloaded by some of the miners. Ike, Ben and Sean Dolan sat on a fallen timber in one of the few shady sections of the area.

"Well, Sean," Ike asked, "what shape's the mine in?"

"Not as bad as I thought."

"Oh?"

"Worse."

"Oh."

"Hasn't been worked since the war started. Whatever time and the weather didn't ruin, the Apaches did. Seems they don't welcome intruders on their land, or in it."

"Can't say I blame 'em too much," Ike said. "This was their real estate for a long time."

"That's one way of lookin' at it."

"It's their way."

"Reckon so. They did their best to knock down all

the shoring and do whatever other damage they could think of—and they thought of plenty. It'll take us a long time before we can do some real diggin' and come out with gold."

"If there's any gold left."

"Son, I can smell gold like a jackass can smell water."

"You're pretty sure of yourself." Ike smiled.

"Who else would I be sure of? At least when it comes to yellow. It's been my life since I started swingin' a pick at the age of eleven. I don't know much else, but I know gold."

" 'Gold! Gold! Gold!' " Ike looked toward the shaft of the mine. " 'Bright and yellow, hard and cold.' "

"What's that?"

"Part of a poem."

"What's the other part?"

"Well, let me see—'Sought by the young, hugged by the old. To the very verge of the churchyard mold . . .' Something like that."

"Yeah, and it's true, with me and a lot of other prospectors. You know, Ike, there's a lot of other ways—if not easier, more certain—to make money, but there's somethin' about that stuff that gets into your veins along with your blood."

"It sure got into yours."

"I can't exactly explain it, but I figure the Almighty put everything on this earth for a purpose, on land and sea. It's funny, there ain't that much purpose for gold. The world could sure get along without it. But there's somethin' about it. . . ."

"I'm not sure what you're saying, Sean."

"Maybe I'm not either, but . . . well, that watch you carry for instance. Let me see it for a minute, will you?"

"Sure."

Ike lifted the watch and chain from his vest and handed it to Dolan, who let it rest in the palm of his calloused hand.

"This timepiece could be made of a lot of other metals and still keep the same time. Right?"

"Right."

"But there's somethin' about its being made of gold that makes it different." He handed the watch back to Ike. "You've got to admit it's beautiful."

"Yes, I do," Ike said as he looked at the watch.

"Same with a gold ring or a gold coin. And there's only so much of it, so people like me have to dig for it and people like you pay us for it—pay for all of us who find it, and even for those of us who don't."

Ike put the watch and chain back into his vest and into his pocket. "I never thought about it in those terms."

"You know somethin', Ike? Neither did I . . . at least not in those exact terms. But everythin' I've got in this world except for some loose change is invested in the Rattlesnake, and these men here, they're workin' for short money—awful short—but also for shares. So, brother, there better be some gold in that shaft. See what I mean?"

"I do." Ike rose. "And we better be getting back."

Ben also rose and spoke for the first time since they had sat on the fallen timber.

"Mister Dolan," he said, "I wish you luck."

"Thanks, and I'm glad to see you workin' with Big Ike. You could do a lot worse."

"I have." Ben almost smiled.

They started back toward the empty wagon. Ike looked at the sign Sean Dolan and the miners had placed above the shaft of the tunnel. He pointed.

"How come they call it the Rattlesnake?"

"Fella shot one up here and split a rock. When he looked at it, it was filled with gold."

"The rattlesnake?" Ike smiled.

"No, the rock. Sure you don't care to stay for supper?"

"Thanks, no. We'll be home for supper."

So Ike thought.

But from a far-above vantage point, Quemada, Secorro and three other mounted young Apaches watched as the wagon with Ike Silver and Ben Brown rolled away from the Rattlesnake Mine.

CHAPTER TWENTY-FIVE

Once again, a veil of silence fell between the two men as the wagon followed the descending sun on the way back to Prescott. Once again, Ike Silver thought it best not to push Ben Brown into a conversation, unless the black man did the initiating.

"On the way over I started to say somethin'. Remember?"

"I do." Ike nodded. "About us having something in common."

"Don't you care to know what that somethin' is?"

"I do. If you care to tell me."

"About the war. You fought in it."

"I did."

"On the side of the North?"

Ike nodded.

"I was a soldier, too. On the same side."

"Is that so?"

"You don't seem much surprised."

"Nope."

"You ever hear of a man, a white man, named Robert Gould Shaw?"

"I did."

"So did I, while the war was goin' on. I heard he was organizin' a unit of black soldiers—the Fifty-fourth Massachusetts. So I escaped from down South, made my way on the Underground Railroad and joined up. I was with him at Battery Wagner."

"Pretty bloody."

"Led us on a charge hollerin', 'Forward, Fifty-fourth!' He got killed there."

"I heard that, too."

"Later on I was in Virginia. Siege of Petersburg."

"That was even bloodier."

"Thirteen U.S. colored troops got the Congressional Medal of Honor. Did you know that?"

"No, I didn't."

"Neither does hardly anybody else. I didn't get no medal. But I did get a mini-ball."

"I got mine at Shiloh."

"So I heard. And that's what I meant about us havin' somethin' in common, Mister Silver."

"I see what you mean." Ike smiled. "And there's something I've been meaning to talk to you about, Mister Brown—if you'd care to listen."

"I'm listenin'."

As the wagon rounded the corner of a brawny boulder, Quemada, Secorro and the three other Apaches dropped from the top onto the moving wagon and started swinging fists and knives at Ike and Ben.

CHAPTER TWENTY-SIX

Three of the Apaches concentrated their attack on Ike and Ben. Fists flew and knives flashed. It happened before the two men had a chance to wield and fire their weapons. Both Ike and Ben fell off the wagon with the three Apaches on them.

Quemada and Secorro rode off on the wagon with the Henry rifle still onboard.

On the ground over and under the bodies tumbled, grappling in the dirt, twisting, with Ike and Ben warding off thrust after thrust of Apache knife blades while delivering blow after blow—smashing noses, jaws and throats of the red men until two of them lay unconscious while Ben grabbed hold of the third and pinned his arms behind him.

Ike drew his gun, cocked the hammer and pointed it directly at the temple of the Apache, who was certain he was about to be killed.

Instead, Ike's other hand clutched the thong at his throat and held out the eagle claw.

Ike said only one word.

"Colorados."

CHAPTER TWENTY-SEVEN

"Hello, Scotty."

"Well . . . hello, Miss Millay. Ain't seen you in here in a long time."

"Haven't been in here in a long time."

"That's what I meant. What can I do you for?"

"I, uh . . . need some . . . yellow ribbon. You carry any yellow ribbon?"

"Sure do. How much you want?"

"Oh . . . couple of yards'll do."

"I'll fetch it."

"Good . . . I didn't see Mister Silver come back into town yet."

"No, none of us have."

"Shouldn't he be back by now?"

"Seems like. Most any time now . . . but here's the other Mister Silver."

Jake had just come down the stairs.

"Good afternoon, Miss Millay, I heard you ask about Ike. Can I do anything for you?"

"Why, no. I needed some ribbon. . . ."

"I'm sure we got all you need."

"Yes, Scotty's getting it . . . and I did want to give

something to Ike. Do you mind if I give it to you and you can tell him it's from me . . . when he gets back?"

"Sure. That'll be fine. What is it?"

She reached into her purse, then handed him a coin. "Just a silver dollar. It's customary for luck when somebody goes into business. Will you tell him it's from me . . . for luck?"

Jake nodded and took the silver coin.

"I'll be glad to. Silver for Silver. I'm sure he'll appreciate it and so do I . . . all of us do."

"And I'd like to talk to the nun if she's around?"

"Sister Bonney? Right through that door. She's fixing things up for the school."

"Thank you. I'll be right back."

Sister Bonney and Melena were hanging up a curtain as Belinda walked into the storeroom.

"Oh, excuse me, ladies. May I come in for just a minute?"

"Of course. I'm Sister Bonney, and this is Mrs. Melena Brown."

"Pleased to meet you both. I'm Belinda Millay. I own one of the saloons down the street."

Sister Bonney smiled. "Yes, Belinda's Emporium. We've heard all about it."

"I guess everybody has by now. I just came over to buy some ribbon. Mrs. Brown, I understand your husband went with Big Ike to the mine."

"Yes, he did."

"Are you going to be staying here in Prescott?"

"I . . . don't know."

"I hope so. Sister, there was something else. I understand you're starting a school."

"Yes. Do you have children?"

"Me? Oh, no. But I know you've been to different places around town for—"

"For whatever help I could get. Yes, that's right, Miss Millay. Desks, chairs . . ."

"Money?"

"That always comes in handy."

"Well, I didn't expect you to come and see me, so I thought I'd come by and see you . . . with some money."

Belinda took a roll of currency out of her purse.

"Would a hundred dollars help?"

"A hundred dollars!" Sister Bonney glanced at Melena.

"I hope you'll accept it even if you consider it tainted. . . ."

"Miss Millay, I consider it a most generous gift from a most generous lady, and I accept it with deepest gratitude and so will all the children. You'll be in all our prayers, especially mine."

Belinda handed Sister Bonney the money. "Well, here then." She paused for a moment. "You know, it's funny. The three of us."

"I don't understand," Sister Bonney said.

"Well, Missus Brown, she's taken a vow to one man. And you, Sister, you've taken a different kind of vow, while I . . . as far as men are concerned . . ."

"Miss Millay, in the eyes of our Lord, the three of us are sisters."

Belinda Millay turned and walked through the door, back into the store toward the front door.

"Miss Millay." Jake pointed at the counter. "You forgot your yellow ribbon."

"Colorados. You give a token of friendship, then send this thief to steal our wagon and horses."

Ike pointed to Quemada standing near the wagon and horses, holding Ike's rifle. And next to Quemada stood Secorro.

Colorados's camp was isolated within a spectral sanctuary between the shoulders of the Bradshaw Mountains. A few wickiups and an assortment of Apaches; men, women and children.

"Quemada was not sent by me."

"Well, who makes up the rules around here?"

"White men take from us," Quemada said, "we take from them. Those are the rules."

"I haven't taken anything from anybody." Ike nodded toward Ben Brown. "Neither has this man. I'm just a small businessman trying to stay in business."

"They take our burial ground,"—Quemada looked directly at Ike—"and you bring them food and guns."

"I haven't brought anybody any guns. But Colorados, I bring you a message from Colonel Crook, who's now in command of this territory. He wants to talk to you—if you'll just listen—"

"My father talked and listened. . . ."

"I know all about that. But there're new leaders now. Grant, Sheridan and Crook. They're soldiers from the great war."

"Now they will make war on Apaches."

"No. They fought so everybody can live in peace. They're sick of war. The whites are learning to live together and with their black brothers. It's got to be so with the red and the white."

"This is the land of the Hassayampa. Apache land."

"That's so, Colorados. For two hundred years. But Crook told me before that it was Pima land. The Apache were stronger and took it from the Pimas."

Colorados nodded.

"Now the soldiers are stronger."

"The fight is not always to win," Quemada said. "It is to hurt back. To—"

"There's land enough for both," Ike interrupted. "Make a beginning, Colorados. So your people will survive. Crook'll start by getting you a pardon."

"Will you sell the bones of your fathers," Quemada asked Colorados, "for a piece of paper?"

"Crook's word is good. Colorados, meet him and make a beginning."

"I will think on it."

Ike reached into his pocket, pulled out a pouch, and handed it to Colorados.

"Tobacco. Colorados, you can smoke while you think. But don't take too long."

Ike, followed by Ben, walked toward the wagon. As they came close to Quemada and Secorro, Ike, in one swift motion, reached out and grabbed the rifle from Quemada.

"And I'll take back my rifle."

Quemada screamed something in Apache and took a step forward.

Ike's left hand held the rifle, his right turned into a fist that first slammed into Quemada's midsection, then whipped into his face, dropping him to the ground with blood leaking from his mouth.

"I'm getting a little tired of looking at your face, sonny," Ike said, then turned to Brown. "Come on, Ben. We got what we came for." He glanced back at Colorados. "Or at least some of it."

Ike and Ben climbed onto the wagon.

Colorados took a step forward.

"Wait."

"For what?"

"You came with a message from Crook."

Ike looked down at Quemada, who wiped at the blood from his mouth.

"I already got his answer."

"Now you will get mine."

"What is it?"

"Tell Gray Wolf that—"

"Who's Gray Wolf?"

"Crook. You did not know that that is how he is known to the Indians? In our language, Nan-Tan-Lupan."

"No, I didn't. What's the message?"

"Tell him Colorados will meet him when the sun is high in three days at a place the soldiers call Spanish Flats."

"I'll tell him."

"I will bring only two with me, without weapons, if he will do the same."

"He will . . . and Colorados, that is a good beginning."

CHAPTER TWENTY-EIGHT

It was late when Ike and Ben got back to Prescott.

The boys were in bed, but Jake, Melena and Sister Bonney were waiting.

Ike provided them all with a brief report and said he would be riding out to Fort Whipple the next day to give Colonel Crook the message from Colorados.

For the first time they saw Ben Brown take Melena's hand as they started to walk toward the stable.

"Mister Brown."

"Yes, Mister Silver?"

"Thanks for all your help. We make a pretty good team, don't you think?"

Ben Brown nodded, Melena smiled and they went on their way.

"Anything interesting happen around here while we were away?" Ike looked at Jake and Sister Bonney.

"No," Jake said. "Oh yeah, I got something for you." He reached into his vest pocket and handed Ike the silver dollar. "Silver for Silver. But you can't spend it. It's for luck from that lady from the saloon."

"Miss Millay?"

Jake nodded. "She came by—she said to buy some yellow ribbon—but she gave me this for you for luck. . . ."

"And," Sister Bonney added, "she also gave a hundred-dollar donation to help with the school. Wasn't that nice?"

"Very nice," Ike said.

Sister Bonney smiled. "Well, it's been a long day. Time to sleep . . . after prayers. Good night."

"Good night, Sister," both Silvers said as she left.

"Did both boys say their prayers?" Ike asked.

"Like always."

"Think I'll go up, kiss 'em good night, and maybe . . ."

"Maybe what?"

"Stop over for a nightcap." Ike put the silver dollar into his vest pocket.

"You'll excuse me," Jake smiled, "if I don't join you."

" 'Alas, poor Yorick! I knew him, Horatio: a fellow of infinite jest, of most excellent fancy: he hath borne me on his back a thousand times; and now how abhorred in my imagination it is! My gorge rises at it. Here hung those lips that I have kissed I know not how oft . . .' "

Instead of a skull at the graveside, Binky held up an empty whiskey bottle on the stage as he performed Hamlet's lament to the saloon audience that paid scant attention.

The late night patrons were more interested in the consumption of whiskey and beer, in the cards they were holding or about to draw and in expectation of their turns up the stairs with either Francine, Alma or Marisa.

Belinda sat at her table with a deck of cards as Rupert Lessur approached with a drink in hand.

"May I join you for a moment or two?"

"Sure,"—she indicated a chair— "sit down . . . for a moment or two."

"Thank you." Lessur sat. "May I buy you a drink?"

"No, thanks. Had my quota for the night."

"Then may I repeat and even raise my offer to buy an interest in—"

"You can repeat and raise all you want, Mister Lessur, the answer still is I'm not in the market for a partner and—"

"And, if at first I don't succeed—"

"Yeah, I know the rest. Speaking of succeeding, you think Gallagher'll succeed in getting back from La Paz?"

"Oh, I think he's got as good a chance as Ike Silver has of getting back from the Rattlesnake."

"You'd better think again."

"How's that?"

"It appears,"—Belinda pointed—"that Ike Silver is already back. Sit down, Ike." She smiled. "We were just talking about you."

Ike sat.

Lessur nodded. "Yes, did you have a pleasant journey?"

"Pleasant enough . . . enough that I'm going to take another journey tomorrow to talk to Colonel Crook about it."

"Is that so? Well, that's a coincidence; I'm going out to Fort Whipple myself tomorrow. Perhaps we can ride out together."

Binky was winding down. " 'Where be your jibes now? Your gambols? Your flashes of merriment? Now get you to my lady's chamber and tell her, let her paint an inch thick, to this favor she must come; let her laugh at that.' "

There was little clapping, laughter or appreciation from the audience as Binky concluded, bowed and walked off still holding Yorick's substitute skull.

"Mister Silver . . ."

"Yes?"

"I said perhaps we can ride out to Fort Whipple together."

"I heard you."

"It must be the material," Binky exclaimed as he came to the table. "It can't be my performance. *Hamlet* is not for these peasants. Methinks I'll try a comedy next. Greetings, all! Glad to see you back, Big Ike." He arched a generous eyebrow at Lessur. "And how is the Prince of Darkness this eve?"

"I don't think you're very amusing, Mister Binkham." Lessur rose. "I hope you have a pleasant journey again tomorrow, Mister Silver. Good night, Belinda."

"Rather an abrupt leave taking," Binky noted after Lessur left. "I guess it was something I said."

"Or something Big Ike didn't say." Belinda smiled.

"Speaking of leave taking, I hope you two will excuse me. I think I see a pigeon." Binky set the empty bottle on the table and made his way to the bar.

"Well," she said, "some of us are glad to have you back."

"Thanks."

"About your talk with Crook tomorrow . . . ,"— Belinda pointed to the eagle claw—"you didn't happen to run into your friend, the Apache, did you?"

"I did."

"And?"

"I feel like a carrier pigeon."

"Well, you sure as hell don't look like one. Want a drink?"

"No, thanks."

"What do you want? You didn't come over to listen to Binky."

"I came over to thank you for the donation to the school . . . and for this."

Ike took the silver dollar from his vest.

"Oh." She smiled. "It's customary when somebody goes into business. For luck."

"We have a custom of giving something back. Something sweet."

Ike removed a small object from another vest pocket.

"What is it?" she asked.

"Oh, just a piece of candy."

"Hoarhound?" Belinda smiled.

"Rock." He placed it on the table and rose.

"Do me a favor?" she said.

"Sure."

She raised her arm, palm up. "Put it in this hand."

He did.

CHAPTER TWENTY-NINE

The flag with thirteen red stripes on a white field and thirty-seven stars on a blue field flapped in the hot morning breeze atop the mast at Fort Whipple.

Ike Silver hitched his horse to a post on the parade ground and entered the wood and adobe building with the sign:

HEADQUARTERS
COLONEL GEORGE CROOK
COMMANDING OFFICER

In the reception room he stopped at a desk that fronted another room and spoke to the sergeant, who looked more like a butcher than a receptionist.

"Morning, Sergeant. Ike Silver to see Colonel Crook."

"Is he expecting you?"

"I think so."

"We'll see if *he* thinks so. He's not alone, but I'll let him know you're here."

"Thanks."

"Ike Silver, that it?"

"That's it."

The sergeant rose, went to the door, knocked, waited for a response, heard "come," opened the door, went inside, closed the door. In less than thirty seconds the door opened.

"Colonel Crook says to come right in, Mister Silver."

Ike nodded and went in as the sergeant shut the door to the reception room behind him. He was—and wasn't—surprised to see Rupert Lessur in the office with Crook and Captain Bourke.

"Morning," Crook said. "I think you know my aide, Captain Bourke, and I know you know Mister Lessur."

"I do."

"I was just telling Colonel Crook and the captain that I'll have a wagonload of supplies from La Paz in a few days—and I thought you'd be interested too, Mister Silver, since we're both in the freighting business . . . aren't we?" Lessur smiled.

"We are." Ike nodded. "Colonel, you were right about my running into a certain party." He touched the eagle claw at his throat. "I've got a message, if you care to hear it."

"I certainly do."

"So do I," Lessur said. "Do you object, Colonel, if I stay and listen?"

"Yes, I do. This is army business."

"But it might concern—"

"Whatever it concerns, you'll find out soon enough . . . if there's a need for you to know. That'll be all, Mister Lessur."

"Very well. Good day."

After the door closed behind Rupert Lessur, Crook looked from Bourke to Ike.

"Well, Ike? How did it go?"

"You said you wanted to make a beginning. I think he does too."

"Good."

"He'll meet you day after tomorrow, with two men, no weapons. High noon at a place called Spanish Flats. You know it?"

"I know it, all right. Did you tell him I'll try to get him a pardon?"

"I told him you'd do more than try."

"I will, if he keeps his word. . . ."

Captain Bourke cleared his throat.

"What is it, Captain? You have something to say?"

Bourke hesitated for a moment. "Permission to speak freely, Colonel?"

"Go ahead."

"Well, sir, I don't think you can counsel with a murderer or rely on his word. I don't think the solution is conciliation."

"What's your solution, Captain?" Crook asked.

"Not just mine. Many other officers who've been here on the frontier agree . . ."

"To what? Extermination?"

"That's one solution . . . another is subjugation. Complete. Unconditional. You can't compromise with savages, I learned that. So did my brother. The hard way."

"Your brother?"

"Yes, Colonel. Did you ever hear of Major Addison Bourke?"

"I don't remember. . . ."

"I do. One of the best soldiers the army ever had. A hero at Gettysburg and Yellow Tavern. He was mother and father to me. . . . but to the Indians he was something else . . . something to be butchered, mangled and mutilated."

"Not by Colorados," Ike said.

"No. But they're all the same breed."

"No, they're not." Ike shook his head. "Not any more than white men are."

"Captain," Crook said, "I'm sorry for your brother, and I'm in no way excusing what happened, but none of that started until they were driven nearly crazy by being lied to and cheated. 'Til their women were beaten, sold as slaves and diseased—"

"Is that any reason—"

"No! But I'm here to see that none of that ever happens again . . . on either side. And I'm going to start at Spanish Flats, and so are you, Captain. You're dismissed."

"Yes, sir."

Captain Bourke saluted and left.

"Well, Mister Silver . . ."

"Well, Colonel, there seems to be a divergence of opinion within the ranks of the United States Army regarding the Indian situation, especially among the officers."

"Mister Silver, you were a soldier in the United States Army and there's one thing you know—an officer always obeys orders. And I give the orders."

"Yes, sir." Ike smiled. "By the way, you know that the Apaches call you Gray Wolf?"

Crook nodded. "I've been called worse."

Outside, Lessur had been waiting.

"Captain."

"What is it, Mister Lessur?"

"Without violating any rules, can you tell me anything?"

"Yes, I can tell you something."

"Please do."

"There isn't going to be any war."

"There isn't?"

"Hell, no. Thanks to Ike Silver, Colonel Crook and Colorados are just going to talk themselves to death."

Captain Bourke made a sharp turn and walked across the parade grounds.

Rupert Lessur lit his cigar and smiled.

CHAPTER THIRTY

At the blaze of noon on Spanish Flats, Colonel Crook and Colorados sat across from each other on rocks, talked and smoked. Nan-Tan-Lupan smoked a cigar and Colorados smoked the pipe that Ike Silver had given him.

"Colorados, it is sometimes harder to keep the peace than to make war. Some of your braves won't like it."

"And some bluecoats won't like it either."

Crook nodded.

"Too many Apaches have killed troopers and too many troopers have killed Apaches."

"Yes."

"But it's got to stop sometime, and this is as good a time and place for both sides to stop. Now, I'm working on getting you a pardon, but it will take time and effort on the part of both of us. The first step in ending a war is to declare a truce. To prove to your people and to my superiors that we can live in peace."

"We know where the white man lives, but where will the Apache live during this time of truce?"

"Right where you are now, and I don't want to know where that is. I will send cattle and supplies to Spanish Flats where you can pick them up."

"Good."

"But you must agree that the Apaches will not strike against the troopers, that the stagecoach and supply wagons and the settlers will pass through the Territory in peace. . . ."

"That will not be easy."

"It must be done—by you and by me. We must show both sides. After a time, I promise that you can have a place where you can live and hunt as you did before."

"A place that the white man chooses for us?"

"No. You will make that choice. This I promise. But know that first this truce must last for many moons."

"How many?"

"Not as many as you spent in prison. Will you agree?"

"Did Gray Wolf bring a paper to be signed?"

"No. Your word and my word is much stronger than any paper."

Two Apache tribal elders watched and heard, along with Captain Bourke and another officer, as Crook and Colorados spoke.

And from a distance, two other men watched but could not hear; still, they had a pretty good idea of what was being said.

Rupert Lessur and Quemada.

"The army talks and makes promises, Quemada, but always it breaks its word and takes what it wants from the Apaches."

"Colorados does not speak for all Apaches. I will walk away and there are Apaches who will follow."

"No."

"Why not?"

"You and I were both better off when Colorados was in prison. It will be so again. The time will come to strike, but let them think it was the doing of Colorados, not of those who walked away."

"And what of the mine?"

"The time will come for that, too. The mine is in business for a profit. Take away the profit and they're out of business."

"And the man who brought Colorados and Crook together?"

"Ike Silver."

Quemada nodded.

"I'll see that he's out of business too."

CHAPTER THIRTY-ONE

"How much do I owe you for those cigars?"

"Well, Mister Mayor, I'm not quite sure," Jake said. "Scotty's making a delivery, and there was no price on the box. You remember how much you've been paying?"

"Well, to tell the truth,"—and he wasn't—"I don't recall. Just started smoking these Wheelings a short time ago."

"I see. Well, ten cigars . . . call it two bits even."

"That's reasonable." Mayor Davis's face lit up as he also lit up a cigar after biting off the end of it, and put the money on the counter.

"Need any matches, Mister Mayor?"

"No, thanks. Say, I . . . uh . . . understand that Colonel Crook had a meeting with Colorados."

"Correct."

"And before that, the colonel talked to your brother."

Jake nodded and pointed to a chair. "Right over there."

"You know what they talked about?"

Jake nodded again, then leaned in and whispered confidentially, "Mister Mayor, can you keep a secret?"

The mayor also nodded, moved even closer to Jake, and whispered even more confidentially, "Yes, I can."

"So can I," Jake answered softly, then smiled and spoke in a normal tone. "But this is no secret. Everybody's gonna know pretty soon."

"Know what?"

"That there's gonna be a truce, thanks to my brother, the peacemaker. Ain't that right, Ike?"

Ike Silver had come down the stairs and heard part of the exchange. "That's not the way it happened, but it looks like it's happening."

"A *truce?*" The mayor was obviously amazed.

"Did I hear somebody say *truce?*" Oliver Knight had rushed in through the open door and hastened toward Ike. "There're rumors flapping all over town that Crook and Colorados had a powwow up in Spanish Flats and signed a treaty. Big medicine!"

"Well," Ike said, "far as I know they didn't sign any treaty, but did come to an understanding."

"To do what?" Mayor John Davis asked.

"What *not* to do," Ike said.

"What do you mean?" the mayor inquired.

"It's what *they* mean. Not to shoot at each other for the time being 'til they can work something out officially."

Knight said excitedly, "I've got to know more than that for the next edition . . . maybe get out an extra—"

"Then I'd suggest you ride out and talk to Colonel Crook," Ike said.

"I'm going to do just that."

"Hold on, Mister Silver," the mayor said. "Is it part of this so-called 'understanding' that the stage will be operating? The supply wagons? And people can go about their business without being attacked by Apaches?"

"I'd say that's a reasonable assumption."

"My God! That's hard to believe."

"Crook and Colorados believe it." Ike smiled.

"That's . . . fantastic! I've got to call a meeting of the city council and . . . and . . . well, I'll see you later."

Mayor John Davis took a deep puff from his cigar and trotted toward the door.

"I'm sure His Honor is going to take credit," Knight said, looking out at the departing mayor, "for bringing peace to Prescott and the entire Territory. By the way,"—Knight removed a folded copy of a newspaper from his coat pocket—"here's the edition of the *Independent* with that story about you on the front page. Sorry I didn't have space to say more—'course, it's out of date by now, anyhow. Well, now that I don't have to worry about Apaches, guess I'll ride out to Fort Whipple and talk turkey with Colonel Crook."

Oliver Knight placed the copy of the *Independent* on the counter and left.

Jake picked up the paper and put on his spectacles. "Listen to this, Ike."

SILVER STRIKE IN PRESCOTT

Isaac "Big Ike" Silver, on his first day in Prescott, took on two drunken locals known as the Keeler brothers, by shooting whiskey bottles out of their grasp while they were firing their forty-fours in front of his store, which also serves as home for him, his two young sons, and his brother.

When the Keelers sobered up, they returned to the scene of the dust-up and apologized for their misconduct. First time in anybody's recollection that the Keelers were ever reasonably sober or ever con-

trite. Ike Silver was born in Russia, educated in En-
gland, served with distinction as an officer of the
U.S. Army at Shiloh in the late unpleasantness be-
tween the states and has settled in Prescott, where
he will operate a general store and start a freight
line in competition with the freighting monopoly
currently extant in the Territory. Welcome, Big Ike.

"How do you like that, brother?"

"How do you think Mister Lessur is going to like it?"

"Who cares? I'm not worried about him. Are we?"

"Well, I don't know how worried he is about us, with just a few patched-up wagons and no contracts to supply the army. . . ."

"Why don't you talk to your friend the colonel about that?"

"I intend to."

"Good."

"But there's somebody else I've got to talk to first."

"How's it going?"

Ike Silver entered the stable, where Ben Brown was working on a wheel.

"Most of the wagons are in pretty good shape, Mister Silver. Ought to be finished by the end of the week."

"That's just fine. Appreciate your help . . . and I do want to thank you for your help with those Apaches."

"Didn't have much choice." For the first time, Brown smiled at Ike. "That Quemada—you sure knocked the wind outta his bellows."

"Speaking of that . . . remember before Quemada and his pals jumped us, there was something I wanted to talk to you about?"

"I remember."

"Well, there don't seem to be any Apaches about,"—Ike glanced around the stable—"so . . ."

"So?"

"Rumor has it—in fact, it's stated right here in the current edition of *The Prescott Independent*,"—Ike pulled the newspaper out of his back pocket—"that I'm starting up a freight line here in the Territory."

"Seems to me I did hear mention of somethin' like that." There was more than a touch of humor in Ben's voice.

"Look here, why don't you forget about moving on . . . about sharecropping?"

Ben stiffened.

"Did Melena . . . ?"

"Mister Brown, I want to make a deal."

"What kind of deal?"

"You'll have regular hours . . . probably work eighteen hours a day, seven days a week, thirty, thirty-one days a month."

"Sounds right so far."

"I need somebody to keep these wagons rolling. To help freight the goods from La Paz to the mine . . . to the army . . . to anyplace. You'll get twenty-five percent of the profits . . . if there are any profits,"—Ike pointed to the ceiling—". . . the roof over your head that you fixed, 'til we can find better accommodations, and all the victuals that Melena can cook for you and Benjie. That's my of-fer. Deal?"

"Would you come with me for just a minute, Mis-ter Silver?"

Ike nodded and followed Ben into the kitchen. "Melena."

Melena turned from the sink. "What is it, Ben?"

"Mister Silver has asked us to stay . . . run the freight line . . ."

"Not run it," Ike said. "Be partners."

"What do you think, Melena?" Ben asked.

Melena managed a mock shrug. "Up to you, Ben, but I'm sure Benjie would like to stay here and go to school with Jed and Obie . . . and . . ."

"I asked for an answer from you, Melena."

"My answer is . . . 'wither thou goest.' "

"All right, then . . ." He turned to Ike and extended his hand.

Ike took it and they shook.

"Deal . . . Ben."

"Deal . . . Ike."

Melena could barely keep from quivering with long-forgotten contentment.

Sister Bonney rushed into the store from the street.

"Ike, I heard the marvelous news about the treaty and the part you played—"

"Truce, Sister, not treaty. And I didn't play much of a part."

"Truce, treaty, what's the difference?"

"We'll find out. A lot depends on Colonel Crook and Colorados."

"It'll work out, I know it will. Ike, I have to ask you something. How soon can I meet with Colorados and the other Indians about sending their children to school?"

"Well, I think that's a little premature, Sister. There are one or two other things that have to be worked out first. . . ."

"Yes, I know, but we mustn't forget the children. Will you talk to Colorados as soon as you can?"

"I'll do what I can when I can, Sister, but in the

meanwhile, you'll be glad to know that you'll have at least one more student in your school."

"Oh?"

"Yes. Benjie Brown. Ben and Melena have decided to stay here with us."

"That's grand . . . and don't tell me you didn't play a part in that either."

"The important part is, they're staying."

"God bless you, Big Ike."

The streets of Prescott were stirring, then swirling with activity as word spread and citizens began to celebrate the truce. For some time, Prescott and its inhabitants had lived in near isolation and susceptibility. Ranchers kept their rifles loaded and at the ready; the stage line was shut down except when it could obtain an army escort; supplies from La Paz, when they did arrive via Lessur Freighting, skyrocketed in price. The blame, with considerable justification, fell on Apache marauders who struck from their hidden lairs, stealing horses, guns, ammunition, cattle and sometimes women to be traded to Comancheros who would sell them in bondage below the border.

Hate hung thick as paste in the Territory. Among the whites, hate for the Indians, who were looked upon as savages knowing no mercy; among the Indians, hate for the whites, intruders who despoiled an ancient culture and subjugated once proud hunters and warriors and turned them into subordinates, dependant on the largesse of invaders.

And there was even hate among the whites for other whites. Before and during the Civil War, Prescott and the Arizona Territory were a hotbed of Confederate sympathizers. As many Arizonians entered that war on the side of the South as did volunteers for the Union forces. And those Southern sympathizers who survived and returned still bore the residual resentment toward loyalist Arizonians and the U.S. Army forces now under the command of Colonel Crook at Fort Whipple and other posts in the Territory.

But for the time being, much of that hate and resentment, if not forgotten, was set aside in the hope that some semblance of normalcy and even prosperity would return to what had been a cauldron of conflict.

All that was becoming evident on the streets and businesses of Prescott with the prospect of peace and industry—if the truce held. The store, the bank, the barbershop and the saloons along Whiskey Row all reflected a renewed vigor and vitality amidst citizens who had lived in a limbo of uncertainty.

There were more than enough customers to keep Jake and Scotty busy at the store as Ike walked out of the stable.

"Hey, Big Ike, look here!"

Claude Keeler held up a copy of *The Prescott Independent* as his brother Charlie stood at his side.

"Did you see what that fella at the newspaper wrote right on the front page?" Charlie said.

"I did."

"Somebody just read it to us." Claude grinned.

"We got our name in the paper right next to yours," Charlie added. "We never figured that'd ever happen unless we croaked. Ain't that somethin'?"

"Yeah, that's something, all right."

"But what does that one word mean? We didn't want to ask the fella who read it to us," Claude said.

"What word?"

Claude pointed.

"Contrite?" Ike smiled.

"That's it. Con . . . trite. What's that mean, Big Ike?"

"It means *peaceable*."

"Peaceable?" Claude looked at his brother. "Hear that, Charlie? Peaceable. I'll be damned!"

"We were just goin' over to your store to pick up some goods," Charlie said.

"Hope you find what you need."

"We will." Claude nodded, still grinning. "And thanks for gettin' our name in the newspaper, Big Ike."

"You're welcome. See you later, fellas."

"You bet. Con . . . trite." Claude folded the newspaper. "How about that!"

"Am I to understand, Colonel Crook, that if we come across armed Apaches, we are not to confiscate their weapons?"

Captain Frank Bourke, along with Lieutenants Jud Gibbs and William Williams, stood in front of the desk where Colonel Crook sat lighting a cigar.

"You officers are to understand and make sure every trooper who is under my command understands that part of my agreement with Colorados—and you were there at Spanish Flats when I made that agreement, Captain—is that he and his men are not to lay down their arms. They are to keep whatever arms and ammunition, which is damn little, currently in their possession."

"Supposing we are attacked with those arms, sir, though damn little they may be?"

"I'm supposing that you won't be, but if you are fired upon first, you will, of course, fire back with accuracy and alacrity."

"I see, sir."

"See this too, all of you officers. Under no circumstances are you to provoke or initiate aggression. Understood, by all of you?"

"Yes, sir," the three officers replied in unison.

"Good. Captain, deliver the cattle and supplies to Spanish Flats and report back to me."

"Very good, sir."

"Questions, Captain?"

"One question, sir."

"What is it?"

"Do you mind if I don't speak to any Apache . . . unless he speaks first?"

"That'll be all, Captain, gentlemen."

"Yes, sir," the officers replied, again in unison.

The sun had fallen like a dying moth.

After their usual prayers and nightly altercation, Jed and Obie were in bed.

"They never let the sun set without a quarrel," Jake said to Ike as the two of them walked down the stairs.

"You know who they remind me of?" Ike smiled.

"Us." Jake nodded. "The difference is that I was always in the right."

"Sure you were."

"And still am."

"Of course. Think I'll walk over to the Emporium."

"Don't play poker."

"I won't—especially with the proprietress. Want to come along?"

"No, I got some bookkeeping to do."

"See you later."

Jake pointed to the gun and gun belt on Ike's desk.

"Aren't you going to take along your hardware?"

"No. I think I'll travel light tonight."

Francine, who sometimes entertained downstairs as well as upstairs, had finished her rendition of "Lorena," and the piano player had segued into a rendition of "Shenandoah" as Francine walked up the staircase escorted by a fellow who looked like a Bible salesman, but who had carnal cravings that were about to be satisfied.

The Emporium was at near capacity with drinkers, smokers and card players—Oliver Knight, the sign painter Tom Bixby, the barber undertaker Antonio Gillardi, and sundry citizens including Rupert Lessur, at his usual table with his usual pile of winnings. Belinda Millay stood behind him watching him win again.

Ike entered through the bat wings, stood for a moment, then walked toward the bar, where Binky in full voice was in the midst of one of his reminiscences for those who cared to listen and even for those who didn't.

"I was touring the Welsh provinces in a second-rate company of players, managed by and starring Lord and Lady Ben Greet. Ben Greet was concluding his curtain speech after our performance of *Macbeth* with Lady Ben Greet as Lady Macbeth and himself in the title role. 'Ladies and gentlemen,' he said, 'we thank you for your generous applause, and I am pleased to announce that tomorrow evening the Ben Greet players will perform Shakespeare's immortal love story *Romeo and Juliet*. I shall essay the role of Romeo, and the part of Juliet will be performed by Lady Ben Greet.' At that, someone in the audience hollered out 'Lady Ben Greet is a dirty whore!' Ben Greet summoned up his full stature and in stentorian tone responded, '*Nevertheless* . . . the part of Juliet will be performed by Lady Ben Greet.' "

Binky removed his bowler, bowed and held up an empty glass.

"Buy you a drink, Binky?" Ike said.

"I would enjoy a libation, sir, and your company." Binky replaced the bowler. "Not necessarily in that order. Henry!'

"Ike Silver!" The bat wings had flown open and he stood just inside—an imposing man, well above six feet, a square-jawed face carved out of granite with a grim mouth and steel-gray eyes that matched the uniform he wore—the Confederate uniform of a major, complete with sash, sidearm, and sheathed sword. There was one thing about him that was incomplete—his left arm was missing.

The sleeve was pinned up just above where his elbow would have been. In his right hand he held a copy of *The Prescott Independent.*

"Ike Silver," he repeated.

The Emporium was smothered by silence . . . and stillness. Nobody moved. Except the imposing man in uniform. He took a step forward.

"Where is Ike Silver?"

"I'm here."

"According to this article,"—the man held up the newspaper—"you were at Shiloh."

"I was."

"So was I. Major Montgomery Rawlins, Third Texas. It says here that you served with distinction at Shiloh."

Ike said nothing.

"How did you distinguish yourself?"

Silence.

"I asked, *how did you serve with distinction?*"

Ike shrugged. "I survived. We lost many brave comrades on both sides."

"I lost something else."

"I'm sorry."

"You're going to be sorrier."

"Major, what do you want?"

Major Montgomery Rawlins dropped the newspaper and drew his sword. "Satisfaction."

CHAPTER THIRTY-TWO

Major Rawlins pointed with his sword at the newspaper on the sawdust floor. "You have the temerity to boast of a bloodbath where we Confederates charged with valor, outnumbered and outgunned, led by our beloved commander, who died on the field that day along with ten thousand brave soldiers of the South—"

"Just a minute, Major." Oliver Knight took a step. "Ike Silver never mentioned—to me or anybody else—anything about his service at Shiloh. That's something I found out myself."

"You just stand back, Mister Knight, this matter doesn't concern you. This is between him . . ."—Rawlins pointed the sword at Ike—"and me. Isn't it, Officer Silver?"

"The war's over, Major."

"Some wars don't end because somebody signs a piece of paper. There're some wars that go on . . . inside. Wars for comrades who fell."

"Fifteen thousand Union comrades fell at Shiloh, Major."

"And tonight one more is going to fall."

Rawlins's eyes were twin torches of vengeance. He widened his stance for just a moment, emitted a wild Rebel yell, lifted the sword, charged, and in a vicious strike swung it down toward Ike Silver, who maneuvered swiftly aside as the sword slashed with devastating effect against the bar, sending shattered bottles and glasses in all directions.

In that instant, Ike's right hand clamped onto Rawlins's wrist, pounding it hard once, twice, three times against the bar until the sword fell from Rawlins's grasp.

Ike shoved Rawlins away, picked up the sword and faced the man who had just tried to kill him.

Rawlins stood erect, almost at attention, waiting for . . . he knew not what.

Ike Silver looked for a moment at the sword he now held in his hand, and then into the eyes of the enemy; then he turned the sword around, held it by the blade with one hand, the sword resting on his other arm with the handle extended toward Rawlins, in the traditional signal of surrender.

Rawlins stood frozen by the unexpected gesture. So did everybody else in the saloon.

"You wanted satisfaction, Major. Take back your sword."

Rawlins remained immobile.

"Go ahead . . . *take it!*" Ike commanded.

Slowly, Rawlins reached out and took the handle of the weapon that pointed once again at Ike.

"Now. Whatever it is you crave . . . satisfaction . . . vengeance . . . reprisal. Go ahead." Ike turned just a bit so his left arm was a clearly exposed target. "Go ahead."

Everybody gasped as Rawlins, sword in hand, slowly began to raise his arm above his shoulder.

"This is your last chance . . . to end the war," Ike said.

They stood face-to-face.

Two survivors of Shiloh.

Two enemies on a long-ago field of battle.

Each remembering the clash of resounding arms.

Bugles in the morning and afternoon. Rifles and revolvers. Bloody bayonets and dripping swords. Muskets and mini-balls. Peach blossoms fallen, red with the blood of the dead and dying. General Albert S. Johnston, the Confederate commander, wobbling in his saddle . . . falling mortally wounded onto the twisted troopers in hell's orchard. Bodies limp and lifeless piling one atop another . . . anguished cries and screams . . . confusion . . . chaos . . . destruction and death, with ever more waves of bluecoat reinforcements whirling out of every direction, wreaking havoc on diminishing ranks of Rebels, until their remaining forces could no longer survive the onslaught, broke and fell back as vultures circled above, then later dove into the grizzly harvest of ungathered dead.

All this and more, both men—Montgomery Rawlins and Ike Silver—remembered as only soldiers can remember . . . and want to forget.

It all came and went in a terrible instant. In a fleeting instant that only the two of them looking into each others' eyes could comprehend.

Rawlins trembled, once again feeling the pain in the arm that was no longer part of his body.

Ike Silver had given him his last chance to end the war . . . one way or another.

Rawlins lowered the sword.

With a barely perceptible nod of acknowledgment and softened eyes, he turned and walked a soldier's walk through the bat wings and into the night.

They all watched—Oliver Knight, Binky, Antonio Gillardi, Tom Bixby, the piano player, the saloon girls, Belinda, even Rupert Lessur—watched and began to breath again.

It was then that Belinda Millay slipped the derringer back into her garter and walked up to Ike Silver.

"Mister Silver," she said, "you are one hell of a poker player."

CHAPTER THIRTY-THREE

Discerning that everyone could use a change of atmosphere and a drink—or drinks—Belinda wasted no time in nodding toward the piano player, signaling him to go back to playing.

He did, hitting nearly as many false notes as true, due to the fact that all his fingers and both thumbs were still trembling.

Francine and her erstwhile customer descended the stairs, the expression on her painted face exactly the same as it was when she ascended. In the customer's eyes was a look of sated satisfaction.

Two of the male customers in need of diversion escorted Alma and Marisa toward the second-story sanctums.

Tom Bixby, the sign painter, and Antonio Gillardi, the barber mortician, did their best to beat each other to the bar, as did most of the other customers. Binky managed to approach Belinda and Ike, removed a flowing kerchief from an inner pocket, daubed the glistening perspiration from his mouth and chin, blinked and finally found his voice.

" 'What stranger breastplate than a heart untainted! Thrice is he armed that hath his quarrel just. True nobility is exempt from fear.' " Binky replaced the kerchief and smiled at Ike. "Noble sir, may I buy you a drink?" Then he looked at Belinda. "On my bar tab, of course."

"No thanks, Binky. I think I'll call it a night."

"In that case, I shall repair to the bar and seek solitary succor . . . unless I can find a pigeon."

As Binky departed, Oliver Knight approached with a half-filled tumbler of whiskey in hand.

"My boy, you have given this newspaperman one of the most miraculous stories I could ever hope to write. A full account will be on the front page of the next edition."

"Mister Knight . . ."

"Yes?"

"I'm going to ask you to do something."

"What?"

"Actually *not* to do something."

"And that is . . . ?"

"Not to write anything, anything at all, about what happened here tonight."

"I don't understand . . ."

"I think you do. I think you can understand that Major Rawlins went through enough here . . . and before, without his having to go through it all over again in a newspaper story, for him and everybody else to read."

"I guess that I'm too good, or too bad, a newspaperman to have thought about it like that." Oliver Knight smiled and nodded. "There will be no such story in *The Prescott Independent* . . . and I thank you, Mister Silver. Good night, Miss Millay." Oliver Knight drained the whiskey from the tumbler, set the empty glass on a table and made his way toward the bat wings.

"And *I* thank you, Miss Millay," Ike said.

"What for?"

He looked down for just a moment.

"The derringer."

"Oh, that. Did you see me draw it?"

"Good night, Miss Millay." Ike smiled and walked away.

"Well, it looks like you won again, Mister Lessur," a card player said.

As Rupert Lessur collected the pile of money, the other card players also rose and left him alone at the table with his winnings . . . and his thoughts.

Lessur, as he often did, had won the hand, but in his mind he knew that he had lost something else, something much more important to him. When Major Montgomery Rawlins lowered his sword instead of striking Ike Silver, Rupert Lessur had lost the opportunity of being rid with one blow of the one man who constituted the greatest threat to his plans in the Territory.

But that blow was never struck, not by Major Rawlins—and Lessur would have to get rid of Ike Silver by other means. He did have other means at his disposal, not as immediate, but in the long run, just as effective. He had to ruin Ike Silver—by driving him out of business; by disgracing him; by making sure that the truce with Colorados was broken; or ultimately by a less subtle, but more decisive and fatal means.

If all else failed, Rupert Lessur had a hole card.

A gunfighter-for-hire, a rabid, unrepentant Confederate who would not be as forgiving, forbearing or as clement as Major Montgomery Rawlins. A man who would take the money and relish killing a Yankee officer.

A man called Cord.

Ike Silver unlocked the door and entered the store. Jake was at the desk going over some papers. He looked up and removed his spectacles.

"Back already. That didn't take long."

It might have taken a lifetime, Ike thought to himself, but said nothing.

"Ike, we're going to have to get more inventory if we're going to stay in business. The goods are flying off the shelves."

"I know."

"We got to send those wagons to La Paz and load 'em up. Coffee, sugar, tobacco, shovels . . ."

"We will."

"You've got to talk to your friend, the colonel, about an army contract."

"I will."

"Did you enjoy your drink?"

"Come to think of it, I didn't have a drink."

"You didn't play cards,"—a note of concern crept into Jake's voice—"did you, Isaac?"

"No. No cards."

"Well, what did you do?"

"I . . . I met a man from Shiloh."

"Somebody who was in the army with you?"

"No. Not with me."

"Against you?"

"Not anymore."

"What does that mean? What happened"

"You'll hear about it soon enough. But don't worry, brother. Nothing happened."

Jake shrugged. "Getting any information from

you is like conversing with a wax cat." He rose. "I'm going upstairs. Turn off the lamp when you come up. Good night."

"Good night."

As Ike reached for the lamp, he paused and looked at the gun and gun belt on the desk.

He wondered if things would have turned out any different if he had taken the gun with him.

He wasn't sure. But he was glad he hadn't.

Ike Silver put out the light.

Melena's deep brown eyes were vessels of tears as she lay next to Ben, both their naked bodies gleaming with perspiration from the passion of their lovemaking.

"Melena, why are you crying? Was it something I—"

"Oh, Ben . . . Ben . . ."

"What is it, honey?"

"For the first time since Benjie was born, I feel like . . ."

"Like what?"

"Like I'm your wife again. Ben, I can't remember when I've been so happy . . . ever since you decided that we stay here in Prescott . . ."

"And live in a stable . . ."

"I don't care where we live. It's been so long since I felt we were both really alive. . . . Oh, Ben, 'I opened to my beloved; but my beloved had withdrawn himself, and was gone: my soul failed when he spake: I sought him, but I could not find him. I called him but he did not answer.'"

"Song of Solomon?"

"No, Ben, song of you and me. . . . You don't know what it is for me not to have to wonder what we're going to do . . . and where we're going to go tomorrow . . . what's going to happen to Benjie . . ."

"I'm sorry, Melena, that I haven't done right by you and the boy."

"You've done all that a man could do and more."

"I'll do better yet. No matter what it takes . . . I'll make a place on this earth where you and Benjie—"

"Don't say anything, Ben. You don't have to. This isn't a stable, Ben, not anymore. . . . My beloved, it's home."

CHAPTER THIRTY-FOUR

Ike Silver had paused at the entrance and looked at the sign on the window:

FIRST BANK OF PRESCOTT
AMOS CANTRELL, PRESIDENT

He sat across the desk in the office of Amos Cantrell, who looked to be in his early fifties, gray-haired, pale and gone to flab, with small eyes the color of currency, a voice smooth and confident.

"I'm pleased to meet you, Mister Silver. I wondered how long it would be."

"How long what would be, Mister Cantrell?"

"Before you came to see me."

"You knew that I would?"

"Everyone who settles in Prescott comes to see me . . . sooner or later. And for the same reason. Money."

"Well, I guess you're right about that."

"Of course I am. By the way, you've already made quite a reputation for yourself since your arrival. First the Keeler brothers, then the incident at that saloon last night. Of course, I don't frequent saloons myself, but word does get around, doesn't it?"

"Of course."

"Yes. Now then, how much?"

"How much what?"

"Money, of course, since that is the purpose of your visit. I understand you paid in full for the Winthrop General Store."

"And stable."

"Yes." Cantrell was about to add an "of course," but stopped short. "I also understand you intend to go into the freight business."

"I do, along with my partner, Ben Brown."

"This Brown is a Negro, is he not?"

"He is."

"I see."

"We're about to make a run to La Paz, pick up inventory for the store and, we hope, supplies for the army."

"What kind of supplies?"

"Coffee, sugar, barley, dried fruits, whatever is available. . . ."

"And to purchase these supplies you need money . . . which you don't have."

"I have some money. We could use some more to fill up all the wagons."

"I see. How much money?"

"Five hundred . . . a thousand dollars."

"Which is it, Mister Silver? Five hundred or a thousand?"

"Well, Mister Cantrell, that's up to you. I'll take all I can get."

"Of course you will."

"I do have collateral, you know."

"Yes, I know. When do you intend to . . . make the run to La Paz?"

"Soon as possible."

"I see. Well, Mister Silver, I appreciate your coming in, but . . ."

"But what?"

"Well, it isn't my money, you know. It belongs to the depositors of the First Bank of Prescott, and I have to do what I think is best for them."

"Sure you do. And what do you think is best? Do I get the loan?"

"Well, I'll have to think it over."

"How long will that take to think it over?"

"Perhaps not too long."

"Uh-huh." Ike got up from the chair.

"I'm not refusing, you understand."

"I understand. Thank you, Mister Cantrell."

Ike headed for the door.

"Oh, Mister Silver . . ."

"Yes?"

"Welcome to Prescott."

As soon as Ike left, the door to an adjacent room, which had been slightly ajar, opened wider and Rupert Lessur stepped into Cantrell's office.

Cantrell rose from his desk and smiled.

"Well, Rupert, what do you think?"

Lessur lit his cigar. "I think it'll be a long, long time before Ike Silver gets his loan."

Amos Cantrell nodded.

"So do I."

Ike had just crossed the street, still weighing the odds of his getting a loan from the president of the First Bank of Prescott and not considering them very favorable, when he heard his name called out.

"Mister Silver! Mister Silver, hold up there just a minute, will you?"

Ike Silver held up.

Mayor John Davis, cigar in hand, wearing a freshly pressed pinstripe suit, approached accompanied by a brawny raw-boned man who looked like he had never worn a suit.

"Good morning, Mister Silver."

"Morning, Mister Mayor."

"I don't think you ever met Race Beemer. Race here is a cousin of mine."

Race grunted, then nodded.

"A distant cousin," the mayor added. "Race was in the Emporium last night. I don't go there myself . . ."

"You too, huh?"

"How's that?"

"Never mind."

"Understand you put on quite a show."

"I wouldn't call it that."

"Some of those damn Rebels just don't know when to quit."

"Or how to quit."

"Yeah, I guess so, but they'll learn. Well, I'm glad everything turned out all right."

"So am I."

"You know, Mister Silver, if those damn Indians quiet down and the truce holds—"

"It'll hold . . . as far as the Indians are concerned."

"Yes . . . well, more people will be coming into Prescott and some of us on the City Council have been thinking of appointing a sheriff."

"Appointing? I thought a sheriff is supposed to be elected."

"Not necessarily. Not according to our city charter. We can do it either way."

"That's interesting."

"If it comes right down to it . . . well, the way you've been handling things since you came to town . . . I was just wondering, mind you—"

"Wondering what, Mister Mayor?"

"If you might be interested in the job."

"No thanks."

"Being a sheriff, that's not against your religion, is it? You being a Jew and all."

"No, that's not it." Ike managed a smile. "I've already got a job. The store. The freight line."

"It'd just be part time—if we asked you, that is."

"My job's already full time, but I appreciate you asking about it."

"Well, it was just a thought. We'll see what happens."

"Very good. Say, why don't you ask Cousin Race? He looks like he'd make a sizeable sheriff."

"Race don't have the temperament. He raises hogs. By the way, Colonel Crook just went into your store. I wonder what he's doing in town."

"So do I."

"Just stopped by to get a good cup of coffee."

"Anytime, Colonel."

"One thing the army hasn't mastered, among other things, is how to brew a decent pot of coffee." Colonel Crook took another large swallow while sitting in his chair across from Ike Silver in a corner of the store. "What's the secret to it, Ike?"

"A clean pot."

"How's that?"

"Keep the pot clean . . . and don't be stingy with the makings."

"I'll pass that along to my orderly. I heard about what happened last night over at the Emporium with that unsurrendered Major Rawlins. You know, we thought that one day he might single-handedly—if you'll forgive the pun—charge the gates of Fort

Whipple . . . but I understand that he's settled down some, thanks to you."

"We came to our own Appomattox."

"Yes, good. Let's hope that Colorados and his Apaches also come to the same conclusion."

"I think Colorados already has."

"So do I, but there's always young bucks afire with the fever of hostility. How's everything else going for you around here?"

"Well, I was just welcomed to this fair city by the president of the First Bank of Prescott."

"Amos Cantrell himself?"

"The same."

"That's interesting."

"Yes, it is . . .'specially in view of the fact that he's going to turn me down for a loan."

"What kind of a loan?"

"Oh, to pick up extra supplies in La Paz."

"That's even more interesting."

"How so?"

"Well, in the first place, Amos Cantrell might be the nominal president of that bank, but somebody else calls the shots there . . . and at a lot of other places in these parts—namely, your competitor in the freight business."

"Rupert Lessur himself?"

"The same. He's slippery as a snake on ice."

"You do a lot of business with him."

"I've had to . . . up to now. He underpays when he buys in La Paz and overcharges when he delivers in Prescott . . . and Fort Whipple. That's because he's had a monopoly . . . up to now . . . which brings me to the second place and why I'm here . . . besides to get a good cup of coffee."

"And that is?"

"Lessur's already bringing in a wagon train of supplies from La Paz and I've got to pay him his price, but I'm prepared to give you a contract for all you can deliver after that. What do you think about them apples, Mister Silver?"

"I think them's good apples, Colonel Crook."

"So does the army. Furthermore, I've brought along a draft of one thousand dollars as an advance payment on that contract . . . along with a list of supplies we're in need of most. So you can forget about that loan."

"It's forgotten." Ike smiled.

"Howsoever, there's one thing we can always use that we're not going to get. At least not for awhile."

"What's that?"

"I'd put in a requisition for a hundred of the latest repeating Winchesters and two thousand cartridges, but I just got a telegraph that those rifles and cartridges are being sent to another destination."

"That destination a military secret?"

"Nope. The Dakotas, along the Platte. Down here there's just a few hundred Apaches. The Dakotas are swarming with six thousand Cheyenne and Sioux."

"I thought the Cheyenne and the Sioux were at peace."

"Not anymore. They're painted again and doing something called a ghost dance . . . following a leader named Wovoka. He's fevered up Sitting Bull, Crazy Horse, Big Foot, Kicking Bear and the rest of the Oglala and Hunkpapa chiefs. There's even talk Sheridan might send Custer up there."

"Custer's in Michigan, isn't he? Retired."

"Looks like he'll unretire. He's only thirty, and the boy general's getting restless."

"He's one hell of a soldier."

"He was at Chickahominy, Gettysburg, Saylor's Creek, Yellow Tavern, Appomattox and at other places, but he's also a powder keg. The whole thing's liable to blow up any time . . . so we'll have to make do with what we've got."

"You'll make do, Colonel."

"We both will. By the way, we made good on that first delivery at Spanish Flats we promised Colorados . . . and so far he's kept his promise." Crook rose and set down the tin cup. "Well, thanks for the coffee, Mister Silver."

"Thank you, Colonel."

"Uh-huh. Just watch out for that slippery snake." No sooner had Ike and Colonel Crook stepped out of the door of the store and onto the boardwalk than they were greeted by the caramel voice and physical presence of the subject of their recent conversation.

"Good morning, gentlemen." Rupert Lessur smiled. "Colonel Crook, I was told you were here."

"I'm sure you were."

"Gallagher will be back with that wagon train of supplies any time now, so I thought you might want to come by the office and make out a list for the next shipment."

"I've already made out the list."

"Good."

"And handed it to Mister Silver."

"You have?"

"I have."

"Well, that's surprising, Colonel."

"Why?"

"We've done an awful lot of business. What's the reason?"

"That *is* the reason."

"What do you mean, Colonel?"

"I mean a lot of that business was awful as far as I was concerned, but then I had no choice. Now I do have a choice. And for the time I choose to do business with Mister Silver."

"I see, and Mister Silver, may I inquire, are you fully funded to keep that ragtag, patched-up freight line supplied . . . and in operation?"

"I appreciate your concern, Mister Lessur—and the answer is, yes I am, no thanks to the First Bank of Prescott."

"Well, gentlemen," Crook said, "I've got to get back to Fort Whipple. But I'm glad to see that the spirit of friendly competition is alive and well—as a matter of fact, thriving—in this part of the Territory."

Ike Silver and Rupert Lessur watched as Crook mounted and rode up the street at the head of a small contingent of troopers that had escorted him into Prescott.

"Does this mean," Lessur asked, "that you'll be out of town a good deal of the time?"

"I don't think so. Jake and Ben can handle a big part of the freight business. By the way, if you know of any good teamsters looking for work, send 'em over. We'll be hiring."

"I'll do that, Mister Silver, and when you're ready to sell out, let me know and I might make you an offer." Lessur smiled.

"That's very good of you, Mister Lessur." Ike also smiled. "And that goes both ways—if you decide to sell out, after the spirit of friendly competition." Ike turned and walked into the store.

Lessur turned and walked toward his office.

Both men knew that the competition would be anything but friendly.

* * *

Sister Mary Boniface was walking south along the boardwalk past the Emporium when the bat wings swung open and she heard her name called out by Belinda Millay, who came toward her with a serious countenance and an upraised hand.

"Sister Bonney!"

"Oh, good morning, Miss Millay. And how are you this fine day?"

"Never mind that. That's not the question."

"Oh, I'm sorry then—what *is* the question?"

"The question is, what the hell . . . uh, what are you doing down here in the Slot?"

"What is the Slot?"

"Part of it is where you're standing."

Sister Bonney looked down and around, then shrugged.

"I don't see anything different from anyplace else I've been standing."

"Well, that's because you've been lucky so far . . . but I wouldn't go any farther, not in the Slot."

"Will you please explain to me, Miss Millay, about this so-called Slot?"

"From that corner you crossed back there,"— Belinda pointed north—"two blocks ago . . . from there on, it's called a lot of things—'Whiskey Row,' 'Deadline,' 'the Slot'—and some other things I won't mention. It's an area not frequented by most estimable citizens, particularly female citizens, night or day. Just take a gander at some of these passersby."

Sister Bonney took a moment to do just that. There was a noticeable difference in the dress and deportment of the almost exclusively male pedestrians, some of whom stared in virtual disbelief at the sight of the slim figure dressed in black.

"Oh, I see what you mean."

"What are you doing down here, anyhow?"

"Well, I was told that a Doctor Zebelion Barnes had an office on this street."

"That's true, because a lot of his patients are from around here, but he makes house calls to the regular folks. Are you sick, Sister?"

"Oh, no. I think Obadiah has a slight fever. I didn't want to disturb Ike or Jake—they're so busy—and I thought, perhaps the doctor . . ."

"That's all right, Sister, I'll get word to Doc Barnes to stop by."

"Thank you."

"Now look, you stay away from this riffraff. Stay away from the Slot. If you need—"

"Welllll! Howdee-doo!" The odor of whiskey accompanied the crackle of the voice out of the pinched, dirty face as he stopped unsteadily, too close to both women. "Hey, Bee-linda. What have you got there?"

"On your way, Windy."

"I am on my way . . . into your saloon."

"No, you're not. Keep moving."

"I got money."

"You got a snootfull. Beat it!"

The little man pursed his rat lips and squinted at Sister Bonney. "Ho! Ho! What is this? You got a new saloon gal! I ain't never seen no whore like this!"

"Windy!" Belinda warned.

"Let's have a closer look, maybe—"

As Windy reached out and wobbled closer, Belinda's knee, in a swift upward movement, crunched into his groin. He buckled in agony, and with both hands, she shoved him hard against the wall, where his head banged, his hat fell, and he followed it down onto the boardwalk as he moaned once and settled into unconsciousness.

"Oh, my," Sister Bonney said. "Shall we go for Doctor Barnes?"

"No, Sister. You just go back to where you came from and I'll see that Doc Barnes comes by . . . to check on Obie."

"If you say so."

"I do."

The bat wings moved slowly open and Binky peered out, then looked down upon the recumbent figure on the boardwalk.

"Ah! He is of a very melancholy disposition."

Once again at Spanish Flats, Colonel Crook and Colorados sat across from each other on rocks, talked and smoked, Nan-Tan-Lupan his cigar, and Colorados the pipe that Ike Silver had given him.

This time, Captain Bourke and Lieutenant Gibbs stood out of hearing distance behind Crook, as did the two Apache elders behind Colorados.

They had been talking and smoking for nearly a half hour.

"And I heard that you have taken a bride, Colorados. Congratulations."

"In prison, you think of two things—freedom and—"

"I know what you mean. I was in a Confederate prison once—and sometimes a fort is like a prison."

"You have a wife, Nan-Tan?"

"Far away in a place called Ohio."

"Why is she not here? A fort is not like a prison in that way."

"She will be . . . if things stay quiet, and I don't get transferred."

"What is 'transferred'?"

"Assigned to some other territory or fort."

"No. It is better you stay here."

"That's not up to me, but in a way it's up to you and your braves. If the truce holds and we sign a treaty, my wife and the wives of other officers and soldiers will come."

"That will happen."

"I hope so. In the meantime, I gave our friend, Ike Silver, a list of the things we talked about and he will bring them from La Paz."

"Good." Colorados inhaled from the pipe. "Tobacco?"

"You bet, tobacco."

"Su-Wan smokes, too."

"Who's Su-Wan?"

"My wife. She is young. Strong. She smokes. Your wife smokes?"

"Mary? No. She doesn't smoke."

"Is she young? Strong?"

"Well, she's twelve years younger than I am and pretty strong."

"Good. I have had two other wives. Both dead. Not strong. The Apache way is hard."

"I know, my friend."

From the mouth of a cave, high in the distance, Quemada, Secorro and four other braves drank home-brewed *tizwin*—an Apache drink that was forbidden by the white man—a drink that has the same effect as whiskey. They drank and listened as Quemada pointed in the direction of Spanish Flats below and spoke in their tongue.

"Colorados has taken a bride, but he has become a squaw to Nan-Tan-Lupan. He is Crook's woman, who does the white man's bidding and makes us do the same. We are not farmers, but they will want us to plant crops, stop us from hunting, and drinking *tizwin*—from moving across our land whenever we choose. Instead, they will have us squat like squaws and do their bidding while they break their promises. While they dig for yellow iron and scar the sacred resting place of our ancestors."

"What will you have us do, Quemada?" Secorro asked and drank. "Will we break away? There are others who think the same and will follow."

"Not yet. We must have more cause and more weapons. Once again, the bluecoats will break their word and I will get us rifles—then more will come with us when we break away as Goklaya broke from Cochise. Now he is more remembered by his new name, Geronimo. The time will come when Quemada takes a new name and breaks away from Colorados."

With help from Rupert Lessur, Quemada intended to do just that, and also take with him Su-Wan, who was to be his bride . . . until Colorados broke out of prison and took her for himself.

CHAPTER THIRTY-FIVE

TRUCE!

So read the banner headline in the special edition of *The Prescott Independent*.

The story, attributed to Oliver Knight, went on to say:

It appears that peace has once again prevailed in the Territory. An agreement has been reached between Colonel George Crook, on behalf of the U.S. Army, and Colorados, Chief of the Mimbreno Apaches.

The Butterfield Stage will once more commence its regular run from La Paz to Prescott, Flagstaff and back again. Under the terms of the truce, supply trains, wagon trains, and travelers of all kinds will move through the Territory without interference from the Apaches, who will dwell hereabouts under the auspices of the U.S. Army, and be supplied with necessities by same.

If the truce holds for sixty days without incident on either side, a formal treaty will be signed by both parties. In the meantime, Colonel Crook, known as Gray Wolf among the red men, is working on getting a full pardon for red man Colorados, and have a mutually agreed upon area set aside for our Apache neighbors.

"My name's Zebelion Barnes, Doctor Zebelion Barnes, and I'm here to see about a potential patient named Obie Silver. Know anything about him?" Doctor Barnes asked Ike Silver at the store.

"Well, I know that I'm his father. Who told you he was sick?"

"Sent here by Belinda Millay, who was told about it by a nun named Sister Somethingorother."

Ike took a good look at Doctor Barnes, who looked like he hadn't washed his shirt or even taken it off in a fortnight. His hands were tobacco stained and so was the rest of him. He carried a medical bag that looked as old as he did—maybe sixty. He spoke with a gruff sandpaper voice that sounded as if he'd never heard of bedside manner. Ike Silver liked him right away.

"Well, he's outside, but he seemed all right to me."

"Who's the doctor around here? You, or me, or somebody else?"

All three boys were doing their yo-yos, two of which were recently fashioned by Ben Brown for Jedediah and Obadiah.

"Which one of you is Obie?" Doctor Barnes asked as he and Ike approached.

All three boys stopped yo-yoing.

"I am." Obie apprehensively stepped forward.

"Oh," Sister Bonney appeared, broom in hand, "are you Doctor Barnes?"

"I ain't the King of Rumania."

"Thank you for coming, Doctor. I know there's fever going around, and it seemed to me Obie had a temperature. I don't have a thermometer, but—"

"Stop right there," Barnes instructed. "I'll do the diagnosin' around here. Stick out your tongue, sonny."

Obie stuck out his tongue.

"Uh-huh. Peel it back."

Obadiah peeled it back.

Doctor Barnes placed his palm on Obadiah's forehead.

"Uh-huh."

"What do you think, Doctor?" Sister Bonney asked.

"I think you've wasted my time. This boy's one hundred percent."

"But—"

"But nothin'. Boys that age run hot and cold. It's part of growin' up. Did he tell you he was sick?"

"No, but—"

"There you go buttin' again. He'll tell you when. Meantime, leave the both of us alone."

"I'm sorry, Doctor."

"Understand you're gonna start a school."

"Yes, sir."

"Don't 'sir' me, Sister. Any your students get really sick, let me know. I mean really sick."

"I will."

"How much do I owe you, Doctor, for the call?" Ike asked.

"Nothin'. No charge."

"How about a good cigar?"

"In that case, make it two."

* * *

"Well, boss, we come through with never a sign of a redskin. Seems like they just melted away into the mountains."

Lessur's men had pulled up their loaded wagons in front of the warehouse. Rooster and the rest of the teamsters waited for instructions, while Gallagher spoke with Rupert Lessur at the side of the lead wagon.

"We heard about the truce. Seems like it's working."

"Yes, but nature abhors a vacuum."

"What does that mean?"

"It means keep your powder dry."

"Huh?"

"Never mind."

"You got a real good deal on those Yellow Boy Winchesters you ordered from New Haven. Three crates, forty dollars a lick." Gallagher pointed toward three oblong boxes, along with several square boxes in his wagon. "And enough cartridges to start a war."

Lessur smiled, but said nothing.

"You want us to take all this stuff to the fort in the morning?"

"No."

"No?"

"I want you to take it out now."

"Now?"

"Are you going to stand there and repeat everything I say?"

"Uh, no, boss."

"Take everything except the rifles and ammunition."

"What?"

"Store those in the warehouse, that's what."

"Who they for?"

"They're for nature's vacuum. And don't ask me what that means. I've got to go to a council meeting."

"Boss, it's been a long ride. Can we stop over and get a drink before we go to the fort?"

"It's going to be a longer ride. You can stop over and get a drink after you go to the fort. You can get ten drinks."

Lessur turned and walked away.

"Ten drinks," Gallagher said under his breath, "is that all?"

SILVER & CO.
"WE DELIVER THE GOODS."

"Ten signs on them wagons. That'll be ten dollars, Mister Silver."

Tom Bixby had just finished lettering the last wagon as Ike, Jake, Jed, Obie, Sister Bonney, Ben, Melena and Benjie watched.

"There you are, Mister Bixby."

Ike dropped ten silver dollars into Bixby's paint-smeared palm.

"Well, partners,"—Ike pointed to the wagons— "how do they look?"

"They look empty," Jake said.

"It's up to you and Ben to go to La Paz and fill 'em," Ike answered.

"And bring them back," Jedediah added.

"That's right, Jed." Ike put his hand on his son's shoulder. "The first of many, many round-trips. Jake, do we have enough teamsters?"

"Brother, we've got a payroll you wouldn't believe."

"Anybody else got a sign they want painted while I'm here?"

They all shook their heads.

"Then I'm out of here."

"Me too," Jake said. "Scotty's in the store all alone and I see customers going in."

"Look, John, if there's no further business to discuss, I move to adjourn this damn meeting. I've got some *important* business to take care of." Lessur knocked the ash off his cigar into the ashtray on the conference table.

The weekly meeting of the Prescott City Council was taking place as usual, whether there was any business to discuss or not, in the office of Amos Cantrell, with Mayor John Davis presiding.

The Prescott City Council was composed of five members, all present—Mayor Davis, Amos Cantrell, Gene Sweisgood, proprietor of the best restaurant in town, and Miles Akins, who owned the Hassayampa Hotel.

Lessur, Davis and Cantrell always voted as a block, following Lessur's lead. The other two invariably went along, since they'd be outvoted anyhow, and besides, Lessur owned the building that housed Akins's hotel.

"I second the motion to adjourn." Cantrell raised his hand.

"Just a minute, Amos. Before I recognize the motion and the second, there was one other matter on the docket to be discussed at today's meeting."

"What's that?" Akins asked.

"Whether we want to appoint a sheriff, 'specially in view of—"

"Of what?" Lessur interrupted.

"The truce and everything. The town's gonna be busier than ever—I even mentioned it to that new fellow, Ike Silver. . . ."

"You did?" There was an edge to Lessur's voice. "Why?"

"Well, the way he handled things since he came to town—"

"That was damn presumptuous of you, John, without consulting the rest of us."

"I was just inquiring about the possibility, and he turned us down, anyhow."

"Not 'us,' John. You. And from now on, don't you go shooting off your big fat mouth without our approval, you understand?"

Mayor John Davis understood that Lessur meant without *his* approval. It was Lessur who had him elected mayor and had the city council packed so nothing would be approved without *his* approval.

"We don't want a sheriff," Lessur went on, "and we don't need a sheriff. Once we start with that, people around here will start talking about hiring other officials and having other rules and regulations here in town—along with taxes to pay for hiring and enforcing those officials and regulations—and most of us here in this room aren't geared for taxes and regulations. Are you?"

"Well . . . no."

Lessur knew that he had effectively made his point and his voice and manner took on a mellower, more modulated artistry.

"Let's just maintain the status quo and see what happens in the next few weeks. There'll be time enough to make changes if and when any changes are necessary. Do we all agree?"

It was evident that they all agreed. Some more reluctantly than others. But they all knew that majority would rule—and majority meant Lessur.

After they all nodded, Lessur once more made his motion to adjourn, and once more Amos Cantrell seconded the motion, which passed unanimously.

He was about to open the door of the bank and

walk into the street when someone opened it from the outside. Binky held it open as Belinda Millay entered carrying a black satchel. Rupert Lessur stepped aside and they both entered. Lessur nodded, smiled and once more reverted to his charming façade.

"Good day, Miss Millay."

"It is a good day." She smiled.

"I think so too," Binky added. "In case you're interested."

"I'm not," Lessur replied without charm, and pointed to the satchel. "Making a deposit?"

"A considerable deposit."

"The saloon business must be good."

"Very good, and I expect it to get even better. To bad you can't raise the rent for the next five years."

"Oh, I can get by very well without raising your rent."

"Can you? How's the freight business now that you've got competition?"

"I hadn't noticed much competition."

"Really? I've got a feeling that you will."

"So have I," Binky said. "In case you're interested."

This time Lessur did not reply.

"By the way,"—Belinda held up the satchel—"business is so good that I just might make you an offer one of these days."

"What kind of an offer?"

"For the Emporium building."

"Two corrections. One, it's the *Lessur* building. Two, Lessur isn't disposing. He's expanding. Good day, Miss Millay."

He brushed by Belinda and Binky and went out into the street.

Rupert Lessur didn't like the way that things were going. Didn't like it at all.

He didn't like the fact that John Davis, a former

hog farmer who had failed at other businesses, and whom he had handpicked to be mayor, was beginning to believe his title—going so far as to talk to Ike Silver about becoming sheriff.

Moreover, he didn't like Ike Silver, an interloper who set himself up in business as a competitor in freighting and brought Crook and Colorados together in an unwelcome truce.

He didn't like some uppity whore lording it over him with caustic remarks in public.

There were a lot of things he didn't like, and it was time to make a preemptive strike—or strikes.

During the meeting, Rupert Lessur had said that he had some important business to take care of. He was on his way to the Butterfield Stage and Telegraph Office to do just that.

It had taken him years to achieve his present position. Years of struggle and infinite loneliness since his mother died. As he walked toward his destination, he thought about those years and about his mother.

Amanda Lessur, it was generally agreed, was the most beautiful young lady in Charleston, perhaps in the entire state of South Carolina and beyond. Delicate, flaxen-haired, blue-eyed—a perfect personification of a Southern belle.

The question was, why did such a desirable young lady marry such an undesirable, unredeemable old man named Marcus Beaudine—a parrot-faced scarecrow of a man, above average in height, with piecrust skin, huge hands and feet? Part of the answer, people speculated, was his money. The other part became evident when she gave birth to a "premature" son seven months later. It was the first time anyone could remember that a premature baby weighed ten and a half pounds.

As he grew older, Amanda Beaudine saw to it

that her son Rupert had every advantage she could accord him; or rather every advantage that Beaudine's money could accord him. The best schools, "lothes and upbringing. Rupert's "father" satiated his lust and barely spoke to his offspring.

For years, Amanda bore the burden of Beaudine's abuse for the sake of her son, until she could bear no more and she became ill and of no service to her husband. At that point, he gratified his venereal appetite with a beautiful copper-complexioned house slave named Selena.

On her deathbed, she told her son what others had surmised and what he was now old enough to understand. She had been in love with a young naval officer. They were to be married when he returned from duty at sea. But he never returned, and she had to have a father for their child. Marcus Beaudine became that father, but in name only.

When Amanda died, Beaudine disowned Rupert, who was barely sixteen, and turned him out without a penny.

Rupert took his mother's maiden name and made his way by wile and wit. He stole. He cheated—and when he was old enough he discovered the illicit slave trade and prospered.

Rupert Lessur had no allegiance to anyone or anything. Not North nor South.

When the Yankees burned Charleston and Marcus Beaudine's mansion and his decrepit body with it, Rupert Lessur smiled for the first time since his mother died. He smiled and turned west with what wealth he had accumulated and put to use his wile and wit in Prescott and the surrounding area of the Arizona Territory.

As he walked, he thought of his mother and recounted the years of struggle and success.

Rupert Lessur had no intention of allowing anything or anybody to stand in the way of his continuing that success.

Not George Crook; not Isaac Silver. And while he was at it, he was not about to allow a reformed whore to stand in his way either.

Lessur thought of an old saying. "Even a hawk is an eagle among crows." Lessur didn't consider his enemies crows. They were hawks. But among those hawks he considered himself an eagle.

At the Butterfield Stage and Telegraph Office he sent two wires.

One to a gambler.

The other to a gunman.

CHAPTER THIRTY-SIX

Like the spokes from the rim of a giant wheel, they had all come to the same hub.

Not only from different parts of the country, but from across the seas, other countries and other continents—fate, destiny or maybe just chance had ordained that they be in this place at this time.

And in this place at this time, it seemed to each of them, he or she was on the right course.

But it was inevitable that those courses would collide—and there would be casualties.

Ike and Jake Silver—after years of travel and travail had come to a place they could call home, sink roots, and cultivate a new life for themselves and the two young boys.

Melena and Ben Brown—born in bondage, now free and working, not as sharecroppers and servants, but as partners with a man they respected and who respected them, were now able to see their son look at them and smile.

Sister Mary Boniface—with an ever-abiding faith, had found friends among strangers to help her carry out her mission.

Belinda Millay—who had "traveled through a land of men, and heard and saw such dreadful things as cold Earth wanderers never knew," was now the sole owner of the Emporium, and would never have to walk up the stairs to degradation again.

Basil "Binky" Binkham—who in his time had played many parts, but had never found a stage that gave him more freedom and suited him better than the proscenium provided by the Emporium, along with liquid fringe benefits.

Sean Dolan—seeker of the cold yellow, poised to leap upon a mountain that held the promise of every digger's dream.

Colorados—who broke out of prison to reclaim his heritage, and whose life had been saved by a man called Silver, and who now was reclaiming that heritage with the help of a soldier called Crook.

Quemada—who coveted Colorados's chiefdom and bride, and who had an ally named Rupert Lessur, an ally to provide him with the means to possess both.

And Rupert Lessur—who had built an empire without regard to conscience or compunction, and who now saw that empire in temporary relapse because of Silver, Crook, Colorados, and even Belinda Millay, with her natting annoyances. But Rupert Lessur was a man with supreme confidence in his ability to destroy the enemies of his empire: The freight line, the truce, the mine, and even the saloon. He had a plan that included them all. A plan that concluded with their destruction, death or conquest.

Rupert Lessur thought of another saying and smiled inwardly.

"The strong take it from the weak, and the smart take it from the strong."

As he crossed the street he smiled, and no longer just inwardly, because he knew he was both strong and smart.

"Well, Big Ike, there it is. From storeroom to classroom." Sister Bonney walked across the room and turned toward Ike. "Thanks to you."

"I just provided a little space. You did all the rest."

"With the help of the good people of Prescott, and, of course, the good Lord."

"Of course."

"Desks, chairs, books, and, as of tomorrow, the most important ingredient—students."

"You've forgotten another important ingredient, Sister."

"And what ingredient is that?"

"The teacher."

"Oh, that." She shrugged.

"Yes, that."

"Would you believe, Big Ike, that already twenty-four children have enrolled?"

"That's twice as many as another teacher had a long time ago," Ike smiled. "When they sat down to supper."

"Oh, please." Sister Bonney was visibly embarrassed at the comparison and wanted to change the subject. "And you do know, of course, that two of those boys are named Silver and another is named Brown."

"Benjie's a little young for school, isn't he?"

"For him it's a sort of preschool. We wouldn't want to leave him out, now would we?"

"No, Sister, we wouldn't. And I must say, I do admire your dedication and determination . . . ."

"It's all a part of what you said to Colorados that night on our journey. . . ."

"Not quite sure what you're referring to."

"I'm referring to 'tribes.' I couldn't help overhearing you mention that the Apaches have many tribes; his was the . . . ?"

"Mimbreno."

"Yes, and you said you were from the tribe of Joseph, isn't that right?"

Ike nodded.

"Well, in my faith we also have tribes. My tribe is called 'Sisters of Charity' . . . and this school is just part of our purpose."

"But how is it that you—"

Ike Silver never finished his question. He was interrupted by the sound of hammering just outside the side door.

"What on earth is that?" Sister Bonney exclaimed.

"Let's go find out."

The two of them walked to the door and opened it.

A familiar group had gathered: Jake, Jed, Obie, Melena, Ben, Benjie, and even Belinda and Binky. They were all watching as Tom Bixby stood on a ladder and pounded the last nail into a freshly lettered sign.

PRESCOTT SCHOOL
FOR BOYS AND GIRLS
TEACHER
SISTER MARY BONIFACE

As Bixby climbed down the ladder, all those assembled, except Sister Bonney, clapped their hands.

"There you are, Sister," Bixby said, "compliments of just some of your friends and well-wishers."

"I'm so happy," Sister Bonney said, "I think I'm going to cry . . . but I do think, Mister Bixby, we ought to paint over that last part of the sign."

"Oh, no," Jake said emphatically. "Everybody's got to know who's in charge. Right, everybody?"

"Right!" everyone responded at once.

"By the by,"—Binky stepped forward with one hand behind his back—"since I am not a student and cannot be accused of bribing the teacher, I would like to present the teacher with a small token."

He bowed and held out a large, shiny red apple.

Sister Bonney accepted the apple—and more applause.

"And whenever you need someone to lecture on Shakespeare, I am available at no charge." Binky bowed again.

"Well, tomorrow's a big day," Ike said. "Jake and Ben are going to La Paz, and Sister Bonney and the young ones are going to school."

"And I," Belinda Millay said, "am going back to the Emporium."

"So am I," Binky added.

"Dad?" Jed asked. "What are *you* going to do?"

"Me? I'm going to take it easy."

"Sure you are," Jake said.

CHAPTER THIRTY-SEVEN

There was a whisper of winter in the air—a whisper that presaged change.

A whisper that grew louder with each passing hour, day and week, as the long October nights dissolved into November and stretched ever longer and darker. Each dawn the sun pushed harder and was slower on its upward climb toward first light above the eastern peaks.

Winter's whisper brought its cooling breath, which promised desert frost would not be far behind.

Bureau drawers that held long-sleeved, knitted sweaters were drawn open and the sweaters unfolded and pulled over, or buttoned onto, first the younger, and then the older members of the family, and then the mothers and fathers.

The extra blanket saw service and so did the fireplace. Lemonade and sarsaparilla were replaced with hot coffee and tea.

But the changes in and around Prescott and the Arizona Territory were not just in weather and wardrobe. The climate change occurred every year. But there were new and different changes this year.

CHAPTER THIRTY-EIGHT

Since the day that the Prescott School for Boys and Girls opened on a crisp late October morning, Jake and Ben had made three round-trip runs between Prescott and La Paz.

On the first trip they rode in separate wagons. On the second trip they both rode in Ben's wagon and, in spite of Jake's garrulous nature, the conversation was on the sparse side. Ben was nowhere near as withdrawn as he had been when they first met in La Paz, or on the journey to Prescott with Ike, or during the early time when they got there, but still, there was a certain residual reserve about him.

But by the third trip, they not only rode together and talked to each other, but more often than not, it was Ben who initiated the conversation. Sometimes about Ike, other times about Sister Bonney or the boys, even about marriage.

Once, when Ben mentioned Melena's name and how, now that things were going better, the two of them hoped that soon there would be a baby sister or brother for Benjie, Ben looked at Jake and asked, "How about you?"

"How about me, what?"

"I know that Ike was married, but how about you, Jake? Have you ever been married?"

"Nope."

"Never been in love?"

"I didn't say that."

"Then I won't ask."

"You've already asked . . . so I'll tell you. It was at Temple, back in England. I was sitting up front, and for some reason something made me turn back and look. There she was, across the way, close to the back. After that first glimpse I couldn't help turning and looking at her again and again. She wasn't the most beautiful girl I ever saw, but there was something about her, mostly her eyes, something that made me feel I had knives in both knees, something that made me tremble and made me try to catch my breath. I knew I had found the woman I wanted to marry. When the prayers were over, I pushed my way through people and went to where she was— but she wasn't. She had left. Outside, I looked everywhere. But she was gone. I never heard her voice and I never saw her again . . . and maybe it's better that way. But you know something? Not a day goes by that I don't remember those eyes, and think of her and hope that sometime, somewhere, I'll see her again. But one thing I'm sure of . . ."

"What's that?"

"It won't be in Prescott."

"You never can tell, but that's some story, Jake."

"It is,"—Jake smiled—"if you believe it."

"Huh? I don't know whether to believe you, or—"

"I'll tell you something you can believe. Something you can see with your own eyes."

"What?"

"Indians. Apaches. On that ridge." Jake pointed. "They been riding along with us for the last mile or so."

Jake took off his hat, held it up high and waved.

"That one up front. From here he looks like Colorados to me."

The Indian up front waved back.

"To me, too." Ben nodded. "But it sure is a different Colorados than we met that first time."

"You're right about that. He's changed. But then, we've all changed some."

"Sure have, Jake." Ben smiled. "Some more than others."

As the loaded wagons with Jake and Ben in the lead wagon rolled by the window of Lessur's office, Gallagher shook his head.

"Well, boss, looks like business is boomin' . . . for them. That's their third trip. . . ."

"I realize you can count to three, Gallagher. Just shut up."

"Sure, boss. Anythin' else you want me to do?"

"Yes, there is." Lessur picked up a sheet of paper from his desk. "I want you to make another run to La Paz. Here's the list."

Gallagher took the paper and glanced through it. "All this?"

"No, you damn fool, just half of it."

"Huh?"

"Of course, all of it."

"Well, I just meant . . . stuff's beginning to pile up in the warehouse and—"

"And things are going to be different around here, and soon. We'll get rid of all we've got stored . . . *and* some other things."

* * *

During that time in November when Jake was away with Ben, Ike would hear the boys' nightly prayers, then sleep on his bed in the room next to theirs for the rest of the night. But when Jake was in town, once or twice a week, Ike would walk over to the Emporium, watch a card game—seldom playing himself—but would listen to Binky's orations, have one or two drinks, sometimes with Binky, sometimes with Oliver Knight or Doctor Zebelion Barnes or Tom Bixby, but usually with Belinda Millay at her table while she kept her fingers mobile with a deck of cards.

Lessur was usually there, usually playing cards and usually winning. Ike never sat in and played against him. Neither did Belinda.

On one of those nights as Ike and Belinda were at her table, she shuffled the cards and slapped the deck.

"Cut."

Ike cut.

She picked up the deck and dealt. Five cards apiece.

"Take a look," she said.

Ike looked at his hand.

She didn't look at hers.

"You'll take three cards. Right?"

"Right."

"Sure you will, because you've got a pair of kings and nothing else." She dealt. "Now look."

He did.

"You feel good because you caught another king. Right?"

"Right!"

"So you'd bet pretty heavy. But don't."

"Why not?"

"Because . . ."—Belinda discarded her top card without looking at her hand and dealt herself a card from the deck—". . . you'd lose. I just dealt myself a flush." She turned over her cards. "All blue."

"I've been in a lot of card games, but that's the most amazing hand I've ever seen anybody deal."

"That's nothing." She smiled. "I'm only *pretty* good. You ought to see some of the gamblers on the riverboats or in New Orleans. They're *really* good."

"What about our friend,"—Ike pointed at a table—"Mister Lessur? *Pretty* good or *really* good?"

"Not *really* good."

"That reminds me. You never did finish telling me the story of your life. How did you get to be . . . *pretty* good? You started to say something about your father. . . ."

"Oh, yes. My father. He was a simpleton. An honest, hardworking Tennessee farmer, but a simpleton. Worked seven days a week all his life and died in debt. But his brother, my Uncle Max, never worked a day in his life and lived in relative comfort all his days, playing cards in and around Memphis.

"Uncle Max made sure not to win so much that the losers would quit playing with him, but enough for his needs. He had a gift with numbers, and nimble fingers that could deal seconds and thirds. He was kind enough to teach his little niece a few tricks while keeping his fingers limbered. By the time I was twelve I could count the cards at blackjack. By fifteen, Uncle Max proclaimed me a poker master. Sometimes I could even beat him . . . but not long after that both he and my father were dead. One in a duel after a card game, the other from hard work and a weak heart.

"But a fifteen-year-old girl couldn't play poker for a living . . . and then, Mister Silver, as the story goes, 'I met a man' . . . and the rest isn't so pretty."

"Good evening, you two." Rupert Lessur had finished his game, collected his winnings, and stopped by Belinda's table.

Both Ike and Belinda nodded, but didn't answer the greeting.

"And I want to thank you, Miss Millay, for a very enjoyable and profitable evening."

"No thanks necessary, Mister Lessur. To me it's a matter of indifference. The house never loses."

"Mister Brady lost the house."

"Mister Brady wasn't good enough."

"And you are?" Lessur smiled.

Belinda cut the deck . . . and revealed the ace of spades.

"Very amusing. I've seen other players do that . . . and still lose."

She replaced the ace in the deck.

"Would you care to try?"

"Oh, no." He smiled and tipped his hat. "Not me. Good night." He reached for a cigar as he left.

"Be careful," Ike said. "I think Mister Lessur's got something up his sleeve."

"Good advice, Big Ike." Belinda nodded. "Take it."

As was his custom each night before retiring, Ike Silver wound his gold watch, pressed the stem to open the lid, listened to the tune it played and looked at the wedding picture pasted to the inside of the lid. This night he thought of the lines in a poem.

Of all sad words of tongue or pen,
The saddest are these, "It might have been."

He thought of what might have been if Rachel hadn't died giving birth to Obie. Of what might have been if they were all there together. His only consolation was that every time he looked at those two boys, in a way, Rachel went on living.

Ike Silver closed the lid of the watch and went to bed.

Once more, Captain Bourke and Lieutenant Gibbs stood at a distance at Spanish Flats, where Crook and Colorados met, talked and smoked.

Lieutenant Gibbs smiled as he spoke to Bourke, who was not smiling.

"Looks like they're getting along like two peas in a pod."

"Far as I'm concerned, they're not two peas. One's a snake and he'll strike whenever it damn well suits him, just like those other snakes struck my brother."

"Maybe not, Captain. Things change."

"Things," Bourke replied, "not snakes."

Crook puffed on his cigar, then tapped off the long white ash. "We're more than halfway there, Colorados. It won't be long before your pardon comes through and we can both sign that treaty."

"Other treaties have been signed."

"Not by you and me."

"That is true, Gray Wolf. You have kept your word. I will keep mine."

"I know that. Then maybe I'll meet your bride so I can give her a wedding present."

"The treaty will be present enough."

"How is she . . . what is her name?"

"Su-Wan. She has brought me much happiness."

"There will be more to come when you have children."

Colorados nodded, smiled and smoked.

Naked, Su-Wan bathed in the cold running stream. She was copper-colored with long blue-black hair, fawnlike eyes set wide apart with curled lashes and narrow eyebrows for an Apache. She was tall for an Indian woman, with wide shoulders, blossoming breasts, a tapered waist and full hips that narrowed into strong, lengthy legs.

She scooped the water with both palms onto her face, shivered just a little and walked gracefully out of the stream, then froze at the sight of Quemada.

His eyes absorbed her nakedness. Still, she did not move. She did not try to cover herself. And in her eyes there was defiance . . . until he turned and walked away.

That night as they lay in their wiki-up, smoky and private, Colorados sensed a difference after they had coupled, and finally spoke of it.

"Su-Wan, is there something wrong?"

"Not as long as we're together," was all she said, then put her arms around him.

"Ben, can this last?"

"Can what last?"

"This. You and me together . . . with Benjie, here in this place, with these people. Every time you leave to go to La Paz, even though I know it's just for a few days . . . I get an ache in my heart . . . thinking maybe something'll happen . . . and you won't come back . . ."

"I'll always come back to you, Melena."

He put his arms around her and drew her close where they lay.

"I'm back now."

TRUCE HOLDS!!!

So read the headline in the new edition of *The Prescott Independent*.

The story, once again by Oliver Knight, went on to say in part:

> ... *this marks the third edition since we first printed the welcome news of a truce between the U.S. Army and the erstwhile hostile Mimbreno Apaches, as agreed to by Colonel Crook and Chief Colorados, thus giving the lie to numerous naysayers and crepehangers who went around Prescott proclaiming the truce had as much chance of succeeding as a flatiron of floating at sea. Well, nuts to you, naysayers, because it won't be but a few more editions before an official TREATY is signed by said parties.*

"I made it my business to deliver this to you personally, Rupert," Oliver Knight said as he placed the newspaper on Lessur's desk and looked at him and Gallagher, "since, as I recall, you were one of the naysayers about the truce."

"Oh, no!" Lessur feigned incredulity. "You must have misunderstood, Oliver. I'm all for prosperity and peace in the Territory."

"Sure you are, Rupert . . . your own prosperity, and a piece of everything you can grab in the Territory."

"Why don't you just go ahead and print something like that, Oliver, and see what happens?" Lessur grinned.

"Is that a suggestion, or a threat?"

"Take it any way you like, Oliver."

"In that case, Rupert,"—Knight walked toward the door—"I suggest you keep reading the *Independent*."

After the door closed, Gallagher looked at Lessur as Lessur lit a cigar and didn't seem at all distressed.

"That little bastard's got nerve, hasn't he, boss?"

"That little bastard,"—Lessur inhaled the smoke from his cigar—"is going to have a couple of other things to write about in the next few editions of his newspaper."

"It won't be long now, Big Ike. The shorin's all done, everything's cleaned up, the diggin's begun, and what we've dug out so far looks as rich as anything I've ever come across."

"Glad to hear it, Sean. You and your men've put in a lot of hard work these past few weeks."

"We're used to it, but I'll tell you one thing we're not used to."

"What's that?"

"Spectators . . . at least they're spectators so far." Dolan pointed toward a ridge, where, outlined against a gray November sky, a half-dozen mounted Apaches could be seen, but not identified.

"I see what you mean."

"Every day, well, most every day, they show up, look down on us for a time, then just disappear. We know about their burial ground between here and there, and believe me, we don't go anywhere near it. They can have their ghosts. We don't want any part of 'em. All we want is pay dirt, and we've already got that."

"Good."

"And speakin' of pay dirt, like I said, it won't be long before we'll be needin' your best and strongest wagon to haul that yellow outta here."

"You'll have it, just send down word."

"We'll do that, but . . . I've got a feelin'. . . ."

"What kind of feeling?"

"Well, that things are goin' *too* good. My sainted mother used to say that she didn't like things to go

along *too* good . . . better that things are just in between . . . that way nothin' can go real wrong."

"Some Jewish mothers seem to have the same
outlook, but in this case—"

"You're right, Ike, they could be wrong."

"They better be." Ike smiled.

CHAPTER THIRTY-NINE

During those weeks, dozens and dozens of strangers came to Prescott from different directions for different reasons. Some to buy ranches, some to find gold and silver, some to start businesses.

But two of those strangers had come for other reasons.

One was a gambler named Sebastian; the other a gunman named Cord.

Each had been sent for by Rupert Lessur.

Milo Sebastian arrived on a stagecoach, Quentin Cord on a statuesque white stallion.

Sebastian was corpulent. So much so that he took up the better part of two spaces on the stagecoach. Dressed in an amber blanket of a suit, with the deepset eyes of a fox peering out of a furrow-browed face, he was unmistakable in any crowd. He damn near was a crowd. Those anywhere near his size were usually of a jovial aspect. There was nothing jovial about Sebastian. He had only one expression—solemn.

Rupert Lessur had booked a room for him at the

Hassayampa Hotel, where they met the evening of his arrival.

"One thousand dollars,"—Lessur placed the money on a table between them—"as promised . . . for openers."

"Go on."

"Since last we met, I know that things haven't been going too well for you in your . . . profession. And the reason is that you're too damn good and too well known to get into any big games with any big players . . . and besides, you don't have a bankroll."

"You call that a bankroll?" Sebastian pointed to the money on the table.

"I said it was for openers. Just put that in your pocket and keep it."

"Then what?"

"Then I'll bankroll you with ten thousand more to challenge a 'lady' named Belinda Millay, who owns a saloon called the Emporium, to a not-so-friendly game of poker. You win the game, keep the ten thousand and I get the saloon."

"Suppose I lose?"

"I'll take that chance, but you won't lose, not with those hands. . . ."

Sebastian put both his hands flat on the table. "These hands aren't as good as they used to be. You can see they've put on a little weight and so has the rest of me."

"They're plenty good enough and so are you. We're talking about some female, an ex-whore . . . and I'm not so sure about the ex. Sebastian, what do you have to lose?"

"You're right. Nothing. But you do. And the last time we met, we didn't exactly part the best of friends."

"That was a matter over a lady friend. This is business. And you're the man for the job. Do we have a deal?"

"We do," said Sebastian.

"Excellent. By the way, do you know whatever became of Myrna?"

"Yes, I do. I married her."

Quentin Cord rode into Prescott alone, as he had done in dozens of other towns throughout the South and Southwest, from the Shenandoah to the Columbia, in desert and high country, and he always rode out alone as well—and left behind a dead body. Sometimes more than one.

He had a hard, narrow face, perfectly symmetrical, with steel-gray eyes and hair, a long, thin nose, a knife-blade mouth, clean-shaven except for close-cropped sideburns that extended well past pointed earlobes. There was a prominent scar high across his left cheek, which might have been caused by a sabre or gunshot. Nobody knew. Nobody asked.

He had killed, some said murdered, more than a score of opponents after insulting each of them publicly and challenging each of them to draw first. And, in front of witnesses, after their pistol cleared leather, he would hook and draw and fire . . . and kill.

Cord had served with J. E. B. Stuart and was still an unrepentant Confederate, still dressed in gray from head to heel.

He rode an ash-white stallion that stood near seventeen hands; he named it Travler, after the mount ridden by General Robert E. Lee.

Cord was tall and limped slightly on his left leg, a result of the war or a gunfight. Again, nobody knew. Nobody asked.

"You! Boy!" Cord looked down from his mount. "You stable horses here?"

"His name is Brown. Ben Brown." Ike appeared alongside the black man. "And no, we don't stable horses."

"Who are you?" Cord asked.

"Name's Silver. Ike Silver."

"This boy work for you?"

"This man and I are partners."

"Partners?"

"There's a livery up the street." Ike pointed.

Without speaking, Cord reined his horse around and moved away.

Ben stared after him.

Ike's hand barely touched Brown's arm.

"Ignore it, Ben."

"Yeah."

"We all have to ignore some things . . . when we can."

"Yeah."

In his office, Lessur looked up and down at Quentin Cord, and for a moment settled on the .44 strapped low at the leg of the man who stood in front of him.

"His name is Silver. Ike Silver."

"I've already met him."

"When?"

"Just a few minutes ago."

"What do you think?"

"I think," Cord said without emotion, "Ike Silver is a dead man."

"Good." Lessur smiled. "Pick your time and place, then—"

"You hired me to do a job, Mister Lessur. Don't try to tell me how to do it."

"I wouldn't think of it, Mister Cord."

CHAPTER FORTY

Ike sat at the table with Belinda Millay.

The Emporium was at near-capacity with the usual customers. But this night there were two new customers, neither of whom had spoken a word to Rupert Lessur since Lessur entered—or to each other.

Milo Sebastian was at the near end of the bar, Quentin Cord at the far end.

"You know those two?" Ike asked.

"I know of one of them," Belinda said.

"Which one?"

"The fat one who's looking this way. Name's Sebastian." Belinda tapped the deck of cards on the table. "He's *really* good."

"Better than you?"

Belinda smiled. "He used to be, but he looks a little out of condition . . . maybe he is, and maybe he's not, but I think we're going to find out."

Sebastian approached the table and bowed slightly.

"Miss Millay. My name is—"

"Sebastian."

"Yes. I understand you never sit in on a game unless you're invited."

"That's right."

"Well, I'm inviting you. Poker. Just the two of us."

"Are you playing on behalf of yourself . . . or somebody else?"

"On behalf of a considerable bankroll."

"In that case, I think Mister Silver will excuse us while you sit down and we go over the rules of the game . . ."

Ike nodded, rose and started to leave as he heard Belinda Millay say, "We alternate the deal, dealer's choice, no limit . . ."

Two hours later there was only one game being played as they all stood watching: Ike, Binky, Lessur, Oliver Knight, Tom Bixby, Francine, Alma, Marisa, and all the other customers who strained to get a look at the players—all except Cord, who stood in place at the bar.

Just before the game started, Ike had managed to speak to Belinda.

"You think he can pull anything fancy against you . . . or vice versa?"

"In a game with just two players like Sebastian and me, each of us is so busy making sure the other one's playing straight, it's just about impossible to do otherwise."

"You know Lessur's backing him."

"I do."

"Then don't play."

"I've got to."

"Why?"

"Rules of the game."

"I don't understand."

"Sure you do."

During all that time with two perfectly matched players, neither making a miscalculation, fortune smiled first on one player, then the other, but most recently on Sebastian.

It would seem going into the third hour in a crowded, smoke-smeared room, a man as heavy as Sebastian would begin to sweat. But there was no sign of perspiration on his brow or anyplace else. He sat with cool confidence and a pile of cash in front of him.

"My deal," Sebastian said.

"Call the game."

"Five cards straight-up. Ten thousand against the Emporium."

"Deal."

Slowly, deliberately, Sebastian began to deal.

A queen to Belinda.

An ace to himself.

A jack to Belinda.

A seven to himself.

A ten to Belinda.

An ace to himself.

A king to Belinda.

Another ace to himself.

Belinda needed an ace or a nine for a straight.

Sebastian needed an ace for four of a kind or a seven for a full house to win either way.

He dealt.

A nine to Belinda.

She had her straight.

But there was still an ace and three sevens in the deck . . . and Sebastian was still dealing.

For the first time since he began his turn at dealing, Milo Sebastian paused for a notable beat, while the people in the room and even the smoke itself seemed to freeze.

Belinda's expression never changed, nor did Sebastian's.

Then someone in the room did move. Rupert Lessur struck a match with his thumbnail and lit the cigar in his mouth, a mouth curved slightly upward.

Sebastian dealt.

A deuce to himself. No help.

Belinda's straight won the pot—the Emporium and Lessur's ten thousand.

A thunder of cheers and applause reverberated around the room. Celebrants laughed and slapped each other's back. All but two.

Cord stood, canting slightly to the left, a statue of indifference.

Lessur stepped even closer to the table as Sebastian rose to his feet with some effort.

Rupert Lessur blew forth a pattern of smoke directly into Sebastian's porcine face.

Sebastian—all three hundred pounds of him—simply shrugged.

Binky leaned in toward Belinda, where she still sat at the table with the straight and the pile of money in front of her.

"Miss Millay, for a moment there, I thought that both you and I would end up as homeless as a pair of poker chips."

Belinda Millay looked up and winked . . . at Ike Silver.

As Milo Sebastian was about to step aboard the stagecoach the next day, a hand pressed against his left arm. The hand belonged to Rupert Lessur, who stood close and spoke just above a whisper while the other passengers were boarding.

"You fat bastard."

"Yes . . . and speaking of bastards, you asked

about Myrna. I did marry her, but shortly after your baby was born dead . . . she hanged herself. . . ."

Lessur's hand dropped from Sebastian's arm.

"Incidentally, in case you're interested, it was a baby girl."

When Milo Sebastian stepped onto the stagecoach, he weighed slightly more than when he arrived.

Ten thousand dollars more, plus the thousand Lessur had advanced.

CHAPTER FORTY-ONE

Belinda confided what had happened to no one.

Except Ike Silver.

When she and Sebastian sat down to discuss the rules of the game, she included an observation and a proposition.

"Maybe you can beat me and maybe I can beat you. Either of us can win or lose. But there's one way we can both win. Make it look good for a couple of hours. Then deal me a winning hand. I'll keep the Emporium and give you back the cash. How big is the bankroll?"

"Ten thousand."

"Lessur?"

Sebastian nodded.

"I thought so. You and I both win and Lessur loses."

For the first time in a long while, the look on Sebastian's face, for less than a second, turned less solemn.

Rupert Lessur's first ploy had failed, but it was a minor ploy compared to the other two. There was still Quentin Cord. And a truce to be broken.

CHAPTER FORTY-TWO

"Ike, he's here for one reason and one reason only. To kill you."

As Ike Silver was passing by, Oliver Knight had waved him into the pressroom of *The Prescott Independent*, saying he had something important to talk to him about.

The *Independent* had come out just the day before, so Matt Crowley, Knight's copyboy/reporter/assistant editor, had the day off, and there was no activity in the pressroom. Nevertheless, Knight had closed and locked the front door so the two of them would not be interrupted.

Knight sat on his swivel chair at the rolltop and Ike stood leaning against the cluttered desk.

"There's a stack of obituaries stretching across six states and three territories, all with the same cause of death—and that cause can be summed up in two words: Quentin Cord. He's not here to see the sights. He's here because he was hired to do a job and that job can also be summed up in two words: Ike Silver."

"You can't be sure about that."

"Just as sure as the turning of the earth. And I'm

just as sure about who hired him and I can sum that up—"

"I know, in two words."

"Rupert Lessur." Knight nodded. "Ike, Lessur's got to get rid of you, and Cord's the quickest, most effective and permanent way."

"It takes two to make a gunfight."

"Not the way Cord does it. The pattern's always the same—he'll goad, insult, disparage, humiliate, mock, slap the shit out of his victim in public, saying he won't draw until his opponent's gun is out of its holster. Then he'll shoot him dead in self-defense. He's done it time and again. Son, I don't want to write your obituary in the next edition."

"I don't want you to either." Ike smiled.

"Good."

"But what do you want me to do?"

"I'm not sure." Knight shrugged. "Maybe leave town."

"For how long? I'd have to come back and he'd still be here—or else he'd follow me and I'd still have to face him . . . and with a gun. If I didn't carry one, he'd provide it, right?"

"I suppose so. . . ."

"And I'd have to use his instead of mine."

"Look, Ike, I know you can shoot. You proved that with those Keeler boys. But they were whiskey-soaked and that was an exhibition, not a gunfight. What the hell do you know about gunfighting?"

"I know some."

"Some's not good enough. Not against Cord. You've got to know everything—and *then some.* Where'd you learn?"

"In the army."

"I never heard of any quick-draw gunfights against Confederates . . . sure as hell not at Shiloh."

"After Shiloh. We were recuperating."

"Who's 'we'?"

"A fellow 'we' called J.B. He was a scout and a spy for the North, got wounded, and while we were recuperating, he kept in practice. Showed me a few things. Even beat him to the draw—once."

"With real bullets?"

"Nope."

"Well, that's what Cord'll be using."

"Oliver, I appreciate what you're telling me, but this is something I have to face alone. And I'd appreciate it a lot more if you didn't say anything about this to anyone—'specially my family—Jake or anybody else who might get in the way, or might get hurt."

"Jake's in La Paz . . ."

"But he and Ben'll be back in a couple days. Will you promise?"

"Sure, sure. But I think somebody else's already figured it out—besides Lessur, of course."

"Who?"

"Belinda Millay. She knows all about Cord. . . ."

"Well, just don't say anything more."

"I won't say anything to anybody, but don't be surprised if Crook knows about Cord. I think he's come across him before. Cord killed an army sergeant—in self-defense, of course. By the way, whatever happened to this J.B. fella? Is he still alive?"

"Far as I know."

"Uh-huh. Well, I'll just close my little editorial telling you that you're a damned fool."

"Oliver, there's an old saying . . . 'even a fool must now and then be right.' "

"Even if he's *dead* right? Ike—"

"I thank you, my friend." Ike smiled. "Now if you'll kindly unlock that door . . ." He pointed toward the entrance.

"All right, all right . . . but I myself would shoot that son of bitch Cord in the back . . . if I weren't afraid of guns."

"Ike," Crook said, "I got a notion to throw that son of a bitch Cord in the stockade. . . ."

"On what charge?"

"I'll think of something while he's in there . . . trespassing on government property . . . spitting in the river . . . gimping . . . some damn thing. . . . The truth is—"

"The truth is, Colonel, you know better. There's nothing you could say or do that'd stick, and you know it."

"Yeah, and I knew Sergeant Bronson, a good man and a good soldier, but not good enough with a gun . . . not against Quentin Cord."

"Colonel, you've got enough on your mind keeping peace in the Territory . . . you weren't sent here to worry about what happens to one civilian named Ike Silver."

"Are you telling me my duty, Ike Silver?" Crook said in too gruff a voice.

"Just a gentle reminder, Colonel Crook, which you're too good a soldier to need, but thanks anyhow."

"If there's any way, any way at all, fair or foul, that you can think of . . . *do it!* That's an order, Captain."

"*Yes, sir,* Colonel." Ike nodded.

"You told me not to tell you how to do your job, Mister Cord," Lessur said, "but there's one thing you ought to know about a friend of Ike Silver's."

"Which friend is that?"

"Her name's Belinda Millay . . ."

* * *

Ike Silver thought about J.B.—6'2", azure-blue eyes, long yellow hair, lean and raw-boned, slow to speak, but panther quick and leather tough when pressed into action. Born an Illinois farm boy, but a natural with a gun, he became a lawman in Kansas by the age of twenty, and then in other places until he enlisted as a scout and spy for the Union.

Ike thought about the times at the hillside of the hospital when J.B. kept in practice while teaching Ike the fine points of the art of gunfighting—and the way J.B. did it was an art . . .

"There's them that keep the hammer on an empty chamber. I'm not one of 'em. Don't you be either. Might need that extra bullet. Now this is important. Never . . . never squeeze the trigger unless you're willing to kill . . . and I mean kill without compunction or hesitation. Got that?"

"I got it, J.B."

"Good. Because an instant of hesitation could cost you your life, because the other fellow won't hesitate, and that's the difference between the quick and the dead. And you'd better be quick or else you'll be dead. Follow me?"

"I follow, J.B."

"And don't do anything dumb like aim to wound. That lets him get off a shot, a shot that could kill you. And never aim for the head. Know why?"

"Too small a target."

"Partly right. The other part is that the head moves quicker than the rest of the body. The chest, Ike, that's the place . . . broader and slower, and that's where the most vital target is . . . the heart. Now, speaking of that, don't give him a broad target by standing square on. The less he has to aim at, the better your odds of coming out alive. Got that?"

"Got it, J.B."

"And forget that shit about watching his eyes. He shoots with his thumb and trigger finger. When that hand *starts to move, you move faster . . . unless you decide to move first . . . and don't worry about being fair—worry about being alive. That's why I say don't squeeze unless you're willing to kill . . . just like war. Only difference is a gunfight is a war between two people. Hook. Draw. Fire. Three elements in one swift, sure motion. Hook. Draw. Fire. Repeat that."*

"Hook. Draw. Fire."

"Good. Now there's just one other element. Accuracy. All the rest is bullshit unless you hit the target. Part is natural. The other part is practice. See that tree over there with that hanging branch?"

"I see it."

"That's a man who's willing to kill you . . . unless you kill him first. The leaf on that branch is that son of a bitch's heart. When I say 'now' his hand is starting to move. You move too. Hook. Draw. Fire. Fast, but not too fast or the barrel won't be level. You ready, Ike?"

"Ready, J.B."

"Now."

A half dozen years later in Prescott, Ike was thinking back on how that unlikely friendship and tutelage began. In the ward of a makeshift hospital that had been Southern University, a tall man lay unconscious with feet extending over the cot next to Ike's. The man had been shot in the back while climbing over a wall on a spying expedition of a Confederate compound. He made it back to his headquarters, gave his report, then collapsed. After the operation, he was taken to the wardroom, became delirious with his right hand trembling like an October leaf.

The doctors and nurses were too busy with other patients, bleeding and expiring, to do any more for this patient.

But Ike, still recovering from his own wound, did do something.

For more than forty-eight hours, Ike held the man's trembling hand, soothing and massaging it, until it trembled less and less and then not at all.

When the man regained consciousness, he looked into Ike's eyes and felt the warmth of Ike's hand as one of the nurses told him what Ike had done.

And the man told Ike that without the use of that hand he didn't have much, or any, future as a lawman.

So it began.

The friendship and the tutelage while they both recovered.

Hook. Draw. Fire.

Both Ike and J.B. went through that swift, sure motion hundreds of times, as hundreds of leaves on hundreds of branches were ripped into and fell onto that hillside, until both men were discharged and went their separate ways, leaving hundreds of spent cartridges among the leaves and grass.

But shooting at a leaf was far different than shooting at a man's heart while that man held a gun and was aiming to shoot you first.

And that's what Quentin Cord would be aiming to do.

CHAPTER FORTY-THREE

That night Ike said his prayers along with the boys, kissed them good night, told them that he loved them and went to his room.

He unfastened the gold watch, pressed open the lid, listened to the tune, and looked at the wedding picture—and remembered.

He knew that soon one of two things would happen: He would come back and kiss Jed and Obie again as they slept, *or . . .* he would be with his beloved Rachel.

Ike closed the lid of the watch and set it on the table next to his bed.

He strapped on the gun belt, lifted the Remington from its holster and checked to make sure there was a cartridge in each of the six chambers, then replaced the weapon into the holster.

Ike stopped by the kitchen, where Sister Bonney and Melena sat drinking coffee.

"I'm going out for a little while, ladies. The boys are asleep. They should be all right 'til I get back. Good night."

"Good night," both Sister Bonney and Melena said.

Both couldn't help noticing that Ike was wearing the gun.

This was the first time Ike had left Jed and Obie while Uncle Jake was away.

CHAPTER FORTY-FOUR

The atmosphere was funereal.

Despite the music from the piano, the smoking, drinking and the card playing, the atmosphere was thick with anticipation.

Everyone seemed to be at the Emporium—Binky; Bixby, the sign painter; Gillardi, the barber/undertaker; Doc Barnes, who for the first time had brought along his medical bag; Oliver Knight, nursing a beer across from Henry, the bartender; Gallagher and Rooster, both leaning, backs to the bar, each with a drink in his hand; Francine, Alma and Marisa, none of whom had any clients that night, because nobody wanted to miss what might happen; Lessur, at his usual table, but with fewer winnings in front of him, looking as if he had something on his mind beside the poker game; Quentin Cord at his place at the bar, with an inscrutable expression on his face and nobody close to him on either side; and all the others, all moving a beat slower, and even speaking a little softer, with eyes and ears that watched and listened for any unusual movement or sound. They all did their best to avoid looking from Cord to Ike and Belinda. They weren't very successful.

Somehow, the word had spread—maybe inadvertently, maybe on purpose—but the word had spread. There was going to be a showdown. And it was going to be deadly.

As Oliver Knight had said, the cause could be summed up in two words.

Quentin Cord was the perfect hired killer. Cord had no feeling—at least none that was ever betrayed or divulged. He was immune to emotion. All that had been left behind with the defeat of the Confederacy.

There was no hint of fealty to family, cause, country, animal, human or anything else. His only loyalty was to himself and to the job he was paid to execute. And execute was the operative word. He could provoke and slay an innocent sodbuster while the victim's wife and children looked on, then walk through the bat wings to finish a drink without taking a deep breath.

He was the consummate killer with no regard for life or afterlife. A businessman whose stock in trade was tailor-made death. One size fits all, satisfaction guaranteed, results permanent, no strings attached. When the deed was done, the doer traveled to another job site and another piece of work.

Cord had been drained of every vestige of emotion. There was no place in any corner or crevice of his mind or body for any feeling of friendship, tenderness, sorrow or sympathy—detachment was the key. Feeling the enemy. Friendship unthinkable.

All of it—feeling, friendship, family—was consumed by Sheridan's torches, and the flame and smoke that rose years ago from the Shenandoah Valley.

Quentin Cord swallowed the bourbon from the whiskey glass, set the glass back on the bar and motioned to Henry, then pointed to the glass.

Henry walked away from Oliver Knight, reached to the backbar for a bottle of bourbon, filled Cord's empty glass almost to the rim, then walked back toward Knight.

Cord looked at the glass for a moment, but his hand did not move toward it. Instead, he took a step away from the bar.

As he did, Binky approached.

"I say, old chap, I wonder if you—"

Before Binky could say more, Cord's right arm shot straight forward and his palm smashed against Binky's chest, sending the little man hurtling against the bar, then down to the floor.

Silence. Utter silence.

No one moved, or, it seemed, even breathed.

Cord paused for less than a second, then moved in a slow, uneven gait toward Ike and Belinda.

"You don't have to do this," Belinda whispered.

"I've got to."

"Why?"

"Rules of the game."

"I don't understand."

"Sure you do."

The words they spoke were virtually the same that they had spoken just before Milo Sebastian had challenged Belinda to a game of poker.

But this was no game. Or, if it was, the stakes had nothing to do with money. The wager was for life or death.

Cord stopped near the table, closer to Belinda than to Ike.

"You. Silver."

Ike did not respond with word or eye contact.

"Look at me when I talk to you."

Still no response.

"I see you're keeping company with the saloon whore."

Belinda sprang up. "Listen, mister—"

Cord slapped her hard with a backhand, grabbed and twisted her, lifted the right side of her dress and pulled the derringer from its garter holster. He tossed the derringer toward a spittoon near the bar, then shoved her away. He glanced toward Lessur, then turned back to Ike.

"Now you haven't got a skirt to hide behind, so stand up and act like a man."

Ike rose. Not fast. Not slow.

He stood facing Cord.

"You're a craven coward," Cord said, "and you're going to get down on your knees and grovel."

No word or movement from Ike.

"Then act like a man. Go ahead. I won't pull until your gun's out of its holster. Draw, you coward!"

Still nothing from Ike.

Cord stood too far for Ike to even think of throwing a punch or leaping toward him. It had to be a gunfight.

"I'm going to say it so everybody can hear. You're a craven coward so get down on your knees and grovel. I want to see you do it in front of everybody here."

Cord took one, two, three steps back.

"Pull, you low-down lying Yankee nigger-loving Jew bastard!"

Nobody watching could tell who drew first, but it was evident who got off the first and only shot.

Hook. Draw. Fire.

Ike's shot hit Cord square in the gun hand. The hand went limp and bloody and dropped the revolver. Cord, stunned, went down to one knee. For just an instant he looked at Ike, then leapt forward, left hand extended toward the gun on the floor. In that split instant Ike knew that he had violated one of J.B.'s cardinal rules—" . . . *never squeeze the trigger unless you're willing to kill a man . . . without compunction or hesitation . . . it could cost you your life. . . .*" This time Ike fired twice without compunction or hesitation.

The first bullet hit Cord's heart. The second bullet hit the first.

At the end of this game there was no applause. No cheering. Just silence . . . and awe.

Doctor Zebelion Barnes, carrying his medical bag, walked over to the man on the floor and leaned down, then looked up toward Antonio Gillardi.

"Dead . . . I'm happy to say."

First there was a murmur, then movement.

Binky walked to the bar where Cord had stood, lifted the glass of bourbon in a mock salute and drank.

Belinda went to Ike's side and touched him gently on the shoulder as he holstered the Remington.

Rupert Lessur sat in shock, realizing that the second part of his plan had also failed.

Ike glanced at the bat wings where Sister Bonney stood holding her rosary. He walked toward her and nodded.

"Come on, Sister. I'll take you home."

"Just a minute." Oliver Knight approached shaking his head. "Ike, who is this J.B. fellow who taught you?"

"The initials stand for James Butler. Last name's Hickok."

"The one they call Wild Bill?"

"I never called him that."

CHAPTER FORTY-FIVE

Being the gentleman that he was, Rupert Lessur paid Antonio Gillardi for the twenty-five dollar funeral and Tom Bixby for the five dollar lettered marker with only Quentin Cord's name and date of death inscribed. Nobody knew or cared when Cord was born—or if the coffin was comfortable.

The thirty dollars was far less than Lessur had agreed to pay Cord if the job had been executed, but Lessur would have been much happier spending the agreed upon fee and being rid of Ike Silver.

First Milo Sebastian had double-crossed him, then Quentin Cord had disappointed him; still, Rupert Lessur counted on the third and most important part of his plan, which would ignite the Territory and eliminate competition . . . along with Ike Silver.

CHAPTER FORTY-SIX

"Ike," Jake said, "it's not the boys who need a nurse-maid anymore. It's my baby brother. Every time I go away you get into trouble. Right?"

"Right, Jake. Next time I'll wait 'til you get back."

"That's not what I meant and you know it. . . . Ike, I heard what that son of a bitch said to you. . . ."

"So did I," Ben softly interrupted.

"Fellas, it's all over. Let's forget about it."

"It ain't all over, brother Ike, not so long as a certain party named Lessur is around."

"Jake's right," Ben agreed, "and you know it."

"We'll take 'em as they come." Ike smiled.

Jake nodded. "Okay, but next time include me."

"That goes for me, too," Ben added.

"All right, fellas, but in the meantime those wagons have got to be delivered to Fort Whipple."

Jake pointed as Colonel Crook and Captain Bourke dismounted. "It looks like the colonel's come in himself to take the delivery."

The rest of the army contingent remained on their horses as Crook and Bourke approached the front of the stable. And as they did, they were joined by Mayor John Davis, who scurried up beside them.

"Good morning, gentlemen," Crook said.

"Yes, good morning," Davis chimed.

Good mornings were exchanged all around except for Captain Bourke, who maintained his silence.

"You come in to escort us out to the fort?" Jake asked.

"No, I don't think that will be necessary, but I heard about what happened over at the Emporium."

"So did I," Davis added.

"Are you all right?" Crook looked at Ike.

"Just fine."

"So's that gunfighter," Jake said, "and right where he belongs. I hope they bury him face down so he can see where he's going."

"I agree," Davis said, "and I still think we ought to have a sheriff here in Prescott."

"Then why don't you do something about it, Mister Mayor?" Jake suggested.

"I'm working on it, but it's got to be done according to the—"

"Yeah, yeah," Jake mocked.

"Did you get everything on the list?" Crook pointed at the loaded wagons.

"You bet, Colonel." Jake nodded.

"Good. I'll be meeting with Colorados at Spanish Flats, and I think we've got something worked out that'll be satisfactory to all concerned."

"That's good news, Colonel," Ike said. "And Ben, after you make delivery, make sure your wagon's in good shape. We'll be bringing in that first shipment from the Rattlesnake."

"It'll be ready, Ike."

"Well," Davis said, "I'd say everything's in good shape."

"Yes, Mister Mayor," Jake remarked, "and we thank you for all your help."

"Uh-huh." The mayor cleared his throat. "Well, I've got to get over to the office. Good day, gentlemen." The mayor walked away as fast as he could without trotting.

Jake nodded toward the departing mayor. "I think the worm is beginning to turn."

"He knows which side his bread is buttered on," Crook said.

"It doesn't matter to him," Jake observed. "He'll eat both sides."

Ike smiled. "Brother Jake, you're a cynic."

"No, brother Ike . . . a philosopher."

"We'll see you at the fort," Crook said. "All right, Captain, let's mount up."

Crook and Bourke headed toward their animals.

"Well," Ike said, "I'll go see how Scotty's doing."

"Stay out of trouble 'til we get back," Jake declared.

"Who, me?"

The slim rubber sling snapped, sending a wad of paper through the air and smacking against the back of Jed's head as he sat in the former storeroom—the present schoolroom.

Sister Mary Boniface stood in front of several rows of students in attendance. Among them were Jed, Obie, Benjie, four Mexican children and other boys and girls of assorted complexions and ages.

"Jedediah," Sister Bonney asked, "did you say something?"

"Uh, no, ma'am—I mean Sister."

Jed launched a threatening look at angelic Obadiah as Sister Bonney continued where she had left off.

" ' . . . A new nation conceived in liberty and dedicated to the proposition that all men are created equal. Now we are . . .' "

The oldest girl in the room, red haired, with a face full of freckles, who appeared to be about twelve, raised her hand.

"Yes, Elizabeth."

"What about women?"

"How's that?"

"I mean, what about us? Why did President Lincoln leave us out of his speech?"

"Well, in the first place, Elizabeth, that line of the Gettysburg Address is a direct quote from the Declaration of Independence. In the second place, the word 'men' actually means 'people.' All people are created equal . . . men and women."

Jed raised his hand.

"Yes, Jedediah."

"Then how come women can't vote?"

The students all laughed.

Jim Gallagher had been passing by outside the open window and paused when he heard the laughter. Gallagher poked his head closer to the window to find out what was so funny. But he did so discreetly, so as not to be seen.

"Jedediah," Sister Bonney said as the laughter subsided, "that is a question I would like to put to the men in the Congress of the United States. But, children, we must remember,"—she looked first at Benjie, then at the other boys and girls in the classroom—"it took time for slaves to be free in the United States and other countries, and in time, and I'm sure it will happen, we women will be free to vote and even run for office. Of course, some of us women, myself included, have chosen another calling. Now then, Elizabeth, Jedediah, does that answer your questions?"

"Yes, Sister." Elizabeth nodded.

"Sort of," Jedediah said, barely audible.

"How's that, Jedediah?"

"Nothing, Sister."

"No, don't say 'nothing.' I heard you say something. Now, whatever you have in mind, speak right up."

"Well, if I ever go to Congress, I'll vote for girls to vote."

"Very good. We 'girls' thank you very much and if you need any assistance in your campaign, I'm sure we'd be glad to help."

More laughter.

"Now, time's up, so tomorrow we'll continue with what President Lincoln, who is now in heaven, said in his Gettysburg Address, 'All men . . . ,'"—Sister Bonney smiled at Elizabeth—"'. . . and women are created equal.' Class is dismissed. Get home before dark."

The boys and girls bounced out of their seats and bounded toward the door.

"We *are* home!" Obie hit Jed on the arm.

"That's two I owe you," Jed said and chased him out of the room.

Sister Bonney leaned over to Benjie, who was still in his seat, and whispered something. Benjie nodded and smiled, then walked toward the door.

When the children had left, Sister Bonney heard Gallagher's voice.

"That's a lot of hogwash, Sister." By now Gallagher was leaning well into the window.

As Sister Bonney reacted and walked toward him, Ike appeared at the doorway of the classroom and stood there without saying anything or being seen.

"What's a lot of hogwash, Mister Gallagher?" Sister Bonney asked.

"That hooey you've been spoutin' to them kids."

"This is a classroom, Mister Gallagher, not a weed patch. What we try to cultivate here is learning, if not wisdom. To what 'hooey' are you referring?"

"That stuff about all men being equal."

"You don't believe that?"

"The point is, Sister, a lot of other people don't, too many other people. There's a lot of signs back East that say 'Irish need not apply.'"

"There's no such sign in the Senate—or in city halls all over the country, and that's why your people came to this country."

"They came because of the potato famine."

"That's one reason, but where else would they, or you, be better off?"

"Aww, come on now, you know we're looked down upon, Sister."

"Nobody can look down on you without your own consent, Mister Gallagher, no matter what your religion or nationality."

"You really believe that, do you?"

"Yes, I do."

"You *are* Irish, ain't you, Sister?" Gallagher smiled.

"I don't know."

"How's that?" Gallagher was genuinely perplexed.

"I said I don't know . . . I was a foundling."

"You mean you don't know who your mother . . ."—he hesitated slightly—". . . and your father were?"

"The important thing is . . . I know who *I* am."

Gallagher seemed even more perplexed.

"Don't you agree, Mister Gallagher?"

"Well, I . . ."

"Think it over, Mister Gallagher, and you're welcome to drop by any time. Now, would you help me shut the window? It sticks sometimes."

"Uh, sure, Sister. Sure."

After the window was shut, Sister Bonney turned and saw Ike smiling near the entrance. He walked toward her.

"I'd say Mister Gallagher is your oldest pupil."

"We can all go on learning at any age."

"I'll try to remember that. And I didn't mean to eavesdrop, but I did learn something about you."

"Oh, about being a foundling? Well, I've never tried to keep it a secret. I'm not ashamed of it. I was just a few days old when left bundled in a basket at the stoop of Saint Francis Orphanage in Baltimore and reared by the Sisters of Charity there."

"Is that why you became a nun?"

"Actually, I'm still 'becoming.' I've a year to go before taking the final vows . . . if I'm worthy."

"Oh, I don't think there's any doubt about that . . . being worthy, I mean."

"It's good of you to say that, Ike, but the answer lies with someone else. And, no, I didn't take this path because of where I was reared."

"No?"

"No. When I was old enough, I left Saint Francis."

"But you went back."

"Not to Saint Francis. To where I decided, with God's help, I belonged, if the Sisters of Charity will have me."

"I think the Sisters of Charity are very lucky . . . and so are we."

"And so am I."

He started to turn toward the door.

"Ike."

"Yes, Sister."

"After we came home, I said a prayer for you . . . and for that Mister Cord."

"I figured you would."

"Hello, Scotty."

"Hello, Miss Belinda. How are you?"

"I'm fine. Haven't seen you around the Emporium lately."

"No, ma'am. And you're not gonna. From now on I'm strictly a storekeeper. Too much excitement for my nerves over there."

"Speaking of excitement, is he around?"

"He is, and speakin' of nerves, I don't think that man has any. He acts as if he just went for a walk in the park last night."

"Well, it was no cakewalk, I'll tell you that."

"So I heard, and so has everybody else. That's all everybody . . . oh . . ."

Ike had just come in the back door as another customer came in the front door.

"There he is now, and there's Mrs. Dalrimple. I'll take care of her, and you two can talk over old times."

Scotty moved toward the front and Mrs. Dalrimple, while Ike walked toward Belinda.

"Howdy," he said.

"Howdy yourself."

"Feel like a cup of strong coffee?" Ike pointed to the pot on the stove.

"No." She smiled. "But I did feel like a shot of strong whisky this morning . . . a double."

"Don't blame you." He looked at Belinda's bruised face. "I see Cord left his mark."

"So did you. Ike, are you all right?"

"Sure."

"I know it sounds silly to say, but I'm glad that things came out the way they did."

"Couldn't have come out any other way . . . between Sister Bonney's rosary and this."

Ike pulled a silver dollar out of his pocket and held it in his palm.

"You still got the silver dollar I gave you, I—"

"You said it was for luck. Didn't expect me to spend my luck, did you?"

"I never expected a lot of things when I met you, Mister Silver, I . . ."

The front door banged open and Oliver Knight charged past Scotty and Mrs. Dalrimple, who was holding a bolt of patterned cloth across her expansive frame.

"Excuse me . . . beg pardon," he rumbled as he brushed past both of them, waving a couple of telegraphs he held in his right hand.

"Oh, hello, Belinda, they told me you were here."

"Who's they?"

"Henry and Binky. Stopped at the Emporium for a snorter on my way over. Great jumping Jehosephat! Never will forget what happened there last night . . . neither will a lot of other people when I write up that story. You'll be famous Ike, and Belinda, so will the Emporium. But first off, look here. . . ." He slapped the papers against his left palm. "I sent out some telegraphs to a couple of colleagues of mine inquiring about James Butler Hickok, and Ike, you'll be pleased to know he's alive and well . . . marshaling in Abeline, where John Wesley Hardin opted to ride out of town like his ass was on fire after Wild Bill gave him ten minutes to say *adios*. Hardin's killed over a dozen men, but he wisely wouldn't face your mentor. Now, about you and Cord, I'm gonna—"

"*Not* gonna," Ike said.

"What?"

"Oliver, I'm asking you for a favor as a friend. Please don't print anything about Cord or me . . . or what happened at the Emporium."

"But Ike, it's a hell of a story. You'll be famous, you'll be—"

"I don't want to be famous, not as a gunfighter. Every story's got to have a finish, and I know how this one'll end."

"Sure. With Cord dead."

"That won't be the end. Just the beginning."

"What the hell do you mean?"

"I mean you might as well paint a bull's-eye on this chest. 'I killed Quentin Cord. Now somebody try to kill me.' That's what that bull's-eye'll be saying . . . to every short-bit drifter looking for a reputation."

"He's right, Oliver," Belinda said.

"I've got a family and a business. Gunfighting isn't my business. So, my friend, I'm asking you . . . don't print that story."

Silence.

Then Oliver Knight crumpled the telegraphs and tossed them on Ike's rolltop.

"I said once that I didn't want to write your obituary . . . besides, what's one more byline, more or less."

Belinda smiled. "Oliver, I'd be pleased to buy you a drink."

"Sure." Oliver Knight nodded. "I got nothing else to do . . ."—he looked at the crumpled telegraphs—". . . now. Ike Silver, that's two stories you stopped me from writing about you. First Rawlins, now Cord."

"But Ike," Belinda said, "mind if I give you a little advice?"

"Go ahead."

"From now on,"—she pointed to the gun and gun belt on Ike's desk, "wherever you go, carry that pistol."

CHAPTER FORTY-SEVEN

The two things that Quemada coveted most were Colorados's coup stick and Colorados's wife.

Quemada was determined to do something about both.

The secret campsite of Colorados and the Mimbreno Apaches was no longer much of a secret. Crook, the officers and troopers at Fort Lowell pretty much knew the approximate location, but Crook had given explicit orders that the U.S. Army was to give the area wide berth. And Colorados had made it clear that the Apaches were not to leave the immediate area with any weapons until an agreement was concluded between Crook and Colorados, and a treaty signed. Neither commander wanted to chance any encounter that might provoke hostility on either side.

But in both camps there were elements of uneasiness, suspicion, resistance and resentment. At Fort Whipple, Captain Bourke and other officers and troopers, who had clashed with Apaches before in bloody campaigns, believed that the only Indian they could trust was a dead Indian.

And at Colorados's camp, despite the fact that the tribe had been provided with food and other necessities better than ever before, Quemada, Secorro and a couple dozen other young bucks were determined to take back the vast territory where they could roam, hunt and raid as they and their forefathers had done since time remembered.

While Crook and Colorados met in the open at Spanish Flats to smoke and come to an agreement, Quemada and Rupert Lessur had met in secret, where Lessur had put forth his plot to help Quemada achieve his goals, and, not incidentally, achieve his own.

The weather was a mite intemperate for picnicking, but the picnickers were determined to picnic, so picnic they did—Ike, Jake, Jed, Obie, Sister Bonney, Melena, Ben and Benjie.

No one was quite sure who had first made the suggestion, an adult or child, but once suggested, the notion was quickly ratified and implemented.

And so, on a Sunday afternoon, the scanty remains of a sumptuous picnic feast rested on a blanket that had been spread on a verdant vale, while the adults sat nearby in various postures of contentment and the three boys busied themselves with yo-yos moving down and up in harmony until the strings somehow became tangled together and Jed, Obie and Benjie went about the task of disentanglement.

Jake, in a dreamy torpor, resting on both elbows, was endeavoring to digest what he had ingested. Sister Bonney and Melena still sat on opposite sides of the blanket with Ben next to his wife. Ike sat leaning against a tree, smoking his pipe.

"Melena," Ike said between puffs, "that was delicious. Thank you."

"You're welcome, and you can thank Sister Bonney too, she certainly did—"

"Much less than you, Melena, but it was a pleasure."

"Yes, yes," Jake said, not moving anything except his mouth, eyes still closed, "we're all very pleased and it was delicious. But someday I'm going to show you both how to make kreplach and matzos."

Ben rose and walked over toward the boys, who were failing miserably in their attempts to untangle the strings of their yo-yos.

"Fellas, from now on when you're doing the yo-yos, stand two feet apart, and if you're walking the dog or going around the world, stand four feet apart."

"That's what I was doin', Daddy. Walking the dog."

"What's 'going around the world,' Mister Brown?" Obie inquired.

"Here," Ben Brown said, "hand me your yo-yo, Benjie, and I'll show the fellas."

He proceeded to do just that.

Sister Bonney rose and walked a few yards to the slight crest that overlooked the tranquil espadrille just below.

Ike watched her for a few moments, then relit his pipe, rose and walked slowly until he stood just to one side behind her. Whether or not it was because of Belinda Millay's advice, Ike had the Remington holstered on his hip.

"What are you thinking, Sister?"

"What? Oh, Ike." She turned.

"You seem to be far away, Sister Bonney."

"Oh, not so far. Just down there a ways."

"What's down there?"

"Nothing . . . now. But someday . . ."

"Someday, what?"

"I was thinking that someday that would be a very nice place to build a school."

"I guess it would. But why out here?"

"It's rather close to town and not far from . . ."

"From where Colorados's people'll be?"

"The Apache children might not want to come into Prescott, but out here it might be different, and I could get one of the older Apache girls to help with the language and—"

Ike couldn't help chuckling.

"Ike Silver," Sister Bonney said, "why are you laughing at me?"

"I wasn't laughing at you."

"Then what *were* you doing?"

"Well, I *was* amused, I guess."

"At what?"

"Sister, you have hardly enough books or proper equipment, a makeshift classroom, barely enough money to keep going, and you're already thinking about building a school. True enough?"

"Well, true enough, but—"

"But?"

"Man's—or woman's—reach should exceed his grasp . . ."

". . . Else what's heaven for?"

"You know your Browning, Mister Silver."

"And I guess you know your business."

"Not business—purpose."

"Well, I'll bet on one thing. . . ."

"And that is?"

"Sister Mary Boniface is going to succeed in her purpose."

"With God's help,"—Sister Mary Boniface nodded—"and yours."

"Ike! Ike!"

Both Ike and Sister Bonney turned toward the sound of Jake's voice.

"Ike, look!"

Jake had run up close to them and was pointing to their right.

"Over there."

Along the ridgeline, a young Indian boy, maybe ten or twelve years of age, was half running, half stumbling down from the rise; then the boy did stumble, fall and lay motionless.

They ran across the field, Ike in the lead, followed by Jake and Ben, then Sister Bonney and the others.

Ike and Ben were the first to get to the boy, who was breathing hard and may or may not have been conscious.

They both bent down and reached out to help the boy.

"No!"

The voice was familiar. They turned and looked toward it.

Colorados, astride his horse, was framed against the rise.

As Colorados prodded his horse forward, the rest of the picnickers also reached the area where the boy lay, still unmoving.

Colorados reined up just a few feet away. They all watched in silence as Colorados looked down, then spoke to the boy in Apache.

"Arida! Varenga!"

It seemed that the boy, at the sound of Colorados's voice, breathed a little harder.

"Arida! Varenga!"

The boy's head moved, slightly at first, then more. He managed to turn face up, open his eyes and look at Colorados.

Their eyes locked.

The boy, seeming to summon an inner strength, struggled to his knees, then managed to stand, pumping air into his aching lungs. He wavered, off balance, as if he might fall again, but looked once more at the stern face of Colorados.

The gaze of his chief appeared to vivify the boy. Without the least acknowledgement of the others the young Indian boy burst forth into a run again.

When the runner was some distance away, Colorados looked for the first time at Ike and the rest.

"The time of his trials. When they are through . . he is a man."

Jake nodded and smiled at Ike.

"Bar Mitzvah."

CHAPTER FORTY-EIGHT

James Gallagher walked from the bar to the table, where Belinda Millay sat with a deck of cards in front of her and Binky next to her.

"Miz Millay . . ."

Belinda cut the deck, lifted the ace of spades off the top, and looked up at Gallagher.

"Miz Millay . . . do you believe that all men—and women too—are created equal?"

It was a toss-up as to who was more startled— Belinda or Binky.

"Would you mind," Belinda said, "repeating that?"

"Well, uh, are all men created equal? I been thinkin' about it."

"Where'd you hear that?" Belinda asked.

"In school."

"That must've been a long time ago." Belinda smiled. "How come you just got around to thinking about it now?"

"No, I just heard it over where that Sister was teaching."

"Are you a student of Sister Bonney's?" Binky inquired.

"No. Just poked my head in the window and heard what she told the kids."

"Well," Binky said, "the conceit is not original by her. I believe it appears in your . . . that is, your country's . . . Declaration of Independence."

Gallagher wiped at his mouth. "So, what do you think, Miz Millay?"

"Why ask me?"

"I had to ask somebody." Gallagher shrugged.

"Well, around the Emporium, all men—and women—are considered equal . . . unless they start acting *unequal*. That's the best I can do for you, Jim."

Binky arched an eyebrow. "My good fellow, if it'll help, the poet wrote 'Death makes equal the high and low.' "

"That don't help much."

"Why don't you ask your boss?" Belinda suggested in jest.

"No. I don't think I will," Gallagher said and walked toward the bat wings.

In the stable on a wagon lettered R. LESSUR—FREIGHTING, Rooster and another employee were loading a long, heavy crate. Already onboard were two similar crates and others of different proportions.

Rupert Lessur watched as Gallagher entered the stable.

"Where've *you* been?"

"Uh . . . just wetting my windpipe."

"Well, if your windpipe is sufficiently wet, I'd like you and Rooster to make a delivery."

"It's almost dark."

"Is there some clause in our arrangement that says you don't work after sunset?"

"No, boss."

Lessur turned to the other employee who had helped with the loading.

"That's all, Gotch. You can go now."

"Sure, boss."

When Gotch had left, Lessur took a step toward Gallagher.

"You know that cave up at Horse Rock?"

"Yeah." Gallagher nodded.

"Put a tarp over the wagon, then take this load up and leave it in the cave."

"But those crates have got—"

"I know the contents of those crates."

"You mean . . . just leave 'em there?"

"Those are my instructions."

"But why?"

"Because . . . ," Lessur said, "those are my instructions."

As Ike entered the stable, Ben was inspecting the front wheel of his wagon while Jake stood by watching.

"Good evening, gentlemen."

"Boys asleep?" Jake asked.

"Who knows?" Ike said. "But they're in bed. Ben, what do you think?" Ike nodded toward the wagon as Ben rose.

"I think we can carry as much as Mister Dolan is ready to load . . . and then some."

"Good. We'll leave for the Rattlesnake at first light. Well, better get some sleep. Good night, fellas. See you in the morning."

"Good night," both Jake and Ben said.

At the entrance, Ike turned and looked back.

"And one more thing,"—he patted the gun on his hip—"don't forget the artillery."

CHAPTER FORTY-NINE

As the December dawn broke over the rim of Horse Rock Canyon, inside a cave a pair of hands reached into a crate that had been ripped open and pulled out a Yellow Boy Winchester.

Quemada threw the rifle to Secorro, reached in again, grabbed another Winchester, tossed it to an eager Apache, then motioned to the dozen other bucks to help themselves. As they did, Quemada leaned over a different box. He dipped in both hands, came up with scoops of cartridges and looked at them as if they were precious stones.

Another Apache entered carrying a clay pot. Quemada let the cartridges fall through fingers, dipped his palm into the pot and brought the hand across his face, smearing it with yellow paint.

> *"Gold! Gold! Gold!*
> *Bright and yellow*
> *Hard and cold."*

The load was not all yellow—not yet. It would have to be refined even more at the El Dorado Mill along the Hassayampa. But it was hard and cold and yellow in spots.

The wagon lettered SILVER & CO.—WE DELIVER THE GOODS was now covered with a secured tarp at the Rattlesnake Mine.

Ike, Jake and Ben, along with Dolan and his platoon of miners, who had been repairing and working for weeks, stood watching as the result of their toil was loaded and made ready to roll.

"That's an awful heavy load," Jake said.

"That's an awful valuable load." Sean Dolan tugged at the brim of his hat.

"Let's get started." Ike tamped the tobacco in the bowl of his pipe with his finger.

Ben climbed into the driver's seat as Jake boarded and sat next to him.

Dolan wiped at his mouth with the palm of his hand. "Ike, are you sure that wagon'll—"

"Sean, I told you six times, Ben's gone over every nut, bolt and spoke—enforced and reinforced and that's the best six-up in Arizona," Ike said, pointing at the horses. "Quit worrying."

"I'm not worrying, but—"

"But what?"

"But I'm coming along, and don't try and stop me!"

"Nobody can stop you." Ike smiled as he mounted the saddle of his horse. "Get on board."

Dolan turned to a miner standing next to him. "Get me a scattergun."

A wooley white mass of sheep bleated and moved together, following the sound of a lead goat's bell along the grasslands of Spanish Flats.

Colonel George Crook and Colorados stood on a rise, Crook smoking a cigar, Colorados, his pipe. The colonel was flanked by a contingent of officers including Bourke and Gibbs—Colorados, by his sub-chiefs, all except Quemada.

Crook pointed west to east, then north to south. "From the Hassayampa to the Verde—from Horse Mountain to Cave Creek. It's good land, Colorados."

"That's why I chose it. But we have been given back our land before."

"I know, they'd give you an apple and take away your orchard. But it'll be different this time. I've said it before to other tribes—I make damn few promises, but I keep 'em."

"We know that Gray Wolf's word has no shadows. But why do you bring us sheep instead of cattle?"

"You'll do better to raise sheep. To get anything out of a steer you have to kill him. But you can use and sell the wool and still keep the sheep."

The Indians who understood the language nodded their approval.

"And," Crook continued, "while sheep'll wander off, they can't get as far as cattle will. If thieves come and run off with some cattle, it's hard to get them back, but sheep travel slow. You can catch up to them . . . and the thieves."

"My friend, Nan-Tan-Lupan, has done well."

"Well, boss," Gallagher said, as Rupert Lessur sat at his desk and lit his long, slim cigar, "anything else you need me to do?"

"No. You can go and wet your windpipe for now. But soon, very soon, there'll be plenty for you to do."

Lessur smiled, removed the cigar from his mouth and exhaled three perfect circles of smoke into the air.

The wagon had moved down from the high country into the open terrain.

Ben held the reins. Jake sat next to him. Dolan

was atop the tarp with the scattergun laid across his knees. Ike was astride his horse alongside the wagon, puffing placidly on his pipe. He heard something from the wagon, looked closer at Dolan, and noticed that in Dolan's hands, resting on the shotgun, there was a rosary—and his lips were moving.

A shrill yell rended the air.

Quemada and his followers, just far enough away to be seen and heard, rode screaming, shooting and charging toward the wagon.

"*Ben!*" Ike hollered. "*Knock on 'em!*"

"*Yaahh!*" Ben lashed the team. "*Yaahh!*"

Jake pulled a rifle up from the floorboard; Dolan shoved the rosary into his belt and took aim with the scattergun; Ike stuffed the pipe into his jacket pocket, drew his revolver and fired as the wagon picked up speed, leaving a wake of dust on the narrow road.

Quemada, Secorro, and the rest of the attackers kneed their ponies and fired shot after shot from their repeating Yellow Boy Winchesters.

Ben gave it all he had, urging the six-up team, but he knew he was losing ground as the bullets flew past, and some slammed into the wagon.

Ike rode hard, still firing back at the pursuers.

One dropped. Then another.

Ben looked across at Ike. "They're catching up! We can't outrun 'em!"

Ike nodded. He jammed the gun into his holster and reined his horse as close to the wagon as he could.

Jake and Dolan were still shooting.

Ike jumped from his horse onto the top of the wagon and landed close to Dolan, who was reloading the scattergun. Ike moved, making his way toward the front, ducking as shots ripped past.

"Where you going?" Jake hollered.

"Get back there!" Ike pointed. "And keep shooting."

He moved up next to Ben as Jake climbed back. Ike pulled up the lid of the seat where Jake had been sitting. From atop the tarp, Jake fired and hit Secorro, who had been riding close to Quemada. Quemada didn't look back as Secorro smashed hard onto the ground.

Ike stooped low next to Ben. He took the pipe from his pocket, put it into his mouth and puffed until he was satisfied that it was still lit.

Jake's eyes widened in disbelief.

"Ike! What the hell are you doing?"

"Keep shooting!"

He reached down into the box inside the seat and pulled up a stick of dynamite. Still ducking low, he stuck the wick into the pipe bowl. Almost immediately, the wick sizzled.

Ike rose just enough to throw the lit stick at the cluster of pursuing Apaches, then reached for another stick.

The first cluster, led by Quemada, rode over the dynamite before it exploded. But the second group didn't make it. Four of them rode directly into the explosion that rocked the ground and catapulted their flaying bodies off their mounts onto the black, hollowed-out ground.

Crook extended his hand and Colorados was about to accept it.

"Peace, Colorados."

The sound of a dynamite explosion reverberated. Then another.

* * *

Quemada and the remnants of his band rode on, trying to avoid the lighted dynamite stick that had landed directly in their path. But before they managed to turn away, the charge went off, blowing apart bodies of horses and Apaches.

Ike had just lit a third stick and was bringing it away from his pipe, as Jake, screaming in triumph, turned and accidentally hit Ike's hand, knocking the sizzling stick into the bed of the racing wagon.

The tube of dynamite rolled far back under the seat, too far to reach in time.

"Jump!" Ike hollered to all aboard.

"The gold!" Dolan screamed.

"Get off!" Jake screamed back. "*Jump!*"

Jake flew off, followed by Dolan.

Ike reached down and released the king pin, freeing the horses from the wagon, as Ben bailed out on one side and Ike on the other, seconds before the blast decimated the wagon. Chunks of gold spiraled into the sky, then cascaded in all directions onto the earth below.

What few Apaches remained on horseback scattered for the hills. A couple of others rose from the ground, staggered and stumbled away.

Jake got to his knees, then rose to his feet, feeling at his elbows and head to make certain that he was still fastened together.

Ben managed to stand up, rubbing his shoulder.

Dolan crawled on all fours toward a chunk of gold. There were glittering gold clods and clumps all around.

Ike rose, looked and nodded toward Jake, Ben and Dolan.

In the distance, they saw riders. Soldiers and Indians led by Colonel Crook and Colorados.

Dolan walked up to Ike, looked around at the remnants from the Rattlesnake, smiled and shrugged.

"Well, it'll take some doing. But I think we can gather it up again."

Some of the soldiers retrieved the team of horses.

Colorados looked down on the broken, unmoving body of Quemada.

Crook rode up to Ike and the others and dismounted.

"You fellows all right?"

"Well,"—Jake pointed to the dead Apaches,— "we're better off than they are."

Crook took off his hat and wiped at the sweat band. "Ike, those were dynamite explosions, weren't they?"

"They were."

"Why were you carrying dynamite?"

"Always do. Clear away boulders that fall on the road."

Crook smiled. "Well, today you cleared away more 'n that."

Colorados rode up, then dismounted with a Winchester he had picked up.

"Quemada is dead."

Captain Bourke stepped forward. "But how many other Quemadas are around?"

"I don't know," Colorados said, "but he got this from a white man." He handed the Yellow Boy to Crook. "And where will we bury our dead, Gray Wolf?"

Sean Dolan looked at the chief. "Colorados, we haven't disturbed that burial ground behind the mine. I promise you we won't."

"And so do I," Crook said, then turned to Ike. "Dynamite, huh. Good strategy, soldier. You shoulda been in my outfit."

"I was."

"What?"

"We were all in the same outfit, weren't we, Colonel?"

"I guess we were." Crook nodded.

"Still are." Ike smiled.

He took the watch from his pocket, snapped open the lid and listened for a moment to the tune.

CHAPTER FIFTY

"I should've known better than to send some stupid savage to do a job."

Behind his desk, Rupert Lessur was again smoking a long, slim cigar, but this time not blowing perfect smoke rings, nor was he smiling as he spoke to Gallagher and Rooster.

"That Big Ike," Gallagher said, "is all grit and catgut."

"We'll see about Mister Big Ike Silver and his grit and catgut. There are several ways to skin a cat."

"What're you gonna do, boss?"

"You two just be back here at midnight and you'll see."

Gallagher started to say something, but changed his mind and turned to Rooster.

"Let's get a drink."

Rooster shrugged and followed Gallagher toward the door.

"Midnight!" Lessur repeated. "Meet me at the stable."

All of Lessur's plans for dealing with his opposition had been unsuccessful. First by Milo Sebastian at the Emporium with Belinda Millay. Then by Quentin Cord in a gunfight with Ike Silver. And now by Quemada with the attack on Silver and the gold wagon from the Rattlesnake. All three unsuccessful. But Rupert Lessur had a fourth and what he hoped was a final plan to eliminate the competition of Ike Silver and Company.

"Ben, one of the first things we've got to do on our next run to La Paz is get you another wagon," Ike said.

"It could've been worse." Ben grinned. "It could've been us in bits and pieces."

"Amen, brother."

"Ike,"—Ben looked around the stable to see if anyone was in hearing range—"I'd like to ask you something. . . ."

"Go ahead."

"You ever notice that wedding band that Melena wears?"

"I have. But what about it?"

"It's made out of copper. Made it for her when we were married, and well . . ." He paused.

"Go ahead, Ben. What's on your mind?"

"I noticed you got some gold wedding rings in the store."

"I guess we have."

"Well, Ike . . . I'd like to buy her a gold one for Christmas."

"No. You're not going to buy any such thing. Compliments of the house."

"I want to pay—"

"Don't argue, partner. It's my gift to both of you."

* * *

"Rooster, what do you figure 'ol Lessur's got in mind for us to do tonight?" Gallagher drained the whiskey from his glass as they both stood at the bar in the Emporium.

"I don't know and I don't care, so long as he keeps comin' across on payday. . . . Say, isn't it about time we got back?"

"We got time for one more. Maybe two. Hey, Henry!"

Inside the store, the big clock started to strike twelve. The store was empty, dark and quiet except for the sound of the timepiece.

Sister Bonney, in her nightclothes, knelt by her bed in a partitioned section of the schoolroom saying her prayers.

Ben and Melena were asleep in the loft that Ben had fixed up in the stable. Benjie slept in a smaller area nearby.

In his bed, Jake snored sonorously.

Jed and Obie were asleep in their room. The door opened and Ike entered with a book in his hand. He walked quietly to the boys' beds, adjusted the disarranged covers, touched each boy's brow, then left.

The door of Lessur's stable opened and Gallagher and Rooster came in, both showing the effects of their visit to the Emporium. Gallagher was in the midst of singing "Who Threw the Overalls in Mrs. Murphy's Chowder?"

Lessur stepped inside and closed the door. "Shut up, Gallagher. You want to wake up the whole town?"

"I don't care." Gallagher shrugged.

"Well, I do, so just shut up and listen."

"Okay, boss." Gallagher shrugged again. "What you want us to do?"

Lessur walked to a corner, picked up a couple of kerosene cans and held them out.

"We're going to get rid of our competition."

Gallagher's eyes widened. "What the hell are you talking about?"

"Big Ike Silver and Company . . . you're going to burn it down."

"There's kids in there!" Gallagher took a step. "And—"

"That's their problem. Lessur Freighting is mine." He set the cans on the floor in front of him.

"Mister Lessur, you're plumb crazy. Look, I've done some things that I . . . awwww, the hell with it!"

Gallagher started toward the door. As he passed by, Lessur grabbed a crowbar and brought it down hard across the back of Gallagher's head.

Gallagher dropped. Lessur turned to Rooster.

"What about you? Do you have any such compunctions?"

"I don't know what that means."

"It means you'll get his job and a fat bonus."

"Yeah, but when he comes to . . . then—"

"He's not going to come to."

Lessur pulled a derringer from the belt under his coat and shot Gallagher in the back, then pointed to one of the kerosene cans.

"Get it going good . . . then meet me at the Emporium. We'll get rid of him later."

"Right, boss."

Rooster picked up a can and headed for the door.

"And make sure nobody sees you."

"Right, boss."

Ike Silver settled himself into the overstuffed chair in the corner of the room near the oil lamp, opened the book and began to read.

"Call me Ishmael. Some years ago—never mind how long precisely—having little or no money in my purse and nothing particular to interest me on shore, I thought I would sail about a little and see . . ."

After Rooster left, Lessur's foot nudged Gallagher for any sign of response. There was none.

Lessur slipped the derringer back into his belt, went out the door and locked it behind him.

He wanted to be somewhere else when the fire started.

CHAPTER FIFTY-ONE

Business at the Emporium was good, both down-stairs and upstairs. Alma, Francine, and Marisa were all in action in their upper chambers, while on the main floor four of the card tables were in action and half a dozen citizens stood at the bar.

Binky had just finished his rendition of Crook-back's cry for "A horse! A horse!" and, drink in hand, navigated toward Belinda's table.

Rupert Lessur entered and headed for the same table.

"Good evening," Lessur said cheerily.

Neither Belinda nor Binky responded with the same cheer, but both nodded as Binky sat down.

Belinda pointed. "If you're looking for a game, there's an empty seat at that table, but the stakes might be too low for you."

It was a low-stakes game because the players consisted of Tom Bixby, Antonio Gillardi, Doctor Zebelion Barnes, Oliver Knight, and Knight's copy-boy/reporter/assistant editor, Matt Crowley, who had most of the meager winnings from the table in front of him.

"No, it's a little late. Thought I'd just come by and have a nightcap. Say, what time is it?" Lessur had pulled a fob and watch from his vest pocket. "Seems my watch has stopped."

"There's a clock on that wall," Belinda said. "Been there for years."

"Oh, yes. Twelve thirty-five." Lessur went through the motions of setting and winding his watch, then tucked it back into his pocket. "Would you two care to join me in a drink?"

"No, thanks," Belinda said.

"I would!" Binky responded.

"Fine. Henry . . . ," Lessur called out as he sat down, "bring over my bottle."

Rooster had made his way along the dark back-streets of town and was soaking rags with kerosene at the side of Ike Silver's store. He set down the can, struck a match, lit the rags, picked up the empty can and skulked back the way he had come.

Ike, still dressed, had fallen asleep in his chair with the book still in his hands.

Flames leaped up the side of the outer wall, crack-ing, then bursting the windows from the heat, and crawled, outside and in, toward the second floor.

Moby Dick fell from Ike's hands onto the carpet. His eyes blinked open, then closed. In a moment they opened again. As he started to rub his eyes, he saw the book on the floor and reached down for it, but abruptly stopped.

Smoke from below had begun to curl into the room.

Inside the store the blaze was spreading. Flames crackled and twisted. Black smoke billowed upward through the building.

"Jake, get up!" Ike shook his brother. "Fire! Get out of here!"

Jake bolted out of his sleep. "The boys!" He
elled.

"I'll get 'em. Get out of here!"

. . . Inside Lessur's stable, Jim Gallagher stirred.
Ie rolled from his back and tried to rise, but failed.
Ie tried again.

Through the swirling smoke Ike had lifted a boy
nder each arm and was carrying them toward the
tairway.

. . . Gallagher swayed to his feet, staggered to the
table door. Padlocked. With his bull shoulder he
mashed it open.

On the street, people rushed from all directions
ward the burning Silver store, with fire and smoke
notting through the broken window panes and
ront door. First Jake, then Ike, still carrying both
d and Obie, careened through the entrance. Ben
nd Melena, in their nightclothes, had come around
he corner from the stable and rushed to help. Ben-
e stood in the street, still half asleep, but safe.

Ike set the boys on the ground as Gallagher
ushed his way through the crowd.

"Ike! Is everybody out?"

"I think so." Ike nodded.

"Where's the Sister?" Gallagher looked around.

"My God!" Melena cried. "She's still in there!"

"Ben!" Ike turned. "Are you sure?"

"She didn't come out!"

Gallagher wheeled and weaved through the door
nd into the store. Like a crazed bull he tore
hrough the store and anything in his way toward
he schoolroom door. Locked—or stuck. He
ammed through, splitting the door apart.

On the street Ike, and by now half the town, in-
luding Belinda, Binky, Knight, Doc Barnes, Bixby,
iillardi, Crowley, Scotty, Lessur and Rooster, were

staring at the inferno. Suddenly, Ike turned and bolted around the corner and down the side street.

"Ike!" Jake screamed.

Jed started after his father, but Jake grabbed and held him.

Ben looked at Melena, then followed down the side street after Ike.

The classroom was choked with smoke. Sister Bonney lay unconscious in her bunk. Gallagher knocked over benches and part of the partition to get to her. He lifted her in his huge arms and began to carry her.

Gallagher had a bullet in his back and his head had been struck by a crowbar, but with Sister Bonney in his arms, it seemed as if a second strength had reinforced every muscle and fiber of his body. Through the flames licking the classroom, he staggered and pitched forward. A beam collapsed just behind them. Then another; the second hit Gallagher, and he went down still holding on to Sister Bonney just as Ike and Ben came through the side street door.

Both coughing and crouching low, Ike and Ben made it to the fallen couple.

"Get her out," Ike said.

Ben lifted Sister Bonney and carried her toward the side door while Ike followed, dragging Gallagher by both shoulders.

Jake, Jed, Obie, Melena, Belinda, Binky, Doc Barnes and a few others had come over to the side of the building.

Ben, carrying Sister Bonney, then Ike, dragging Gallagher, came through the door as another flaming beam crashed behind them.

The cold night air revived Sister Bonney and she looked up at Ben.

"Can you stand, Sister?" he asked.

"Yes." She nodded.

Melena came to her side as Ben set her on her feet.

Doc Barnes moved near and whispered something to Sister Bonney. She looked at him for just a moment, then they moved together, his arm around her, to where Gallagher lay on the ground braced by Ike.

Ike withdrew his hand from Gallagher's back, his palm smeared with blood. Sister Bonney knelt at Gallagher's side. His eyes opened in recognition of the nun whose life he had saved.

"Sister . . ." Gallagher tried to smile.

It took all his ebbing strength, but he raised his hand. She took it in both of hers and leaned closer.

"Please . . . ," he uttered.

James Gallagher coughed and began to whisper the Act of Contrition as Sister Mary Boniface prayed:

"Eternal rest give to him, O Lord: and let perpetual light shine upon him. A hymn, O God, becometh Thee in Sion; and a vow shall be paid to Thee in Jerusalem: O Lord hear my prayer; all flesh shall come to Thee . . ."

A pause; Gallagher was dead.

Ike looked at Sister Bonney and said softly, "He can't hear you, Sister."

"He can hear me. '. . . Eternal rest grant unto him, O Lord, and perpetual light shine upon him.' "

A shadow passed over Gallagher's face. The shadow of Rupert Lessur, who stood as an innocent spectator to the events with Rooster next to him.

Ike rose and Ben stood beside him.

"How'd it start?" Ben asked.

"It started," Ike said.

Lessur, trailed by Rooster, moved away.

"What's the difference?" Jake said. "We're licked. We've lost everything."

"Not everything." Ike took a breath. "And we're not licked."

"The store, the money,"—Jake sighed—"the merchandise, the wagons . . . all gone."

Fire reflected in Ike's eyes.

"We'll build the store up again. We'll borrow money and we'll get merchandise. Ben'll fix the wagons. We're here and we're going to stay here."

CHAPTER FIFTY-TWO

A star had been drawn with crayon on both sides of a paper bag by Obie and stuck atop a small Christmas tree, which had been placed on a crate and decorated with other homemade ornaments in the stable that was singed and scorched, but still standing, and sheltering Ike, Jake, Jed, Obie, Sister Bonney, Ben, Melena and Benjie, who were doing their best under the circumstances to celebrate Christmas.

Whatever had been salvaged from the fire had been stacked or piled against a wall.

A few gifts had been exchanged, mostly presents for the boys, crafted and carved by Ben—new yo-yos, flutes and sailboats.

In the middle of the stable there was a small fire inside a perimeter of stones that served as a stove, where Melena stirred a big kettle of boiling beans while Sister Bonney sliced bread on a wobbly table.

Unseen by the others, in one corner, Ike took something from his pocket and extended his hand toward Ben.

"Here, Ben, I found this when I was going through what's left next door."

He placed the gold wedding band into Ben's palm.

"Ike . . . I . . ."

"Never mind. Just give it to her."

There was noise and a knock from outside the stable door . . . then more noise and knocking.

Jake walked over to the entrance and opened the door.

"Merry Christmas!" was voiced by the dozens of people standing at the entry.

"Come in! Come in!" Jake smiled. "That's what doors are for!"

And in they streamed.

Belinda Millay, Binky, Henry the bartender, Oliver Knight, Doc Barnes, Tom Bixby, Antonio Gillardi, Matt Crowley, Mayor John Davis, Scotty Simpson, Miles Akins from the hotel and half a dozen more people with members of their families entered . . . and they had not come empty-handed.

"Your Honor! Everybody!" Jake grinned. "What're you all doing out on a night like this?"

"We're not *out!*" Binky exclaimed. "We're *in!*"

The mayor laughed. "Yes, yes, we came by to say Merry . . . uh, well, some of us thought . . . it was Miss Millay's idea . . . that . . . we, well, we brought over some things that you might need."

"There isn't much," Obie said, "we don't need."

"Obadiah!" Jake admonished.

"Cider." The mayor held up a jug. "Pretty strong."

Binky took a whiskey bottle from Henry's hand.

"And something a little stronger for those of us who are so inclined!"

"Just what the doctor ordered." Zebelion Barnes nodded.

Everybody laughed and the visitors set down gifts they had brought, some wrapped and some not. Pots, pans, plates—necessities and non-necessities.

Jake walked close to his brother and made sure nobody heard. "Ike," he said, just above a whisper, "you know something?"

"What?"

"Maybe that caravan wasn't so cockeyed after all." Jake turned, wiped at his left eye and walked away. As he did, Scotty Simpson came up to Ike.

"Mister Silver," he said, "you been awfully good to me and I . . . well, I just want you to know . . . if there's anything I can do . . ."

"There is, Scotty. Just don't leave town. We'll be opening sooner than later. And you're still on the payroll."

"Oh . . . no."

"Oh, yes."

"Half salary, then."

"Full salary. Report for work on Monday. There's a lot to do and you're going to help us do it."

"You damn betcha, Mister Silver! And tonight I just might have a wee touch o' that cider."

"Good idea."

A few minutes later, Jake reappeared carrying a scorched and slightly bent menorah with all seven candles lit.

"Wait a minute," he said, "besides being Christmas . . . it's Hanukkah."

"Well,"—Mayor Davis raised a glass, not of cider—"Merry Hanukkah . . . whatever that is."

"Merry Hanukkah!" the crowd responded.

"Uncle Jake," Obie said, "I remember last year at Hanukkah we all danced."

Jake nodded. "So we'll dance this year too!" Jake set down the menorah and picked up a flute. "Come on, Obie, lead the way!"

Uncle Jake began playing the hora on the flute. First Ike, then the others clapped in rhythm.

Obie grabbed Jed, who grabbed Benjie, who grabbed Sister Bonney and started to dance in a circle around the fire in the center of the stable. A dozen other revelers joined in the dance. Antonio Gillardi produced a harmonica from his pocket and accompanied Jake's flute.

Oliver Knight walked up next to Ike. "Mister Silver, this is one thing you're not going to stop me from writing about."

"I wouldn't dream of stopping you, Mister Knight." Ike smiled. "I wouldn't dream of it."

Rupert Lessur stood smoking a cigar and looking out the window of his office with Rooster just behind him.

"Damn fools . . ."

"Yeah." Rooster turned, walked to the door, opened it and looked back. "Well, Mister Lessur, Merry Christmas."

Colonel Crook stood at the door with Captain Bourke beside him. In Crook's hand, a Yellow Boy Winchester. "And an unHappy New Year," he said.

"Ben, what are you doing?"

Ben removed the copper ring from Melena's finger and replaced it with the gold wedding band. "Merry Christmas, Melena."

"I was perfectly happy with the old one," she said.

"I wasn't."

"I do want to make you happy . . . and Ben, I hope this makes you happy, too." She leaned closer and whispered, "Benjie's going to have a little baby brother or sister."

"Happy? Melena . . . happier than a saltwater clam at high tide."

Now Jed, Obie and Sister Bonney stood near Jake

and Antonio Gillardi, while a dozen citizens of Prescott, including Mayor Davis, did their best to dance the hora.

Binky decided he had been offstage long enough. He raised a tumbler of bourbon.

"To paraphrase a countryman of mine," he declaimed, "not the best of times—not the worst of times!"

Jed tugged at Binky's sleeve. "Mister Binkham, he also wrote 'God bless us, everyone.'"

"Amen." Sister Bonney nodded.

"Ike,"—Belinda Millay placed a coin in his hand—"here's another silver dollar for the new store . . . and for luck."

He smiled. "Thanks, but I'm already pretty lucky."

"We all are . . . Big Ike."

Ike Silver walked a few steps away from the others. He took the gold watch from his pocket, clicked open the lid, looked at the wedding picture and listened for a moment to the tune from the past that could be faintly heard amidst the night's celebration of Hanukkah and Christmas.

LOUIS L'AMOUR
SHOWDOWN TRAIL

Collected here are two of L'Amour's classic novellas, appearing in paperback for the first time in these restored versions. "The Trail to Peach Meadow Cañon" was originally published in a magazine, then substantially changed and expanded when it appeared as a full-length novel years later. "Showdown Trail" also appeared first in a magazine, but was reworked and expanded into the novel *The Tall Stranger*, which was the basis for the classic movie of the same title starring Joel McRea. This edition presents these brilliant novellas in their original magazine versions, as they were first written.

Dorchester Publishing Co., Inc.
P.O. Box 6640
Wayne, PA 19087-8640
___5786-7
$6.99 US/$8.99 CAN

Please add $2.50 for shipping and handling for the first book and $.75 for each additional book. NY and PA residents, add appropriate sales tax. No cash, stamps, or CODs. Canadian orders require an extra $2.00 for shipping and handling and must be paid in U.S. dollars. Prices and availability subject to change. **Payment must accompany all orders.**

Name: _____

Address: _____

City: _____ State: _____ Zip: _____

E-mail: _____

I have enclosed $_____ in payment for the checked book(s).

CHECK OUT OUR WEBSITE! www.dorchesterpub.com
_____ Please send me a free catalog.

MAX BRAND®

BAD MAN'S GULCH

One sheriff and two deputies have already disappeared in the rough-and-tumble mining town of Slosson's Gulch. The same fate awaits any other man who crosses the cutthroats and thieves who thrive there. Pedro Melendez is a gambler and a drifter, trying his best to put his gunslinging days behind him. But he'll need all the sharpshooting he can muster to help a vulnerable young woman find her missing father—because there are plenty of miners eager to make sure Pedro is the next one to go missing.

#51
WILDERNESS

COMANCHE MOON

David Thompson

In the untamed wilderness of the majestic Rockies, Nate King has often seen that the line between life and death is a thin one. So far he's managed to stay on the right side, but all that could change on a rare excursion to Bent's Fort. While there, he finds a greenhorn couple looking to settle in the heart of Comanche territory. Unable to leave them helpless, Nate puts himself right in the middle of the warpath. But when an old enemy steals all his supplies and weapons, Nate's left utterly defenseless against a band of vicious warriors who want nothing more than to see him dead.

Dorchester Publishing Co., Inc.
P.O. Box 6640
Wayne, PA 19087-8640

_____5713-1
$5.99 US/$7.99 CAN

Name: _____

Address: _____

City: _____ State: _____ Zip: _____

E-mail: _____

I have enclosed $_____ in payment for the checked book(s).

CHECK OUT OUR WEBSITE! www.dorchesterpub.com.
_____ Please send me a free catalog.

SHANNON:
U.S. MARSHAL
Charles E. Friend

Clay Shannon has decided he's done carrying a star. All he wants is the peace and quiet of a small ranch he can call his own. But then the government names him a U.S. Marshal. Suddenly he finds himself mixed up with a mysterious gambler who has the look of a gunfighter and a man named "King" Kruger, who's determined to grab land any way he can. From back-shooters to bushwhackers, cattle rustling to murder, Shannon may find he's resting in peace much sooner than he planned.

PAUL S. POWERS
DESERT JUSTICE

Sonny Tabor leads a rough life. Wrongfully accused of a string of murders, he has a price on his head and is relentlessly pursued by the law. The four novellas in this volume, collected for the first time in paperback, showcase riveting action and high drama as Sonny is forced into a life of continual flight and constant danger. In one story, he's left handcuffed to a lawman in the middle of the desert without food, water or horses. And in another, he's captured with an outlaw and sentenced to hang. Sonny is desperate to prove his innocence—but that means he'll have to live long enough to find the real killers.

CHASING DESTINY

STEPHEN OVERHOLSER

Thousands of dollars stolen. A man murdered on his own ranch. The crimes were enough to form a posse hell-bent on vengeance and ready to shoot at anything that moved. When their bullets caught a fugitive square in the face, they didn't spend much time identifying the body before pronouncing the man guilty. But some folks in town don't believe the real culprit is six feet under. Some folks think the real murderer is hiding out, still counting all his gold. But they'll have a lot of dangerous hard work ahead to prove whether they're on a fool's errand or...*Chasing Destiny*

RIDERS OF
THE PURPLE SAGE
ZANE GREY®

Zane Grey's masterpiece, *Riders of the Purple Sage*, is one
of the greatest, most influential novels of the West ever
written. But for nearly a century it has existed only in a
profoundly censored version, one that undermined the
truth of the characters and distorted Grey's intentions.

Finally the story has been restored from Grey's original
handwritten manuscript and the missing and censored
material has been reinserted. At long last the classic saga of
the gunman known only as Lassiter and his search for his
lost sister can be read exactly as Zane Grey wrote it. After all
these years, here is the **real** *Riders of the Purple Sage*!
